I0760549

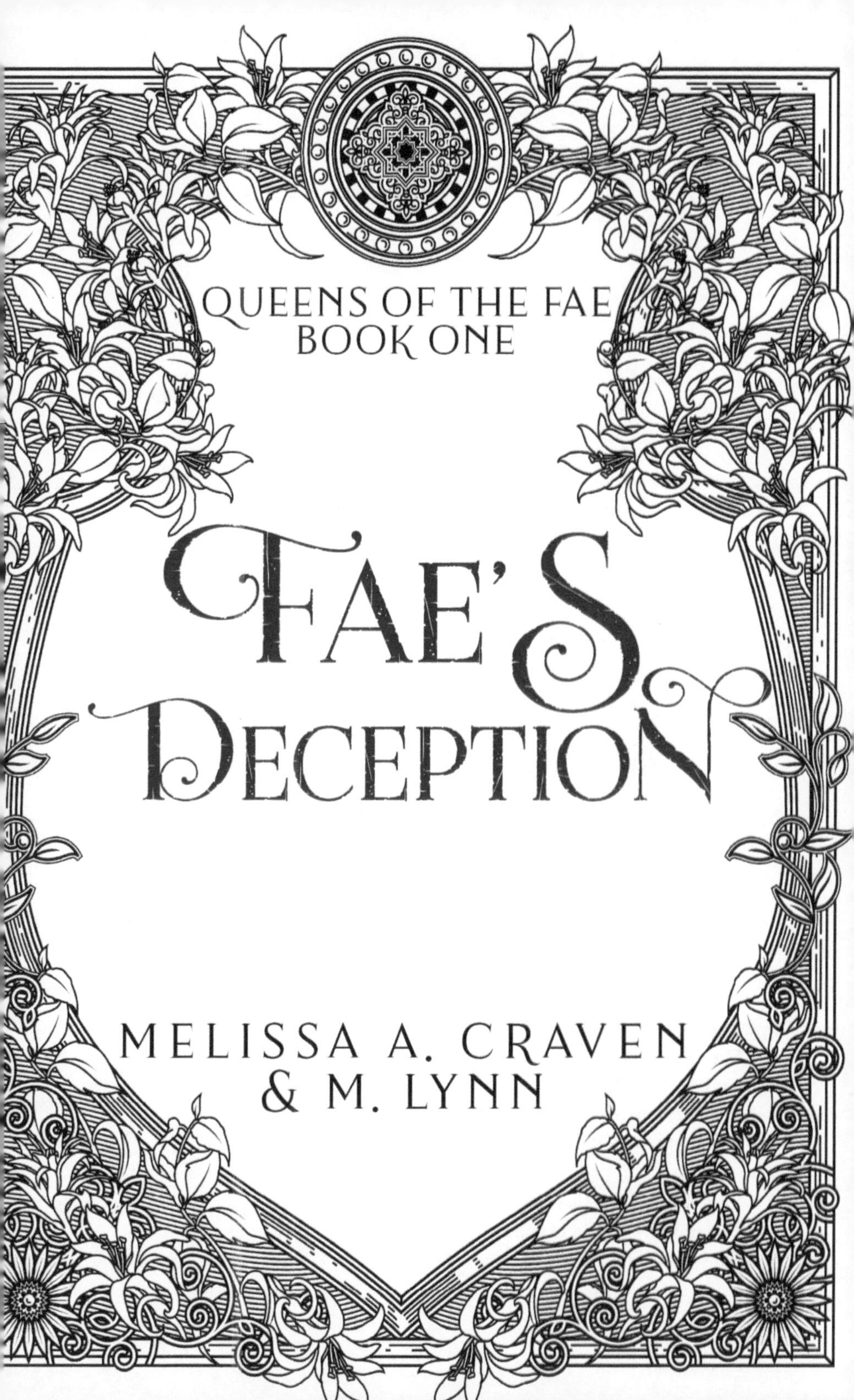
QUEENS OF THE FAE
BOOK ONE
FAE'S
DECEPTION
MELISSA A. CRAVEN
& M. LYNN

Edited by Cindy Ray Hale
Proofread by Caitlin Haines
Cover by Maria Spada

For our advanced readers.
You made us feel like this story matters.

PRISON REALM

NORTHERN VATLAN

LOCH VILLANDI

FARGELSI KINGDOM

SOUTHERN VATLA

DRAGUR FOREST

VINDUR CITY

ISKALT KINGDOM

EASTERN VATLANDS

ELDFAL

SANDUR

SOL LOCH

DUR KINGDOM

TEOTANN OASIS

ELDUR DESERT

CH LANGT

RADUR CITY

Prologue

Alona Cahill

"Your Highness, please, you must allow me to do my job." Rowena rushed to help Alona with her hair.

"Rowena, in less than a year, I'll be serving as Lady Driscoll's maid way out in Sandur. How does anyone expect me to dress and style a great lady if I can't even manage my own hair?"

Rowena leaned down behind her until Alona could see her maid's reflection in her hand mirror. "My Lady, before you leave for Sandur, I will teach you everything you need to know. Until then, I intend to treat you as the princess you are." She ran a brush through Alona's blond mane. "Whatever traditional nonsense dictates, you were born a princess of this kingdom, and it makes no sense you should ever have to be anything less than what you are."

"I am not above the law, no matter who my mother is."

"She will get you out of this. I have faith. You will rule as your mother's heir one day."

"I was born without magic, just like you. I'm almost eighteen now, soon I'll join the serving class. There's no use pretending it isn't so. Now, show me how you do my hair in that twisty thing."

"Very well, my Lady." Rowena guided Alona through the steps to secure her hair in a neat updo, perfect for traveling. "You seem nervous."

"I'm more than just nervous. I'm petrified. What if Lady Driscoll asks me to serve her tea or something else I don't know how to do yet?"

"She wouldn't dare. Not a minute before your eighteenth birthday and probably not even after."

"What do you mean, not even after?" Alona secured her traveling cloak in place with a jeweled broach her mother gave her last year.

"My Lady, I can't imagine anyone will actually make you serve."

"Then what am I to do with my life?" Alona's eyes widened in alarm. For seventeen years she'd prepared herself for a future as a lady's maid. She'd even had days when she couldn't wait to get started in her new life. But if she wasn't allowed to serve as her mother's heir, nor allowed to serve as a maid in more than just name only, then how would she fill her days?

"Don't trouble yourself, my Lady, I believe you will become more of a companion to Lady Driscoll than an actual servant. After all, you may be destined for the serving class, but you are still the queen's daughter. That will never change."

Alona couldn't imagine a more boring task than to entertain an old lady waiting around to die. Lady Driscoll was a widow friend of her mother's. She'd always believed the Lady would treat her well, and she knew her mother and Lady Driscoll had schemes to marry her into the merchant class after she'd served a few years as a maid. But Alona wanted to embrace her new life and the freedoms it brought. One of those freedoms was the right to make her own choices in a way she'd never been able to as a princess.

"Are you quite certain you don't want me to go with you, your Majesty?"

"I can manage without you for a few weeks," Alona insisted.

If the whole point of this trip was to meet her future employer, then she didn't think it made sense to travel with an entourage befitting a princess. She'd had to argue her point with her mothers, but even they saw the sense in her request eventually. She still had to travel with the queen's guard—the head of the guard no less. But Alona looked forward to spending time with Eamon Donovan, the captain of the palace guard and a man who'd been like a father to Alona. He would escort her safely north to Sandur, an exotic city along the coast of Eldur's wasteland. She'd never traveled to the northern half of their kingdom before and was looking forward to the trip.

"Are you all set, sweetheart?" The queen consort peeked into her daughter's rooms with a forced smile on her face.

"Yes, Mama, you two can come in now. I know you've been lurking in the halls for the last half hour. And I know you both have better things to do with your time."

"We have nothing so pressing that we can't wish our daughter a safe trip." The queen crossed the room, taking a moment to adjust the broach at Alona's throat. Both Queen Faolan and Queen Consort Tierney were her mothers in every sense of the word, but Faolan gave birth to her, hoping for a strong heir—something that was not in the cards for their little family.

"Lady Driscoll will take good care of you, my dear." Faolan squeezed her hands.

"I think it's supposed to be the other way around, Mother." Alona smiled.

"Not yet."

Her last year as a princess of Eldur would be filled with many 'not yets.' Her mothers wanted her to enjoy her last year at court, but Alona wanted to get it over with.

"I'll be back before you know it, Mother." She hugged the queens, leaving them behind to comfort each other.

For the first day and a half of her journey, Alona did as she should and rode in the carriage as befitting her current station. But on the afternoon of the second day, she chose to ride with Eamon and his men on horseback. She wanted to catch the first glimpse of Sol Loch's crystal clear waters and the hot springs there. The air already smelled of sulfur, and the heat of the day caused Alona to travel with a cotton veil over her head and face to shield her from the sand and the heat. Had she been born with the power of the Eldur Fae, the sun would have strengthened her the way it did for all Eldurians. They were the strongest of the Fae, yet they were limited to using their magic only during the day. At night, Alona stood among equals.

"Just a little farther, Alona, and we'll break for the evening at the hot springs," Eamon said. "Maybe we can even find one of the mud springs where you and Finn used to have good old fashioned mud fights when you thought I wasn't paying attention." His grin was infectious, and so like his son's. She'd grown up with Finn Donovan among the other children in residence at the palace.

Finn was just two years older than Alona, but most of the

time he acted like he was seven—and probably still would when he was seventy.

"If we find a mud spring, I'll be taking a mud bath. I believe I've outgrown mud fights."

"You know, Lona, pigs take mud baths." Eamon flashed a mischievous smile at her.

"Oh, you know very well the Ladies of the Eldur court pay good money for that mud."

"You're all nutters. Every last one of you refined sort."

"Well, in a year I won't be quite so refined."

"You will always be a refined lady, my Lona." Eamon's handsome smile routinely melted the hearts of most of those 'refined ladies' at court. "Even covered in mud like a pig."

"Oh, you just hush now." She laughed.

"Morgan and O'Mally, ride ahead and find the lady a mud spring. And while you're at it, put up her tent so she can rest before dinner."

"Yes, sir!" The two youngest soldiers of Eamon's unit took off ahead, eager to do their commander's bidding.

"Thank you, Eamon. I shouldn't allow such luxuries, but I am tired, and I haven't enjoyed the hot springs in ages."

"We will get our first glimpse of Sol Loch just over the next rise. The waters there will be soothing this time of year. Hot, but not too hot."

"Sounds wonderful." Alona leaned forward in her saddle, eager to set her eyes on the crowning jewel of Eldur for the first time in years. She'd grown up at the palace in the capital city, Raudur, that lay along the rocky cliffs of the Dalur River. It was cooler there and beautiful in its own way. But Sol Loch was breathtaking in its wildness. She would love to spend her days here among the many lakes and hot springs, but it was far too close to Eldfal, the massive volcano in the northern wastelands. The stability of the land here was always in question.

"I would live here in a heartbeat if the land was fruitful." Eamon gazed across the rolling sandy hills to the oasis that was Loch Sol in the distance.

"And if the water was drinkable," Alona added. "We could have a little cottage near the springs and live out our days free of palace gossip and Eldur hierarchy."

"We can dream." Eamon winked. "If we ride ahead of the carriage, we'll be there in half an hour."

"Race you." Alona dug her heels into her mount's sides and flew down the hillside, laughing the whole way.

"Alona Cahill, I didn't help raise a cheater!" Eamon called behind her.

"Finn taught me!" She galloped over the desolate hills and valleys, but Eamon quickly pulled ahead of her. His men surrounded her, keeping pace with her mount until they reached the rolling green hills of Loch Sol.

"Winner, winner, doesn't have to cook dinner," Eamon taunted.

"If you expect me to cook dinner, we are in for a sorry night indeed. I can't draw my own bath, much less cook a stew over a campfire." Alona felt so useless in these moments. She hated that she needed servants to take care of her.

"It's all right, Princess. You are far too intelligent to waste your talents cooking for a bunch of raggedy soldiers."

"Talents?" She laughed.

"Sir, my Lady," Morgan interrupted their playful banter. "We've set up camp just along the trail ahead. We've found hot springs as well as a mud spring for the princess."

"Thank you, Morgan. I appreciate your fine scouting skills." Alona nodded to the soldier.

"Thank you, my Lady." Morgan's ears turned pink at her praise.

"My men will set up camp, Lona. I will take you to the mud

spring and keep watch while you enjoy the rest of the afternoon. I know you must be weary from traveling all day." Donovan slid off his horse and tossed the reins to Morgan.

Alona dismounted from her horse, feeling every aching muscle in her body cry out for the soothing balm of Sol Loch's healing waters. The unforgiving Eldur sun seemed to have sapped all her strength. The mud would ease the aches and pains and leave her skin silky smooth. When she finished bathing in the hot springs, she would feel a thousand times better.

Alona stripped down to her shift and sank up to her knees in the sun-warmed mud bath. Sitting down, she made herself comfortable for a nice long soak. The magical properties of the natural spring eased the aches and pains of traveling across the unforgiving desert.

A rustling noise brought Alona out of her sleepy stupor brought on by the steam.

"It can't be time to go already." Eamon would die before he would let any of his men near the springs where she bathed, but she wasn't certain they still wouldn't try.

Alona was about to turn when a dirty hand clamped over her mouth. A blinding pain ripped through her head, and her mind went dark.

Two Months Earlier

Brea Robinson was a lie.

Okay, not in the truest sense of the word. Brea was really her name, and Amanda and Jack Robinson were her parents. Parents who would never understand her.

This life was what felt like a lie. She'd never fit in this world of high school hallways and concrete jungles. That was what her school was. A jungle. A wild place, unsafe for anyone who didn't fit.

"I can't believe I'm back here." She sighed as she hiked her backpack higher on her shoulder.

Myles, best friend extraordinaire, sported a giant grin, one she couldn't match.

"Why are you so happy today?"

He lifted his hands to the blue sky above. "It's a beautiful day, Brea." He never said her name with only one syllable like everyone else. Since they were kids, he'd called her Bree-ya.

"It's..." She lifted her eyes to the building they'd tried improving with brick columns and colorful banners flapping in the breeze touting the Southern Ohio school's many accomplishments. "A day. A freezing day."

"Don't be so glum, chum." He draped an arm over her shoulders and squeezed. "I'm just glad you're back."

Back. Because she'd been gone. How could she forget? Mentally unstable Brea Robinson missed the first month back from winter break because she was at the Clarkson Institution for Troubled Teens. It was where they put you when you had a freak out on Christmas morning.

Her ever-eloquent mother named the episodes freak outs. Brea wasn't really sure what they were. All her life, she saw... things—for lack of a better word. Sometimes when she looked at a person, she saw features that weren't there. Pointy ears, flashing eyes, bright colors.

Sometimes they were the stuff of nightmares.

The psych-dude she saw when she was young claimed she was having night terrors, but during the day.

It wasn't just seeing things though. When she got angry or sad or even happy, it was like she lost control of the emotion, and it expanded within her, overcoming every thought and even manifesting as this weird energy beneath her skin.

An energy begging for release that sometimes got her into trouble.

"Do they all know?" She climbed the front steps, walking under a banner proclaiming the school as the football state champs.

Myles hesitated before he spoke. "I mean... there were rumors." He pulled open the glass door and waited for her to enter.

But how was she supposed to do this? Face them? It wasn't the first time she'd been two-sleeves short of a straight-jacket.

If her mom had any say, they'd have lost the key to her room.

Sucking in a deep breath, she repeated her personal mantra. "I'm not crazy. I'm not crazy."

Myles reached for her hand, threading their fingers together. "No one thinks that."

He overestimated the kids in their nowhere town. The people of Grafton, Ohio loved gossip. It entertained their small minds.

He squeezed her hand tighter as if sensing she didn't believe him. She looked down at their joined hands. "You know, this is why everyone has thought we're a thing since like the fifth grade."

"And since when do we care what they think?" He never had, but as she walked down that hall, Brea couldn't think of anything else.

Maybe her mom was right. She did belong at Clarkson permanently, somewhere that could help her rid herself of the hallucinations and surges of anger and fear she couldn't control.

"If you didn't spend all your time with me, maybe you'd have more friends." She pulled her hand free, pretending to adjust the strap of her backpack.

"Why do I need other friends?" He stopped at her locker and leaned against the pale metal. "Who else is going to dissect every scene of *The Witcher* with me? Have you finished season one yet? I'm dying to tell you all the parts you missed by not reading the books."

"Myles." She shook her head in exasperation as she turned the rusted dial. It stuck on the last number—like it always did—and Myles hammered it with his fist until it popped open. She slid her coat off and shoved it in. Opening her bag, she stuffed the books for her first classes inside.

"We've been over this. I'm not a reader." But she was a watcher. She watched every single fantasy movie and television show multiple times and discussed them with Myles. "I don't need to read when I have my very own walking-talking Encyclopedia of fantasy to tell me all the parts that didn't show up in the movies."

"You're missing out." Myles shook his head.

"Speaking of missing out, what did you do while I was in prison?"

"You weren't in prison."

She rolled her eyes. With how closely the staff watched her, she may as well have been. That's what happens when you shove your mom across the room and into the Christmas tree. She still couldn't explain why or how she did it, but that didn't matter.

"Okay, fine. While I was in the hospital spending all my time in therapy, did you hang out with anyone else?"

He only shrugged and propped one Converse-clad foot against the locker. Guilt gnawed at her, but that wasn't a new feeling. She appreciated how loyal Myles was to her. Throughout her life, he was the only person she'd ever been able to count on. But he deserved more than a messed-up girl who saw inhuman freaks everywhere she went.

She met Myles in fifth grade when his family moved into the farm next door to hers. It was a love-at-first-sight kind of thing. Another lie. Love. But not with Myles. It was never romantic between them, but they'd bonded over their love of horses and desire to be anywhere but on their respective farms.

He was an attractive boy, and she knew for a fact the girls in the school liked him. It was one of the reasons they hated her so much. He could have been popular. All he'd have to do was make that short walk across the cafeteria at lunch and slide onto the bench with the rest of his football teammates.

Yep, that was right. Brea Robinson's best friend was a football player.

They walked to his locker so he could grab his books.

"Are you ever going to answer my question?" She tried to ignore the students hurrying down the hall, trying to get to class like it was any normal day. For them, she supposed, it was.

They didn't have to try and re-integrate into a place of whispers and accusing glares. She hadn't missed those.

Myles slammed his locker shut, and the sound reverberated down the emptying hall. The tardy bell rang, and he grinned. "Ooh saved by the bell."

She hurried after him. "We have the same first period, doofus."

They entered English Lit and walked to their usual seats near the back.

"Hi, Myles. You can sit by me." Ellen, a senior cheerleader, sent him a wave.

Brea had never until that moment disliked Ellen. She'd always been the sweet one on the team, unlike the rest of the girls who accused Brea of being some sort of witch—ironically, of course.

Myles grinned and puffed out his chest—ew—before sliding into his usual seat and leaning back. "Sorry, El. My girl needs me."

"El," Brea whispered with a shake of her head. "For the record, I don't need you."

His smile only widened. "Sure you do. You love me."

God help her, she did. Her parents weren't big on the love word—probably because their hearts were made of stone. But Myles let his feelings loose whenever he thought she needed it.

"Are you ever going to tell me what you've been up to?" She folded her arms on top of the dark-stained wooden desk.

"Cap had her colt."

Brea sat up straighter. Captain—named for Captain America—was the pride and joy of the Merrick farm. "Why didn't you tell me the moment you picked me up this morning?"

He shrugged. "I knew you'd yell at me because I've spent the last month in the company of beautiful beasts who aren't big on the talking." He reached over and flicked her hair. "Hey, they kind of sound like you."

"I'm not a beast," she grumbled. Or beautiful. Beauty was another one of those lies she hated so much. It was just an illusion.

He threw his head back with a full-throated laugh that had more than a few heads turning their way.

Brea leaned across her desk to Myles. "They're staring at me."

"That's because they missed you."

She snorted. "Yeah, okay." Most days, she wished the kids at her school didn't know she existed. But it was hard to ignore the crazy girl. That was an awful term—one people at the institute chastised her for every time she used it. But it didn't mean it wasn't how she felt.

Mental illness, they'd told her, was not something she could control, or deserved. They said it was an illness like any other, and nothing to be ashamed of.

But some days, shame was all she felt.

Mrs. Epstein walked to the front of the room, her gray hair pulled back into a severe bun. She started talking to them about whatever boring book—oops, literary classic—they'd been assigned to read.

Brea wasn't a reader. She subscribed more to the "do as little as possible" philosophy. Unlike Myles who was already bent over his notebook scribbling notes.

His perfect grades meant he'd eventually go on to some fancy college, leaving her behind. It was inevitable.

He wanted to be a large animal vet focusing on horses and cattle.

And he'd be amazing at it.

She watched her friend as a lock of caramel-colored hair fell into his eyes, wishing she could have just an ounce of his confidence.

His life wasn't perfect by any means, but then, perfection was only an illusion.

Another lie.

Throughout the day, Brea heard many variations of the rumors about her absence. She'd met an older man and run off with him, only to be dragged home.

She'd left to have a baby. That one stung a little. Had she really looked eight months pregnant before she left?

Then there was the story of the drugs she'd gotten hooked on, thanks to the sketchy characters who worked her family's farm. She thought she seemed pretty good after only a month in rehab.

It was Riley Anders, Captain of the boys' soccer team, who hit closest to home. As she'd walked by him at lunch, she heard the words "wacko" and "asylum" thrown into the atmosphere as if they didn't hold the power of a thousand knives.

Myles waved to her from their usual table, but she stood frozen in the center of the busy cafeteria. Classmates swarmed around her, as if not seeing the girl in the middle of a major crisis.

Her feet wouldn't move, like they were stuck in mud, swirling, sucking mud.

But the white tile floor was clean—or at least as clean as a school floor could be.

Nothing held her in place except a heart-splitting fear. This was her life now. Her breath came in short gasps as she tried to calm her shaking hands.

Energy buzzed underneath her skin, growing louder as the anxiety swirled out of control. She couldn't do this, couldn't be here.

The lies she told herself ate at her. She was okay. It was just a phase. Nothing was wrong.

Nothing was okay. This would never end.

And it was all so, so wrong.

Brea Robinson was a lie.

"Brea." Myles appeared at her side, lifting a hand to grab her arm.

She twisted away from him, forcing her legs to push through the quicksand of her fear.

"Brea!" Myles called after her as she ran through the cafeteria, shoving people out of the way.

She burst through the double doors into the hall, but it wasn't enough.

"I can't breathe," she said to herself as her head whipped from side to side searching for an escape.

"Where are you going, weirdo?"

She didn't know who said it, but a crowd of people stood in the doorway watching her.

Myles pushed through them, trying to get to her, to reach her.

But he was too late.

Brea's sneakers squeaked against the tile floor, and the hall became a blur of lockers. A hall monitor tried to stop her, but she kept going until she reached the front door of the school.

A blast of winter air struck her the moment she crashed

through the doors. She gulped a breath as if she'd never feel its icy chill again and ran down the steps.

Snow coated the walkway in front of her, leading to the student parking lot where a fresh dusting covered the cars.

Snow made the world look so new, but even that was a lie. It only covered up the grime underneath.

A chill raced down her spine, and she hugged her arms across her chest, wishing for the jacket that sat snug in her locker.

Wacko.

That was what they thought of her. She couldn't face this school any longer. But where could she go? Her parents thought much worse things of her. Tears froze in her lashes, and she wanted to scream. Not even her tears could thaw her.

"Where are you going?" Myles' voice behind her was soft.

She didn't turn to him. "Leave me alone, Myles."

"Brea, you have to go back in there and show them nothing they say matters."

"But it does. It all matters." She whirled on her heel, narrowly missing a patch of ice. "You can't tell me you don't think it. Just a little."

"Think what?"

"That I should never have been released from the institute."

"I'd never think something like that."

A warm tear tracked down her icy cheek. "No, you wouldn't say it, but everyone thinks it. My parents. Them." She gestured to the school. "This version of me, the one who exists inside that school instead of in a sterile room. It's not real. I finally see it now. The Brea Robinson you see is the lie."

"Don't say that?"

Anger burned through her. Why couldn't he see this?

The doors opened behind them, and a few of Myles' teammates piled out of the building. They stopped when they saw them.

"Lover's quarrel?" Carson Freemont asked.

As the quarterback, most people wished he'd speak to them. But he'd been tormenting her since middle school, and she just wished he'd go away.

"This is none of your business, Freemont." Myles drew himself up to his full height—which was about an inch taller than Carson's six feet.

Carson laughed. "Touched a nerve, did I?" He looked to his friends with a grin. "So, Brea, heard you were in the nut house. Almost killed your ma."

And it all made sense. How some of the kids at school knew. Carson's mom was in a church group with Brea's.

Her tongue stuck to the roof of her mouth, kept there by some invisible force. A tingling started in her fingertips, and she rubbed them together, trying to rid herself of the feeling. She knew what it meant.

Brea was about to lose control.

She breathed deeply, trying to push away the emotions swirling in her chest. Shame. Guilt. But most of all, anger. She was so freaking angry at this world, this school, these kids. The list was long.

"Not about to go psycho on us, are you?" Carson lifted a brow and stepped toward her. His frame loomed over her smaller one, and she stared down at her feet.

He wasn't finished. "Come on, Robinson. I want to see some of that legendary temper. You can be a grand prize winner of a lifelong stay at the Clarkson Center."

He even knew the institute they'd put her in. The Clarkson Center dealt with delinquents with mental disturbances.

Memories flashed through her mind of the first night she'd arrived there when she was just a child. They'd strapped her to a bed. She'd thrashed against the restraints and screamed about how nothing was real.

After that, everything she'd done had been monitored. Even now, she was expected to go straight to her therapist after school.

Her fists clenched at her sides, and she squeezed her eyes shut. *Don't lose control,* she told herself.

But it was no use because she'd never had control in the first place.

Carson forced her chin up. "Look at me," he growled. "You don't belong here."

Not news to her.

"You never ha—" His words cut off as Myles barreled into him, knocking him to the concrete.

Carson tried to pop up, but Myles was bigger and stronger.

Brea stepped back until she teetered on the edge of the curb. She'd never seen Myles so angry… or violent.

She needed to stop it, to help him. Carson managed to roll them over, his fist pounding into Myles' face.

"Myles," Brea whispered, desperation coursing through her.

Her friend's hand went limp, but Carson didn't stop.

"You can't do this." Her voice was so quiet no one heard her. Carson's friends only watched in fascination as blood poured from Myles' face.

He couldn't get away with this. Searing hot rage ripped through her, filling every cell with its fury. Her jaw clenched as heat pooled in her hands. Her eyes blazed as she became more than the girl on the sidelines.

She tilted her head to the side, trying to hold back whatever was happening. But this was Myles, and that only amplified every emotion in her.

"Myles is good," she bit out. He deserved only good things.

Unlike her. It was in that moment Brea realized she wasn't good, she was fire to his ocean, rage to his joy.

The way he saw the world may have been a lie, but it had to be preserved.

Light poured from her before she knew what was happening. Pain exploded in her temple as the power split her in two. She tried to call it back, to make it stop, but it kept coming.

Her knees buckled, and she fell forward. She didn't sense the impact as she hit the ground or feel whatever that power was snap back into her.

Her eyes found Myles motionless on the ground with the others nowhere to be found. She reached for his hand, struggling to grasp his icy fingers.

Whatever this was, it was just another lie. Another illusion. She'd wake up soon to find everything as it should be.

Part of her hoped it was a dream and she'd open her eyes to find the blank white walls of the Clarkson Center caging her in once again.

A hand pressed Brea to the concrete as her eyes slid open. Flashing red and blue lights reflected off the snow. They didn't belong there, but then, neither did she.

"Am I going back to the Clarkson Center?" she wheezed out.

No one answered. By now, half the school probably watched from the windows.

She lifted her head, searching for Myles and only finding splatters of blood where he'd been before.

"Myles?" Still, no answer. Any minute, he'd walk out of the school to wrap his arms around her. "Where's Myles?"

Whoever held her down took pity on her finally. "The boy who was here? They've taken him to St. Mary's."

"The hospital? Is he..." She swallowed. "Is he going to be okay?"

"I'd be surprised if he survived the ambulance ride."

She shook her head. It couldn't be real. Just another one of her delusions. Myles was fine. He had to be. He was the best person she knew, the only one who'd ever loved her.

It should be her in that ambulance.

The man hauled her up, and her legs wobbled beneath her. She turned her head, catching sight of his police officer's uniform. He nodded to where three other officers waited beside two police cruisers.

"Brea Robinson, you are under arrest for the attempted murder of Myles Merrick."

"No, I couldn't have hurt him. Not Myles." She tried to remember everything that happened, but it didn't seem real. They really thought it was her that did this?

The officer continued reading her rights, but she couldn't hear him over the ringing in her ears.

"You'll be able to call your people from the precinct."

Her people? He meant her parents, but they'd never been her people. That title had always rested solely with Myles, the boy next door.

And she'd killed him.

Brea Robinson was a lie.

A horror story.

But the truth? She wasn't sure if that even existed.

The cop shoved her into the back of his cruiser, her hands cuffed behind her back.

She leaned her head against the seat and stared at the ceiling, wishing she could see the blue sky Myles loved so much. A tear escaped, but she couldn't wipe it away. "I'm sorry, Myles."

CHAPTER TWO

The door to Brea's cell opened. For the last twenty-four hours, the only person she'd seen was her therapist, Doctor Cochran—and his sedatives. He claimed that seeing her parents or anyone else right now would only upset her further.

"Sedation is my friend," or so he said. The doctor just didn't know how good Brea was at tricking him and the nurses into believing she'd swallowed the pills. She had a growing collection of them under her bed, just waiting for the moment when someone finally told her she had actually killed Myles. Her best friend. The promise of those pills were her only comfort now.

"Brea Robinson?" An officer she didn't recognize stepped into her pristinely white cell. "You're being transferred."

"Transferred? Where?" Brea sat up on her cot.

"Dunno." The officer scratched his head, checking the clipboard in his hand. "That fancy doctor of yours signed orders to send you to some big city prison in Columbus with a psych ward, where you'll wait for your arraignment."

"How is Myles?" Brea clutched her clothes to her chest as she followed the officer from her cell.

"Dunno." The officer hitched up his pants as they walked down the long corridor to the main office.

"Do my parents know where I'm going?"

"Your parents signed over their parental rights to your therapist. Looks like they might have washed their hands of you." The officer held open the door for her to pass through.

Brea shuffled forward, unable to make sense of the last twenty-four hours. Everything was a blur. "I need to know how Myles is doing." Her voice sounded distant to her own ears as the precinct officers filed her transfer paperwork, completely ignoring her. No one ever seemed to listen to her. "Please, is he okay?"

"Quiet," another police officer said behind her. Brea turned, startled to see him there. She looked up, and up, to find he had the most striking midnight blue eyes she'd ever seen. "We will leave in a moment, keep your mouth shut." His tone was curt, and he looked like he didn't know how to smile, but his presence sent a wave of warmth through her, calming her fears. Everything would be fine soon. Once she got settled in the psych ward, her doctor would explain everything. That was the familiarity she needed now.

Brea followed the handsome officer with the beautiful eyes and stony frown outside into the freezing night. She didn't even have her coat. Wasn't it odd to transfer prisoners so late at night?

She ducked her head into the backseat of the police cruiser, wondering why the officer hadn't handcuffed her for the transport. The ride to Columbus would be a few hours. Maybe he thought she'd be more comfortable?

Brea's thoughts whirled from one thing to the next, like she couldn't focus on any one thought long enough to question her newest circumstances.

"Myles?" She leaned forward. "Can you tell me anything about Myles? Can you call the hospital and check on him?"

"You're better off forgetting him and whatever he might have meant to you." The voice was like warm hot chocolate. She didn't like his words, but he somehow managed to make them sound like the most soothing of responses.

"What about my parents? Did they really sign me over to Dr. Cochran?"

"As far as your parents are concerned, they never had a daughter named Brea Robinson. Now just sit back and enjoy the ride."

Brea yawned. "I don't think I like you." His voice sent an unwelcome warmth racing through her, but through the fog of her confusion, she couldn't quite work out why that was a bad thing.

It was dark when Brea woke, still in the backseat of the police cruiser—still with no idea what was happening. A spark of fear curled in her gut, and she latched on to it. It was the only true emotion she'd experienced since leaving her cell.

Gazing out the window, Brea expected to see highways and cars heading for the city. Instead, she saw trees and vast stretches of farmland. They were the only car on the dark country road. Panic seeped into her bones as she watched the man behind the wheel. She caught his gaze in the rear view mirror, his dark eyes flashing like sapphire jewels in the night. She'd seen eyes like those before.

I'm not crazy. I'm not crazy. Brea squeezed her eyes shut tight before she dared to chance a second glance at the officer.

His normal midnight blue eyes peered back at her through the mirror. *Exactly, I'm not crazy.* She breathed a sigh of relief. It was never a good thing for Brea Robinson to see things that weren't there.

"Where are you taking me?" She tried to keep the accusation from her tone, but Brea did not have a good feeling about this gruff man who claimed to be a police officer.

"Somewhere safe. Just relax. We'll be there soon."

Once again, his words had a mesmerizing effect on her. Part of her wanted to do something drastic to try to escape, but the other part of her wanted to sit back and relax like the officer suggested. Brea resisted that second part of her subconscious mind trying to tell her everything was fine when it clearly wasn't.

When the driver turned down a long winding dirt road, Brea knew what she had to do. Breathing deep and even, she calmed herself. After nearly a half-hour on the dirt road, the officer finally stopped in front of a small farmhouse in the middle of nowhere. Brea had seen her fair share of psych wards and rehabilitation centers. Not one of them looked like this dilapidated place.

The officer turned to peer into the backseat. Just before he spoke, Brea stuffed her fingers in her ears and rocked back and forth, banging her head against the back seat. It was her best impersonation of a crazy person, which she was *not*. Whenever that man spoke, strange things happened in her mind. The calm he exuded was deceptive.

"Enough of that, Brea. You aren't crazy."

He stepped from the driver's side and she repeated her mantra—and her fit. "I'm not crazy. I'm not crazy."

The moment he opened the back door, Brea shot out of the car like her hair was on fire. She ran down the dark and desolate road, the cloudy night sky offering little to light her path.

"Brea, get back here, now!" The stranger shouted after her, and Brea resisted the unnatural urge to do as he said. "I will drag you back by your hair if I have to, but you're coming with me, girl."

She didn't know where she was going, but she had to get away. If she ever wanted to know the truth about Myles, she had to go back and face the consequences of what she'd done to her best friend. If that meant spending the rest of her life in a padded cell, then maybe that was where she belonged. Maybe her parents were right to give up on her.

The stranger was gaining on her, so she darted into the woods, branches and briars lashing against her face as she ran harder and faster than she ever had before.

"Brea, you don't understand. You're making this harder than it has to be. Come back to the house before you hurt yourself."

Brea stuffed her fingers in her ears as she ran, stumbling from the dense forest into a wide-open field.

"Brea, you're acting like a brat," her assailant called. She darted a glance over her shoulder and ran right into something warm and solid.

"Get behind me. Brea, Lochlan is dangerous." The second stranger of the night shoved her behind him.

"What is this? Who *are* you people?"

"You can call me Griff, and when we get out of here, I'll explain everything, I promise." He put himself between her and the man chasing her. Griff smelled like springtime and fresh-mown grass.

"I'm not crazy. I'm not crazy, I'm not crazy," she murmured, darting her eyes around the field, looking for an escape.

"No, you aren't crazy. You're just the girl we've been looking for, but I need you to trust me, even though you have no reason to. I'm not going to trick you with mind games." He grabbed her hand and warmth spread through Brea's body at his touch.

"Hand her over, Griff." The not-police officer darted into the clearing. "She's coming with me." He moved like a predator, and Brea stumbled back to put some distance between herself and these strange men.

"You can't treat people like pawns, Loch."

"That's rich coming from you." The one named Griff moved to block her from Lochlan.

Brea watched the two men talking about her like she wasn't even there. She should run, but there was nowhere to hide. She didn't even know where she was or if any of this was even happening in reality.

"I'm not crazy. I'm not crazy." The clouds parted and the field flooded with moonlight.

"Griff, don't do it. You know I'll find you."

"Brace yourself, sweetheart." Griff pulled her into his arms and turned toward the moon. The air smelled of lavender and jasmine—two things one did not smell in the dead of an Ohio winter. The air rent in two, right before her eyes, like a piece of fabric cut with scissors.

"Oh, I'm definitely crazy." Brea closed her eyes and everything went dark.

Chapter Three

The man's—Griff's—hand clamped down on Brea's arm as the world twisted and bent around them. A wave of dizziness washed over her, but his grip kept her upright.

She tried to speak, to breathe out the protests and the questions swirling in her mind, but nothing came out.

Everything disappeared. The snow, the bare winter trees covered in a thin sheen of ice.

Even the police officer faded into the background before she couldn't see him at all. Loch, Griff had called him. His smooth voice echoed in her ears, calling after her with a mixture of fear and fury until even that was gone and all that remained was a heavy silence.

Warmth. It was the first thing she noticed. Gone was the dreary Ohio winter. She pried her eyes open to find the sun breaking through flowering trees overheard. It was the dead of night a moment ago.

Neither of them moved for a long moment before Brea finally lifted her eyes to her abductor.

His violet eyes flashed when they met hers, and that was how she knew.

She'd never left the Clarkson Institute. It was all in her head. The first day back to school never happened. She never attacked Myles, never went to prison. It was all just a terrible nightmare.

Ripping her arm from his grasp, she walked backward. "You're not real. None of this is real." She squeezed her eyes shut, hoping when she opened them, she'd see the sterile walls of her room and know she was safe.

Well, as safe as she could be when her own mind played tricks on her.

But it didn't go away. The fresh smell of spring permeated her nostrils, so different from the icy air that filled her lungs only moments ago.

"Come on, Brea," she whispered to herself. "Wake up. You're safe."

The man continued to stare at her and cocked his head, one corner of his mouth lifting into a half-smile. "Are you talking to yourself?"

"No," she huffed. Why did she even respond to him? He was just a figment of her imagination.

His lips parted into a full grin. "I hate traveling to your realm in the winter." He brushed the dusting of snow from the sleeves of his shirt.

Brea's eyes followed his movements, taking in the clothing that looked straight out of one of the fantasy movies she and Myles always watched together.

Myles. She choked on a sob and turned her back on the stranger. That part was too fresh in her mind not to be real. Her best friend was dead because of her. What had she done? The guilt opened up a chasm inside her, but no tears came. It was Brea's curse. Girls were supposed to cry, weren't they? To let their emotions out. At least, that was what Myles always said. But of the two of them, he'd been the crier.

She'd never wished for tears more than in that moment. Myles deserved every bit of emotion she could muster.

Her back shook as she tried to force them out.

"What are you doing?" The man put a hand on her back, and she jumped away from him with a yelp.

"You're not supposed to be able to touch me."

"What are you talking about?"

"Before... when I've... seen things..." She sucked in a breath. "You know what, I don't have to explain anything. You're not real." She walked forward, hoping she could find some way out of this nightmare.

Around her, blooms flourished among the trees. Her feet crunched through the crisp green grass, but they weren't the only ones.

The man followed her.

"Brea, wait."

"I'm ready to wake up now." She reached a clearing and lifted her face to the sky, begging for some higher power to make this all go away.

"You're not asleep, and you're not imagining things."

She turned to face the man who'd called himself Griff. He was ridiculously attractive—if you were into that kind of thing. His long auburn hair was tied back away from the flawless skin of his face. Intense green eyes—no longer flashing violet—locked on her, but she refused to meet them, focusing instead on the pointed tips of his ears.

"You're a delusion."

"I'm not." He crossed his arms over his chest.

"I just want to go home." To wake up in the twin bed she'd slept in since she was a kid and start this day all over again. "I never left the institute. Myles isn't dead."

Griff's expression softened, and he took a step toward her. "I'm sorry about your friend. But it wasn't your fault. You don't know how to control what's happening to you."

"Nothing is happening to me except my mind imagining things." But she felt it, the energy within her. There was no denying how it kicked her heart up a notch and latched onto her anger, her sadness.

Among all these lies, that felt like the only truth she had.

Something was very wrong with her.

Without thinking, she turned and started running, ducking back into the trees. Branches whipped her face, causing a trickle of blood to drip down over her parted lips as she crashed through the woods, trying to get away from the man pursuing her.

She panted as she leaped over a fallen tree and burst past the tree line, stopping dead in her tracks at the sight before her. Rolling green hills stretched into the distance like a painting of a lonely land, untouched and wild.

Clear blue skies topped off the picturesque landscape without a cloud in sight.

"Beautiful, isn't it?" Griff stopped beside her.

Her jaw clenched. "No." Lies, illusions, were never beautiful.

She could barely make out a house in the distance surrounded by pastures where horses grazed.

"That's home." Griff pointed to the house. "I tried to get the portal as close as I could without scaring the horses with the energy it emitted."

"Portal?" She shook her head. None of this made any sense. She walked back into the woods and sat down on the fallen tree she'd jumped over while trying to escape only moments before.

The events of the day played in her mind like a movie.

Returning to school and facing the stares of her classmates. Myles'... death. The word sat heavy in her mind.

Then the police station and the man who took her away from there. How did it all fit together?

Griff dropped to the log beside her. "I know this is all a little much, but I promise you it's real. I just need you to come with me."

"I don't even know him," she whispered to herself. On her many stays at the institute, she'd spent hours and sometimes days with no company but herself. When she got scared or nervous, she talked to herself. At school, she worked hard to hide the habit, but now the words tumbled out. "What does he want from me?"

"I'll explain everything in time." He nudged her shoulder like they were old friends, like Myles would have done.

She scooted away so he couldn't do it again. "I'm not going anywhere with you. Where's the police officer? I want him." Policemen were supposed to keep people safe, right?

Griff's congeniality dropped away and he stood. "That was no human." His eyes narrowed. "Lochlan is not to be trusted, do you understand?"

"And you are? I don't know you. I don't know where I am or how any of this is possible if I'm not just imagining it."

"You don't have a choice, Brea."

"How do you know my name?" Back in the wintery forest, he'd said her name when he pulled her away from Lochlan.

"You'll learn in time."

Anger burned through her. In time? She deserved answers right away if he wanted her to trust him. Unable to control herself, she lunged from the log, springing toward him and taking him by surprise as she tackled him to the ground.

"I want to go home," she yelled. A home she no longer had

if her parents truly had signed over their parental rights. A home that no longer included Myles.

Griff struggled beneath her before finally flipping her off and rolling them over so he pinned her to the ground. "Calm. Down."

"No." She jerked her knees up, connecting with his crotch. His face twisted in pain, but he didn't release her.

"Brea, stop."

Light exploded from her just as it had before. The pressure on top of her vanished as Griff flew across the clearing.

Unlike her mother with the Christmas tree or Myles outside the school, Griff didn't collapse to the ground. Instead, he landed in a crouch before straightening.

"Well." He grimaced. "That's something we will have to get a handle on. Get up, Brea."

She refused. Her chest heaved as she stared up at him with wide eyes. "What's happening to me? What did I do?" She buried her face in her hands.

She truly was a freak.

Griff sighed. "Cut it out with the self-pity. I want to make it home before dark."

She lifted her face to him. "I'm not going to your home." She had to find a way back to hers.

Griff shrugged. "Suit yourself. Just be careful of the wolves." He turned and started walking away.

"Wolves?" She scrambled after him.

"These woods are dangerous at night. I wouldn't want to be caught in them after dark."

"At least tell me where we are?" she pleaded.

He didn't stop walking. "The world of the fae welcomes you, Brea Robinson."

Fae? She truly had lost it.

"Why am I doing this?" Brea mumbled as she followed Griff. He even had a name that sounded like one of those characters Myles used to pretend to be when they were kids.

Why hadn't she read more fantasy books? Or paid attention to her best friend's every word about the worlds he disappeared into every night? No, instead, she nagged him about all the reading he did and waited for the movies and TV shows to come out.

During the summer, they'd hang out in one of the fields with Captain America, alternating between riding the horse and sitting against the base of a giant oak tree at the edge of the property. Myles always had a book propped up in his lap while Brea busied herself picking at the blades of grass and imagining shapes in the clouds overhead.

But that was before.

Before some kind of power she couldn't explain lived inside her.

Before she told anyone about the pointed ears and flashing eyes she saw amid crowds of people.

Before she killed Myles.

"You're going too fast." She struggled to keep up with Griff. They'd been walking for way too long, and her feet ached. "How much longer?"

"Oh, so you're talking to me now?" Griff flashed her a grin. "Your protest didn't last long."

"I just want to know how far we have to go." She tried to see the house in the distance, but as they'd descended into a valley, it disappeared from view.

"We've only been walking for half an hour."

"No way, it's been longer than that." Her foot hit a small hole in the ground, and she pitched forward.

Griff caught her before she fell. "Graceful." He laughed. "Just what I'd expect from someone raised in the human world."

Brea righted herself and pushed away from him. "What does that even mean? There's only one world."

Griff shrugged. "Maybe for those with small minds. Do you have a small mind?"

"No." She clenched her jaw. She may not have excelled at school or basically anything else, but she wasn't an idiot.

"All right, Brea Robinson, let's clear something up." His eyes locked with hers. "I will not lie to you. That is my promise. So, when I tell you something, I need you to believe it."

His voice held such sincerity she wanted to trust him, but she'd only trusted one person in her life, and he was dead.

She shifted her eyes to her ripped jeans, focusing on the patch her mom had sewn in the knee instead of buying her a new pair. Things like that reminded her who she was--a farm girl from Ohio with a history of mental instability.

Also, a girl with nothing to go back to.

"I want to believe you," she whispered. She wanted to believe there was more out there than the life she'd been living. "I just..."

His fingertips brushed her chin and tilted her face up. "Look at me, Brea Robinson. You have questions, and I will answer them in time. For now, I need you to know you're not imagining this." His touch flittered along her cheek, and she swallowed, mesmerized by his swirling eyes.

"This is real." The words released on a breath, as if breaking free of some deeper part of her.

She lived her life in lies, but as she breathed in the fresh air of a new life, a new... world?... she hoped this was anything but.

A smile tilted his lips, different from the wide grin before when he'd laughed at her. This time, there was kindness in his expression, an openness she couldn't help but be drawn to.

He reminded her so much of Myles.

"So," she swallowed as she tested the next words in her mind. "Two... worlds?"

He withdrew his hand and nodded. "You're now in the fae world. It parallels the human world you knew."

"But... how did we get here?"

"A portal." He winked. "Magic."

Her mind stuttered on that word, and Griff turned to keep walking.

She ran after him. "Magic?"

Glee shone on his face. "You have no idea."

"What is magic?"

"Why does this place look like a freaking fairytale?"

"Why is it warm here when it was so cold at home?"

"And why would you bother bringing me here? I'm nobody."

Griff grunted and turned to face her as they crossed the fields leading up to the small stone cottage that looked like it belonged in a storybook.

"I think I liked you better when you wouldn't talk to me." He pursed his lips.

She'd been peppering him with questions as they walked. It was the only thing preventing her from focusing on seeing Myles hit the ground. "Is it still the same day I was arrested?"

"No. You were arrested yesterday. You spent a day and a night in your cell before Lochlan tried to intercept my plans to get you out."

"Are you going to answer any of my other questions?" Now that she'd let herself consider he was telling the truth, she needed to know more, to know she wasn't crazy. Maybe she never had been.

He turned and gazed up at the cottage. "Have you ever wondered why they're called fairytales?"

Her eyes widened. "You're a fairy?"

"Never call me that," he growled. "I told you this was the fae world. What did you think I was?"

She shrugged. "An elf."

"An elf?" He ran a hand through his hair in agitation.

Brea barely knew this man, but she'd seen him as jovial and calm. Riling him up was fun. She crossed the stone wall encircling a small paddock in front of a barn. Hopping up, she let her legs dangle over the side. "Do you have any dwarf friends?"

"What? Dwarves don't exist."

"Sure they do. If elves are real, why can't Gimli be hanging around here somewhere?"

"I don't know who Gimli is." His eyes narrowed. "I told you this is the fae world. Why would you think I'm an elf?"

She shrugged. "No wings."

"Wings?"

"In the movies fae have wings. Like tinker bell."

He stared at her, his jaw dropping open. "Tinkerbell," he said the name slowly.

She nodded. "She's a fairy."

"I know who Tinkerbell is!"

"Wait, really? Is there a TV in that house?" A Netflix night was just what she needed to ignore the hole inside her, the guilt and doubt she'd felt since she woke up that morning.

Pushing away from the wall, she barged into the house, ignoring the thud of the wood as she let the door swing back in Griff's face.

A small room greeted her, with stone walls and a matching floor covered in sky-blue rugs. Wooden chairs faced a giant fireplace where flames lit up the room and an iron pot hung over the fire.

A door opened to her right and an older man shuffled out, stopping when he saw her.

Griff entered behind her with a chastisement she didn't hear as she stared at the new man with his pointed ears and intensely blue eyes.

She looked from him to Griff. "It's not just you. There are more." She practically fell onto a bench behind the oak table, speaking to herself. "I'm not crazy. I'm not crazy. I'm not crazy." For the first time, she started believing her mantra.

Everything she'd seen as a kid... A realization struck her. "There are more of you in the human realm." They were the reason she'd been at the institute.

The older man raised one eyebrow before moving to the fire to stir whatever he had cooking in the pot. Her mouth watered as she realized she hadn't eaten anything since breakfast.

She pointed to the pot. "Is that for me?"

"Brea, this is Leith, a loyal servant." Griff lowered himself into a chair with an exhausted sigh.

Leith offered her a kind smile before spooning the stew into a ceramic bowl and setting it in front of her. "Welcome to Fargelsi, Miss Robinson."

"Far-what-see?" And how did everyone seem to know her name?

"Fargelsi is the forest realm." Griff leaned his head back. "We just call it Gelsi." He took a bowl from Leith. "Thank you."

Brea poked at the stew with her spoon, not knowing what the chunks were. She'd never been picky, eating whatever cheap food her parents put in front of her. With a shrug, she dug in, shoveling stew into her mouth like she hadn't eaten in weeks.

It was the best thing she'd ever tasted, but that was probably the hunger speaking.

Leith sat beside Griff and the two men spoke in low tones. The older man obviously deferred to Griff, but she wanted—needed—to know why.

Her mind drifted back to the police officer, the one who'd flashed her an unnatural look just like Griff's before hiding his eyes. His hat had covered his ears, but somehow, she knew—he too was fae.

"That man..." she started, unsure of how to continue. "The one who..."

"Lochlan?" Griff's gaze darkened as he shared an indecipherable look with Leith.

She nodded. "You... I can't figure out if you saved me from him or abducted me."

"The answer to that won't change anything. You're here."

"And I'm guessing you won't let me leave?"

He smiled in apology. "It's too dangerous. And yes, one of those dangers is Lochlan. You will learn soon enough, Brea, this realm holds many perils, including the three rulers vying for power. Lochlan's master is the Queen of the fire realm—Eldur."

She pushed her bowl away, suddenly not hungry anymore as the reality of her situation struck her. "What do you want with me?"

Griff stood and crossed to the table to sit on the opposite bench from her. He reached out and brushed the back of her hand, sending a calming wave of energy straight through her. "It's okay, Brea. I won't let anything happen to you, that's why my queen sent me to find you."

Her eyes drooped as she suddenly grew sleepy, but he hadn't answered all of her questions yet. Shaking off the weariness, she sat up straighter. "I'm nobody, nothing. Why am I here with two fae trying to pull me into their world? And what could a queen possibly want with me?"

"That's where you're wrong, Brea Robinson." He said her name like a blessing, and she couldn't help but lean in, wanting to hear more, needing his words to calm her racing heart. "You're everything."

Brea woke the next morning with no recollection of how she got into the small barren room to begin with. The last thing she remembered was eating some kind of stew and listening to Griff's mesmerizing voice.

You're everything.

When he said it, she believed him. There was something about the beautiful fae that tugged on her limited trust, making her want to know him, to know his world.

A crack of thunder ripped through the air, and her head

jerked up off the feather pillow. Rain hammered on the glass panes of the window overlooking the barn. A sliver of sunlight breaking through the clouds cut across the dark wool carpet spanning the room.

"Fairytale, my butt," she grumbled. If this was a fairytale world, the bed would have been as soft as clouds and she'd have been awakened by singing birds instead of a roaring storm.

Lightning flashed across the room, illuminating the tiny wooden bed, small table in the corner, and single chair.

That was it. No decorations or other comforts.

As she sat up, wild ebony hair fell across her shoulders and into her face. She searched the bed for the rubber hair tie she'd used to hold it back the day before, but it wasn't there.

That was when she noticed it.

The sleeping gown.

Her hands grabbed frantically at the silk garment covering her small frame. Where were her clothes? "He undressed me." Her cheeks flamed as she imagined Griff's smooth hands sliding the faded jeans down her legs and his intense green eyes taking her in.

She jumped from the bed and searched the room for her clothes, finding none.

The white gown only reached mid-thigh and a chill raced through her.

She was going to kill him. Was murder acceptable in this new world? Maybe if she got arrested again, a human would come save her and take her home.

A strangled laugh escaped her lips at the thought. Griff abducted her after she killed Myles. The guilt she'd tried so hard to ignore, clawed at her, ripping through the shreds of sanity she had left.

She had to get out of here.

Sprinting the short distance across the room, she yanked on the cold metal door handle.

It didn't budge.

She pulled again.

Locked.

Slamming her foot into the door, she tried to control the anger rising up in her. "Griff, you let me out of here right now." He'd taken her from her home, turned her entire world upside down, and now locked her away.

Just when she'd started thinking he might be the good guy...

"Griff!" she screamed.

The door handle rattled seconds before Leith opened it. "Good morning, Brea." He smiled kindly. "I thought you might like some breakfast."

"Where's Griff?" She crossed her arms.

"He had some business at the palace, but he'll return soon."

"The palace?" She swallowed.

He nodded. "Griffin is a loyal companion of Queen Regan of Gelsi. I'm sure you'll meet her in time."

A queen? Brea wasn't the kind of girl to meet anyone important. But she didn't say that. Her stomach growled and she pointed to the plate Leith held. "Is that mine?"

He nodded and entered the room to set it on the table. She was ready to attack the stack of perfect, fluffy pancakes covered in some kind of green berry she didn't recognize.

"Try the Gelsi berries." He winked. "You won't regret it."

He left before she had a chance to say anything else. Giving in, she slumped into the chair and took a tiny bite of a berry. A mixture of sweet and sour juices exploded in her mouth. "Oh, goodness," she groaned, taking another bite.

Before she knew it, the plate sat empty and she wished there was more.

As the storm continued to rage outside, weariness clouded

her mind. If Griff was gone, she might as well crawl back into bed and pretend for just a few more hours everything was as it should be.

"Myles!" Brea screamed, shooting up in bed, her chest heaving.

He was a prominent figure in every dream she'd had since arriving in the fae world. She didn't know how long ago that was or why she just wanted to stay in bed. Dr. Cochran probably would have told her she was depressed, but she just felt so tired.

Every time she woke, she found a plate from Leith, but she hadn't seen him since he brought the first meal. None of the meals since had anything like pancakes. Instead, he seemed to think she could live on nuts and fruit. No matter how good the fruit was, it was never enough.

More than anything, she wanted a hamburger.

But something told her she couldn't just ask Leith to head over to Wendy's.

"Ughhh," she sighed. "I want a Frosty." Instead, she ate what he offered.

Each time she tried to open the door, it was locked, but the anger she'd been known for didn't come. In fact, few emotions did. It was almost like her world of vibrant colors had turned into shades of gray.

She'd even tried summoning whatever that light blast thing was so she could get out of this room and away from the people imprisoning her, but to no avail.

Each day Griff didn't return was another she hoped he never did.

He told her to trust him, that he'd never lie to her.

But this room was a prison just like her room at the

Clarkson Institute and the actual prison cell she'd occupied before Lochlan showed up.

She sniffed the sleeping gown she'd been wearing since that first night and wrinkled her nose. Her hair was matted across the back of her head.

And still, the storm outside raged on, never ending, never quieting.

Lying on her bed, she rested her head on the pillow and tried to summon some kind of sadness or fear or guilt. Just... something.

It didn't come.

"I want to go home," she whispered to herself. She wanted to return to a mom who gave up on her, a dad who didn't understand her, and classmates who ridiculed her.

Yet, that desire for normalcy was an abstract feeling, not one she could grasp or hold on to. It was always just out of reach.

"I hate you, Griff whatever-your-last-name-is."

Even those words had no power behind them.

Wherever she went in life, she was a prisoner, held down by her circumstances. The world she'd known didn't exist for her anymore, yet neither did this one. It couldn't.

So, why had nothing ever felt more real?

In this world that was nothing more than a fairytale, why did her prison hurt more than it had before?

Her appetite gone after so many days in the same room, Brea knocked the plate from Leith's hands the moment he appeared.

"I can't eat any more of that stupid fruit." For the first time in days, her anger returned in small waves.

Calmly, Leith bent to clean up the mess, and Brea saw her

chance. She darted past him into the main room, searching for a way out. Lunging for the front door, Brea stumbled into a world recovering from the storms.

A spotted horse lifted its head to regard her, and she met familiar brown eyes. No, not familiar because she knew the animal, but only because horses were one of the few creatures she understood, and riding was one of the few activities she'd ever been good at.

Considering her options, she looked from the horse to the path leading away from the cottage. Making a quick decision, she climbed over the low stone wall and approached the horse.

"I'm a friend," she whispered. "Please help me get out of here."

The horse stamped its foot and neighed.

"Stop!" Leith yelled.

As if that word held power, Brea's limbs immobilized, stuck in a current that threatened to drag her under.

She tried to free herself, to get away, but the servant approached with sad eyes. "I'm sorry, Brea, but I have orders. I can't let you leave."

"You can't keep me locked away forever!" she screamed. "What does Griff want from me?"

His expression told her he wanted to answer, or maybe even that he wanted to let her go. Instead, he drew a circle in the air with his hand, and Brea's entire body turned, moving closer to the house.

"I cannot disobey orders." He lowered his gaze. "Not even for you."

What did that mean? She tried to ask, but her lips wouldn't move as the invisible force pulled her back into the room she thought she'd escaped. Leith stood looking at her as the door shut, but he didn't say another word.

The power released Brea, and she slumped against the

door. Banging a fist weakly against the wood, she called out. "Please. Let me go." Her knees gave out and she sank to the hard floor. "Please."

A rattle sounded, but the door didn't open. Instead, a slot appeared at its base and a new plate of fruit slid through the opening. Brea lowered herself to her side and picked at the fruit, knowing it wouldn't fill the emptiness inside her.

During her long nights locked up at the Clarkson Institute, she'd known there was someone waiting for her to get out, someone who cared.

Now, she was totally and utterly alone.

The only person left to save her was herself.

If this was a fairytale, Brea Robinson had to be both the damsel and the knight, because there was no one left to come for her.

Chapter Five

It was the fruit.

It had to be. That was the only thing that made sense. Over the last several days since her escape attempt, the only thing Brea looked forward to were the Gelsi berries Leith brought her at every meal. The tart fruit was good, but it wasn't *that* good. She shouldn't crave it like she did. She was never particularly hungry after those first few days, but Brea *needed* those berries. Her body trembled whenever Leith was late.

Brea had grown to like the numb feeling she'd experienced since her latest incarceration. The distant, detached feeling that made her so sleepy she didn't have the energy to contemplate her situation. Crazy. Not crazy. It didn't matter.

Brea rolled onto her side, thinking about getting up. Leith would be here soon with her breakfast. It was the highlight of her morning. After, she'd go back to sleep until lunch. Unless she didn't eat the Gelsi berries today. She'd told herself yesterday she wouldn't eat them. Or was that the day before?

"That's different." She sat up, blinking to make sure she

wasn't seeing things. Not like that would be unusual for Brea Robinson, but the door appeared to be open. "Leith?" she whispered, stumbling across the room to the doorway and peeking into the hall. No one was in the hall outside her door.

Still wearing her soiled sleeping gown, Brea crept into the front room and bolted for the door when she found no one waiting to haul her back to her cell. She didn't waste a moment this time. Brea ran across the yard, not even bothering with the horse. She wasn't going to screw this up again.

The too-green grass was like a plush carpet beneath her feet. Brea, weak from her days of sleeping too much, stumbled into the cover of the forest, gasping for breath. Casting a look back at the cottage, she saw that still no one followed her. It was odd, but she wasn't sticking around long enough to find out why.

Brea's feet skimmed over moss-covered stones and massive tree roots along the pathway through the woods. She'd never seen such a forest, bursting with energy like a living, breathing thing, watching over her.

"Now, you're really losing it, Brea."

Sunlight dappled the ground through the tall, sweeping branches above. Species of trees she couldn't remember ever seeing before flourished in this fairytale forest. Exotic blooms in a riot of colors sprouted from every available surface. There was so much to see, Brea didn't know where to look first. It was breathtaking. Still, she watched over her shoulder. As beautiful as it was, the forest gave her a creepy vibe. Like if she looked under the surface, she'd find something dark and twisted waiting to strike. It was eerily quiet. It took her a while to figure it out. There were no birds singing in the trees. The only sound in the forest was the wind whistling through the branches.

After all she'd experienced in the last few days, Brea no longer trusted anything she saw. She no longer trusted anyone, least of all herself. She had no idea where she was going. She only knew she needed to get away from her jailor and his freaky fruit long enough to clear her head and make a plan.

With that thought in mind, she kept going, following the pathway through the forest. She had no doubt Leith and Griff could track her and drag her back, but she had to try.

Finally stumbling from the forest, Brea found herself in a clearing beside a beautiful lake. Beautiful was such an arbitrary word to describe what she saw. If the forest was breathtaking, then the lake was out of this world. A laugh bubbled up inside her at that thought. She clapped a hand over her mouth to keep her laughter in check. Clearly, she wasn't in Kansas anymore.

Azure water rippled in the cool breeze. As Brea peered into the lake, she realized it was deceptively deep. She could see the rocky bottom like it was only a few feet away, but her eyes played tricks on her. Brea wondered how strong the current was as she watched leaves drift and swirl a little too fast on the calm surface.

Impossibly high mountains bordered the lake on the far side, with a cascading waterfall crashing down from the snow-capped peaks. Behind her lay the forest and the prison-cottage she'd left behind, but to the south lay rolling green hills dotted with trees and Gelsi berry bushes as far as she could see. She could walk for days in either direction and not meet another living soul.

Brea walked along the edge of the lake, hopping from one moss covered boulder to the next, contemplating her next moves. Catching a whiff of herself in the breeze, she almost choked. She couldn't remember the last time she showered, and the lake called to her. The water was so clear under the sparkling sunshine, she wanted nothing more than to dive right in and not come up for air until she was clean. Edging closer to the water, Brea caught her reflection in the surface.

Gasping, she knelt, staring at herself. "I'm seeing things again," she whispered, reaching to touch the tips of her ears. Her pointed ears. Tucking her hair behind one of them, she leaned in closer.

All her life she'd caught glimpses of the people with pointed ears. They always had fathomless eyes too. And she'd convinced herself they weren't real. But now she was seeing those same features in her own reflection. She knew she should be freaking out right about now, but the only thing Brea felt was a weird sort of... relief. Finally, here was physical proof she wasn't seeing things that weren't there. If she could see it and feel it for herself, it had to be real, right?

Feeling suddenly giddy, Brea stood and lifted her foot. She wanted to see how cold the water was before she waded in.

"I wouldn't do that if I were you." The voice caught her by surprise, and she almost fell in right there. But Griff reached out and pulled her away from the water. "Loch Villandi is beautiful but dangerous."

"Dangerous?" Brea couldn't seem to break her gaze away from the water.

"Beautiful things often have a sharp bite." He lifted her chin, forcing her to meet his eyes. "The Villandi waters have claimed many lives. On the surface, she looks harmless and inviting, but underneath lies a heartless current that will sweep you into the bottomless depths never to be seen again. It is best to leave her be."

"I wish you'd leave me be." Shrugging out of his grip, she ran back to the relative safety of the forest. But she wondered how dangerous it was. If Loch Villandi was treacherous, then the forest surrounding it must be too.

"And where would you go if I left you to your own devices?"

"Home." Brea lifted her chin.

"And how would you get back to the human world?"

"I... I will find someone to help me do that portal thing you did."

"You'll be looking from now until forever if that's your plan. Only those of my clan can open a portal between realms to bring fae or humans through, and most of them are long dead."

"What do you want from me?" Brea stomped her foot in the grass. "I'm nobody."

"You have never been *nobody,* Brea Robinson. I thought I told you that already."

"Then tell me what's so special about me that you stole me away from my home at the worst possible moment?"

"I thought it was rather good timing seeing as how you were recently arrested and in the company of a dangerous man." Griff scratched the stubble on his chin. She'd thought elves were supposed to be all smooth-skinned and hairless, but he had a handsome ruggedness about him.

"I'm tired of your games, Elf. Either take me home or leave me be."

"I told you, I am fae. I am not an elf, a fairy, or a nymph, or any other such creature the humans dreamed up."

"Fine, Fae-man-person. Whatever you are. Take me home."

"I can't do that. But I can take you back to the cottage, offer you a hot meal and a warm bath. Fresh clothes and answers to your questions. And you may call me Griff."

"What about your cage? There is no way I'm going back in there, and you can keep your freaky tranquilizer fruit for yourself. I'm done with that stuff."

"I am sorry about that, Brea, truly. I did not mean to treat you like a prisoner. My queen summoned me, and I must go to her when she has need of me. There was no time to explain everything you need to know. I only wanted to make you comfortable and safe while I was gone."

"Here's a little note for the comment card. The next time you have a guest at your little fairytale B&B, don't lock them up."

"I don't know what most of that means, but if you will remember, I told you I will never lie to you. Come with me, and I will explain everything."

"Fine." Brea crossed her arms over her chest. "You can start by explaining how I suddenly have pointy ears."

"You've always had them." He set off for the forest path, gesturing for her to follow. "You were glamoured so neither you nor anyone else could see them."

"Glamoured?" Brea walked beside him.

"It's a Fae thing. Someone didn't want you or anyone in your life to know what you are."

"Which is what? You're saying I'm Fae?"

"You are a human-Fae hybrid. That, among many other things, is what makes you special." He paused. "Yet you don't seem at all upset by this revelation."

"It explains a lot." Brea couldn't seem to stop touching her new ears. "So you're saying my mother had an affair with a Fae person? That makes zero sense. If you knew my mother, you'd agree. She's not the adventurous sort."

"I don't know how it happened, but your birth father was Fae."

"Was? So he's dead?"

"Unfortunately."

"That still doesn't explain why your queen seems to have an interest in me." Brea's stomach growled. She hadn't had anything to eat all day.

"Here, have a silver fig, I picked them fresh this morning." He pulled a handful of figs from his bag.

Brea's eyes widened in alarm when he tossed her the fruit.

"No strange side effects, I promise. I'll have one myself." He proceeded to peel back the silvery skin of the fig and made a show of eating it to prove it wasn't freaky like the berries.

"Fine." Brea was too hungry to argue with him. "But you still haven't answered my question." She peeled the shimmery skin from the fruit and tried not to moan at the taste of the fig. She swore she could taste the sun in that first bite.

"That's a complicated question with a long answer." Griff scratched his head.

"I've got nothing but time it seems. Start talking."

Griffin walked ahead of her, staring up into the clear blue sky for a moment before turning back to her. "The Fae realm is ancient. Ages older than the human world. Within it, there are three distinct realms. We are in Fargelsi now. Gelsi is an exotic realm of lush forests and wild lands. It's warm and sunny almost all year here. To the north lies the Iskalt kingdom. It is very cold there with massive mountain ranges and frozen lakes. It's a rather bleak and cruel land, but beautiful in its own way.

"The third realm to the east is Eldur, by far the largest. It's the fire realm. Desert wastelands in the north and hot springs and marshes to the south. Between each of these realms are the Vatlands. Neutral territories you never want to visit.

"Across Loch Villandi and beyond the deserts of Eldur, lie the Eastern Vatlands, also called the fire plains. The Northern Vatlands separate Iskalt and Fargelsi. Vast rocky mountain ranges where you could get lost for the rest of your life. The Southern Vatlands are the marshlands and putrid swamps filled with frightening creatures."

"Great geography lesson, but that still doesn't answer my question. Why does a Fae queen have any interest in me?"

"As you can probably imagine, the three realms have not always gotten along." Griff kept walking and talking, seemingly bent on not answering her question. But at least she was learning something. The most important being that she had never been crazy at all.

"The Eldur queens have always believed they should rule over all the realms and that Gelsi and Iskalt should serve them. Naturally, the Gelsi queen and the Iskalt king don't feel the same."

"So you're at war or something?"

"Not at the moment. But there have been wars over this issue throughout the ages. The Eldur queen wants all the power for herself, but we are determined to maintain our independence."

"What does any of this have to do with me?"

"I'm getting there." Griff shot her an impatient look. "We are a people steeped in ancient magic. Here in Gelsi, its people draw their power from the forests and nature. In Eldur, the sun fuels their power, but only during the day. Iskalt is a dark and icy realm, and it's people draw their power from the moon, but only at night."

"What does—?"

"Patience, Brea. I'm trying to explain magic to someone who just learned magic exists."

She inclined her head. "Fair enough. Go on."

"Each realm has their own strengths and weaknesses. But one thing we all have in common is the gift of prophecy. Our histories are littered with prophecies."

"So all Fae can see the future?"

"No, not all. Only a select few true seers are born into each realm every generation, and they are greatly revered."

Brea didn't like where this was going at all. If Griff was about to tell her there was some kind of prophecy about her, she was getting the hell out of this place.

"All of the seers of the last three generations have spoken

about a young girl, born of a human mother and a Fae father. Left to live in the human world, never knowing what she was until she came of age and was unable to control her power any longer. This Fae-human hybrid has the power to save Fargelsi from the encroaching fires of Eldur. She has the power to thwart the Eldur queens and bring peace to our world forever."

"And you think that's me?" Brea wanted to laugh but she also felt the hot burn of tears in her eyes and her throat constricted in panic. This was insane, and she had a lot of experience with insanity.

"You fit every single criteria of the prophecy, Brea. That the Queen of Eldur sent Lochlan after you only proves it. She will stop at nothing to get her hands on you. I almost missed it, Brea." He stopped walking at the edge of the forest. The cottage was in view now, but Brea just shook her head in disbelief. "I almost let him take you, and I will never forgive myself for it. You are far too important to fall into the hands of Eldur."

"I'm nobody, Griff." Her voice came out small and shaky. "I'm not important."

"You belong to Fargelsi. This is your home, Brea. Your father was our queen's oldest brother. She is your aunt, and she's gone to great lengths to find you and bring you home safely."

"My aunt is a queen? A magical fae queen?" Brea couldn't wrap her head around such madness. "But I don't have powers." She couldn't be this prophecy girl who was supposed to be some kind of savior.

"I beg to differ. You aren't of age yet, so your true power has not fully manifested, but it's strong already. Have you ever felt like your emotions spiral out of control without warning? Like you feel things so much stronger than others? Like if you make one wrong move, you might drown in a sea of those emotions?"

"Yes," she whispered. "It's like that all the time. Like if I let myself really feel things, there's this energy brewing just under the surface. It scares me."

"That's what happened with your friend, Myles. Unfortunately, he got in the way at a pivotal moment when you weren't in control. That is why you have to come with me, Brea. We have to teach you how to master your emotions so you never lose control like that again. And we have to do it before you come of age on your next birthday. If we wait any longer, it will be too late."

"Myles died because I lost control of something I didn't even know I had? How could she do this to me?" Brea wanted to rage at her mother. "She knew I wasn't fully human but she just let me think I was crazy!"

"Take a deep breath, Brea. You can't get upset now. It's likely your mother never knew the man that fathered her child was Fae."

"I'm so mad I could just..." She wanted to tear the world apart with her bare hands. Even now she could feel the energy buzzing just below her skin. She couldn't let her emotions get the better of her.

"We can talk more later. Right now, let's get you inside and comfortable. You can have a hot bath, and Leith will have a big meal waiting for you when you're done. And if you want, you can have some more Gelsi berries. I really wasn't trying to drug you. The berries will help keep your power dormant so you don't hurt anyone."

Brea nodded. "Perhaps that is best." The last thing she wanted was to hurt anyone like she had Myles. She was beginning to realize how lucky she was that Griff had found her when he had. She shuddered to think what might have happened if Lochlan had taken her to the Eldur Queen.

Griffin O'Shea was unlike anyone Brea had ever met. In a way, he reminded her of Myles with his sneaky grin and twinkling eyes. There was a certain joy in his demeanor. He was also different from her best friend though. Myles never took anything seriously. It was one of the things Brea loved about him, even when it frustrated her.

Griff… After only a few days with him, Brea came to realize he internalized everything, never trivializing. There was a depth to every word he spoke, a meaning behind every action.

Including imprisoning her. He'd said it was for her own good, and she was starting to think he truly had wanted to keep her safe.

She sat atop the stone wall watching Griff work with one of his horses. If she discounted the leather knee pants and loose linen shirt he wore, she could almost imagine they were back home on Myles' farm.

The Robinsons hadn't kept horses since she was a kid. Her parents sold Bellamare, her horse, claiming poverty. It probably wasn't a lie, but some part of her had always thought they did it to get back at her for not being the daughter they wanted.

Had her dad known she wasn't his daughter? In the two days since her conversation by the lake with Griff, she'd gone over every memory she had of him. They'd never been close, and she blamed herself for that. He'd never known how to deal with her problems—like seeing things that weren't there. What would he say if he found out she hadn't been imagining things after all?

She laughed at the thought. He'd never believe her. Just like he hadn't believed her when she said she hadn't meant to hurt her mom on Christmas.

Was there more to it?

She lifted her face to the sun that had been a constant companion during the day ever since the storm. Heat brushed down her bare arms, and she wiped her hands on the blue sheathe-dress Griff had found for her. He'd laughed when she insisted on wearing pants under it, but he'd fetched her a pair before watching her tie the dress at her waist.

There were a lot of things about this place that didn't make sense. How did he have clothes in her size? Where did he obtain the food they ate? She doubted there were grocery stores or shopping malls nearby.

And how on earth had he gotten her into the sleeping gown she'd first woken up in? She hadn't thought about that until it was time to change into something else.

"You look like you're thinking too hard." Griff led his stallion toward her perch.

"Griff, how did I end up in a sleeping gown?"

He lifted one brow. "I did not change you if that's what you're asking." He winked. "Magic."

That word sent a shiver down her spine.

He smoothed the creases on her brow with a finger. "Stop second guessing everything."

"Just trying to figure this place out."

"Well, when you do, fill me in." He grinned. "I'd like to figure it out myself."

She raised an eyebrow. "Haven't you lived here your entire life? You're connected to the queen, of all people. I think you're fine."

He tied the horse's lead to the gate and hopped up beside her, swinging his leg over the stone wall to straddle it and face her. "Don't let us scare you."

"What?"

"I threw a lot of information at you about wars and all that jazz."

"Don't say all that jazz."

"Why not?"

"You're some fantasy creature. You should be speaking all formally or something."

His smile widened. "First of all, I'm not a creature. Just think of me as someone from another country."

"Fat chance of that."

"Second, I've picked up a few phrases from the human realm. That one is my favorite." He cocked his head. "You wouldn't happen to know what it means, would you?"

A laugh broke past her lips. "It's just... never mind. Too much for your fairy mind."

"Nothing is too much for my mind." He jumped from the wall, landing in mud. "Come on. If we have to sit around while waiting for the queen to summon us, then we can at least have some fun."

"Fun?"

"Yes. I'm going to teach you how to ride a horse. Once the queen calls us, you'll need to be comfortable on a horse."

Her lips twitched. Yes, this would be fun. She may not have had her own horse since she was little, but she'd spent more time at Myles' farm than her own, and he'd had plenty.

Her heart squeezed at the thought, but she ignored the feeling as she'd been doing since he died. Myles and high school felt like a different life now. One that belonged to someone else. If this was her new reality, she had to embrace it. She couldn't help but think that was what Myles would want her to do.

Hopping from the wall, she avoided the mud and approached the nearest horse. "What's his name?" The horse bucked up with a neigh, kicking his feet toward her.

"Mack." Griff pulled her back. "Careful, he can be a bit difficult."

Brea bit back a smile and nodded seriously. "I'm going to need help handling such a wild horse."

"Oh no, you won't be riding him. I've got the perfect mare for you." He clucked his tongue and called, "Maisie." A beautiful gray mare approached from the barn. She was on the smallish side with a white streak stretching from mane to nose. "Maisie is an easy girl. She'll take care of you."

Okay, she'd play his game to see how far she could take it. It was her first day not eating any of the Gelsi berries, and the energy within her burned for release. She had to do something.

Griff saddled both horses quickly and led them to the gate that stood open to the rolling hills beyond. "I don't want to go into the forest with a new rider, so we'll head toward the hills."

Brea looked to her hands. "I'm going to need your big strong muscles to help me get up into the saddle."

"Hey." Griff bumped her shoulder. "Don't be embarrassed about needing help. Humans are hopeless when it comes to this kind of thing. You have your steel motor things."

"You mean cars?" She laughed.

He helped her into the saddle, and she grabbed the reins, waiting for him to climb up onto Mack.

"Maisie will follow Mack," he said. "Just work on keeping your balance. Use your thighs. We'll take it slow."

"I just hope I don't fall off." She looked away as a smile came unbidden to her lips.

Griff reached toward her, patting her hand. "You won't. I promise you'll be okay."

His sincerity made her almost feel bad for taking the lie so far. Almost. For the first time since watching Myles hit the ground, she was enjoying herself, and she didn't want it to end.

Griff nudged Mack forward, and they took off slowly down into the lush valley of swaying grasses and wheat fields. If she closed her eyes, she could imagine she rode beside her best friend, enjoying summer in their small Ohio town.

She focused on the familiar feel of the horse beneath her, the fresh scent of the spring day. Only, it wasn't spring, at least, she didn't think so. Did Gelsi ever get cold, or was it just an idyllic land full of singing birds and blooming flowers?

She wondered if she could ever be content staying here. There certainly wasn't anything for her in Ohio, no family she missed, no friends to call her home.

Running a hand down Maisie's neck, she spoke to the horse. "You're lucky this is your home, girl."

She hadn't meant for Griff to hear her. "It can be yours too."

Her head snapped up, but she didn't respond.

Griff went on. "You're the queen's niece. Gelsi is just as much your home as it is mine. You've already accepted this is real."

"How do you know that?"

"When I look into your eyes, the doubt that used to cloud your every thought is gone. If you let yourself admit it, everything I've told you makes sense. Queen Regan is going to welcome you into her court, and if you choose, we can be your people."

Her people? Other than Myles, she'd never had people before. Unless you included the countless psychiatrists and institute employees.

Griff's gaze held so much hope. Why did he want her there? The question never passed her lips because as she lifted her eyes to the most beautiful landscape she'd ever seen, she realized she didn't want there to be any ulterior motives.

So, she decided to trust. In Griff. In this unknown queen. In life's karma, because she'd been through so much crap, she'd earned a little good—even if that came in the form of elves taking her away from her home. If karma did truly exist, Legolas was here somewhere ready to confess his undying love. She just hoped he truly did look like Orlando Bloom.

She laughed to herself.

"What's so funny?" Griff asked.

"You wouldn't happen to be spiriting me away to Mordor, would you?"

His brow scrunched in confusion. "No. We're just riding horses."

She swallowed another laugh. "Okay, good."

Brea didn't know when Griff packed food into his saddlebags or how she didn't see him do it, but he kept producing wrapped parcels like the bags were one of those clown cars where the creepy clowns just kept appearing.

"You spell those saddlebags or something?" She sat underneath the single tree atop the hill where Griff had brought her.

Flowers spread across the valley on the other side, an explosion of yellows and reds.

Griff gave her a what-are-you-talking-about look. "We don't do spells. That's not how our magic works."

"Calm down. It was a joke."

He set a blanket down and placed a loaf of bread at the center, along with several hunks of cheese and dried meat, and a wrapped bunch of figs before plunking himself down. Brea reached forward for some cheese but jerked her hand back when grasses grew up over her lap.

Jumping to her feet, she backed away. "What the heck?"

Griff shrugged, a small smile playing on his lips.

Flowers popped up from where there had been none before, and the faint breeze turned into a wind tunnel aimed directly at Brea. She started running, but it followed her, blowing her hair across her face.

Only moments ago, she'd marveled at how amazing this place was. Now, she didn't like it one bit.

"Griff!" she yelled. "I know you're doing this. Stop!"

"Stop it yourself!" he called back.

How dare he? Dark anger fizzled down her arms, pooling in her hands. This wasn't funny. Power seeped out of her fingertips.

"Release it, Brea."

"I don't know how!"

Light shone underneath her fingernails as she flicked them toward the wind tunnel, wanting, needing it to work.

Nothing did.

So, she did the only thing she could think of, the one thing she was good at.

She ran.

Mack stood closest, and she launched herself into his saddle the way Myles taught her to without any help. Digging her heels into his sides, she urged Mack into a run and took off down into the flowering valley, thundering across the beautiful landscape, leaving trampled flowers in her wake.

Story of her life.

It took her a moment to realize the wind tunnel hadn't followed her. She pulled back on the reins, and Mack reared up as he neighed. She squeezed her thighs to keep her seat as he thudded back down and turned back to the hill where Griff stood watching her.

As she neared him, the shock on his face sent a wave of satisfaction through her. He deserved it after trying to force some kind of magic out of her, a magic she hadn't known about until a few days ago.

That was the one part of all this that still didn't feel real.

"You lied to me." His jaw clenched.

She shrugged and jumped down from Mack, landing gracefully. "It's called hustling." She bumped his shoulder as she walked past him to get to the food. "Maybe if you weren't so bent on helping the poor weak human girl learn basic things, you'd realize I'm more than you think." She sat down and ripped a hunk of bread off the loaf.

He kneeled across from her. "But... that... I don't even ride that well."

"That sounds like a you problem." She laughed at his stunned expression. "I grew up on a farm, Griff, of course I know how to ride horses."

He still hadn't taken his eyes from her. "What more don't I know about you, Brea Robinson?"

She met his gaze. "This magic—or whatever cheesy way you weirdoes describe it—I can't do it. I can't control it. The next time you try to make me, I'll throw you in that deceptively beautiful lake. And I won't cry when the mermaids eat you."

"What's a mermaid?"

"Seriously? Don't all you fairytale people know each other?" She wasn't sure what existed or didn't exist anymore, but this fae world made her realize anything was possible.

Griff smiled. "I think I like you."

She grunted. "Well, everyone has their flaws."

Waiting sucked. Brea started losing track of the days since Griff pulled her through that portal. Not much changed in the cottage she'd considered idyllic at first. Now, it was mostly boring.

She spent most of her time with Mack and Maisie, enjoying their stoic silence. Leith was like a ghost. Tasks got done, but they rarely saw him. Each evening, Brea sat at the table across from Griff to eat dinner. It was becoming her favorite time of day, the only time he wasn't busy and would sit there for hours talking to her about anything and everything.

She'd never been much of a talker with anyone other than Myles, but something about this man brought it out of her. She told him stories of the human world, though he knew the basics since he'd traveled there a few times on missions for his queen.

Even the topic of Myles came up. He assured her what happened wasn't her fault, but if she couldn't blame herself, then who? It was easier not to think about it, and Griff made that easy. His charming smiles and gregarious stories filled her with a kind of laughter she'd rarely experienced in her life.

One night, he leaned across the table, meeting her eyes. "Let's go outside."

"Why?"

One corner of his mouth curved up. "Do you have to question everything?"

"Yes." Despite her protests, she stood and gestured for him

to follow her out into the warm night air. A full moon shone brightly overhead, surrounded by a scattering of stars.

"I used to watch the stars a lot at home." She sat on the ground and leaned back against the side of the cottage. "We had a barn behind the house. I'd climb into the loft and out the window to pull myself onto the roof."

She hadn't even brought Myles there. It was a place that belonged to her alone. And now Griff.

"Sounds dangerous." There was no chastisement in his tone, only curiosity.

"I know you think humans are so... breakable, but trust me, it was better than being inside my house."

"Why?"

She didn't want to explain the sordid details of her family or her parents' constant berating to a man she barely knew, no matter how much she'd started to trust him. "That's a story for a different time." She leaned forward against her knees and drew in the dirt near her feet. "So... elves... do you all like live forever and stuff?"

His lips quirked at the term elves, but he didn't correct her for once. "Not forever, but we do live longer than humans."

"Let me guess... you're over a hundred years old."

He laughed. "Thanks for that. I didn't think I looked a day over sixty. No, I'm nineteen."

She looked up. "Only two years older than me. I... didn't expect that. How come you live out here all alone then?"

"I'm not alone. I have Leith, Mack, and Maisie."

She leveled him with a stare.

He looked away, and she wondered what he was hiding.

"You don't have to tell me."

A sigh rattled through his chest. "It's just... I didn't have the best upbringing. Queen Regan saved me after my parents died. She raised me, but she also realized court life wasn't for me. I need space to think, to just be me. That probably doesn't make any sense."

"No." She reached for his hand, threading her fingers through his. "It makes perfect sense." She'd never done well around other people, preferring animals and a desolate farm to parties and class. Griff could have lived in a palace surrounded by opulent things, but he would have had to change who he was to do it.

He squeezed her hand. "You know... when my queen found out the Eldur queen's dog was going to the human realm to bring you here, I prayed she wouldn't send me after him, after you. Humans hold little interest for me, but you... you're different." Silver light reflected off his dark eyes, giving them an ethereal glow. "I'm sorry I imprisoned you."

"I understand why you did it," she whispered. This place was dangerous, and he'd known she'd try to escape. If he hadn't locked her up, she'd probably be dead.

He tapped the back of her hand with his thumb. "Don't agree with me."

"Why?"

"Because I enjoy your biting tongue."

She laughed. "Fine. You're an idiot who did an idiot thing."

"That was weak."

"If you ever try to lock me up again, I'll rip off your man-bits and feed them to Mack."

"Whoa..." He crossed his legs. "Too far."

"Sorry."

"You should be."

She bumped his shoulder, and he turned to face her. The lines of his face looked smoother in the shadows, his stubble hidden by the dark. Griff was a character from a book, not someone who should exist in real life. And yet... there he sat in front of her. Close enough to touch. Close enough to...

His fingers brushed her cheek, and she sucked in a breath. Myles once told her a kiss is a part of someone you hold forever. He romanticized everything, and she'd always laughed it off. But now, as she sat in front of the most perfect boy she'd ever met, she wanted something of him, something to keep forever even if this adventure had to end.

"What's that?" he whispered.

Brea strained to hear whatever he heard, but there was nothing save the sound of crickets in the night. Then it became clear. Hooves pounded into the dirt path, coming through the valley.

Griff stood and brushed off his pants.

"Who would be traveling after dark?" Brea asked, getting to her feet. She didn't bother brushing dirt from her pants as she strained to see the rider.

Moonlight glinted off silver hair as he rode closer.

"That's a messenger of the queen." Griff drew himself up to his full height.

As the rider neared, Brea could make out a crest of flowers and wolves on the man's uniform.

He slid from his horse and approached, bowing. "My Lord, Griffin."

"Fraser." Griff stretched out a hand, and the other man straightened and clasped it. "Good to see you. Come in."

"I'm sorry, I cannot." He reached into the saddlebag and procured a letter with a wax seal. "From her Majesty. I am due back at court and must ride through the night." He issued one more bow before pulling himself back onto his horse and riding away.

"What is it?" Brea asked.

Griff didn't answer as he went back inside and retrieved an oil lantern from the table. He scraped his thumb under the seal and broke it before unfolding the letter.

After a moment, he looked up, a faint smile on his face. "Finally. We have been summoned to the palace. We leave tomorrow."

Brea swallowed. The palace.

The outcast girl from Grafton, Ohio was going to meet the queen.

Crap.

CHAPTER SEVEN

"How far is the palace?" Brea nudged Maisie to go a little bit faster. The sweet horse had two speeds. Slow and stop. Not that Brea was in a hurry to get to where they were going. She was curious about her aunt, but she was not at all confident she could do this whole meet the queen thing.

"We will be there by nightfall." Griff set an easy pace across the rolling hills just beyond the cottage.

"Is it a for real palace?" Brea chewed her bottom lip.

"As opposed to a fake one?" Griff shot her an amused smile.

Brea shrugged. "I saw this movie once where the queen and king didn't care too much for fancy things. Their palace was a cozy log cabin."

"Your aunt enjoys the finer things. Her palace is grand—and like nothing your human eyes have ever seen."

"Like how?" she pressed. Brea didn't like surprises. She needed to be prepared for whatever was coming her way.

"You will see soon enough. Queen Regan's palace lies along the Villandi River in the forest city of Vindur."

"How can a forest be a city?" Brea leaned into her saddle, hoping her fat little mare would make it to Vindur. At the rate she was stopping to eat grass, it might take them a week to get there.

"You will see soon enough."

"Anyone ever tell you you're infuriating?"

"Frequently." Griff pushed Mack into a trot and Lazy Maisie followed.

"Look at you go, girl! You do know how to run." Brea patted the gentle horse.

Brea enjoyed the warm fresh air and bright sunshine. It was invigorating to finally get away from the cottage and jump into the next phase of her new life. She liked Fargelsi. Sometimes she even thought she felt a connection to the verdant green hills.

"So... what happens when we get there?" Brea asked. "And so help me if you say 'you will see soon enough' I may sic my horse on you. She's a hungry girl, you know."

Griff's laughter was a deep, throaty sound she really liked. "When we arrive it will be late. Servants will show us to our rooms, and you'll likely meet the queen tomorrow or the next day. She's a very busy woman, though she is anxious to meet you."

"What is she like?"

"She is a kind and generous ruler. You should strive to be yourself with her, Brea. Well... perhaps save your biting sarcasm for me." He winked. "I can take it."

"Is there nothing but rolling hills between here and there?" Honestly, she'd grown quite bored with the trip so far. She'd expected to see more. People. Towns. Something.

"We will reach the Dragur Forest soon."

"Dragur? That doesn't have anything to do with dragons I hope."

"No, no dragons."

"What does Dragur mean?"

"Haunted."

"We're going to the haunted forest? Like with ghosts?"

"It's not actually haunted. At least I don't think it is anymore."

"Oh, well, that's just peachy." Brea glanced back over her shoulder.

"Why do you do that?"

"Do what?"

"You're always looking behind us like you think we're being followed." Griff shook his head, as amused with her as ever.

"I don't even know I'm doing it. There's just a vibe I get sometimes. Like not everything around me is as harmless as it seems."

"Probably just your human caution rearing its head. Gelsi is a strange new world for you. Of course you're naturally curious and suspicious of things you don't understand."

They stopped for a break around midday in a beautiful low-lying glen. To the east, the rolling green hills gave way to green mountains with rocky peaks. To the south lay the entrance to the Dragur Forest. As Griff cared for the horses, Brea explored their surroundings, taking the opportunity to stretch her legs. After hours of riding through the hills, Brea was happy to see something that wasn't green. Gorgeous purple flowers bloomed on shrubs at the lowest part of the glen. Orange wildflowers hung in clusters among the tall grass.

Brea picked some of the orange flowers and braided them into a daisy chain for her hair. She even found what looked like bubble-gum-pink strawberries growing on a vine-covered fallen log. She picked enough to go with their lunch, placing them on a napkin on the picnic blanket they'd brought with them.

"I wouldn't do that," Griff came up behind her as she was

about to pick some of the purple blossoms. "You'll be dead before we reach the palace. Even more dead if you eat those berries you picked."

"What's wrong with the berries?" Brea stood up, taking a few steps away from the poisonous flowers.

"One or two would just make you sick. More, and you'd fall asleep and never wake up. Some healers make a tea from the berry leaves for a sleeping draught, but even that can be dangerous."

"What about these?" Brea's hand went to the flowers in her hair.

"Harmless. And quite charming in your dark hair."

"No purple flowers. No swimming in Lake Villandi. No pink berries and no Gelsi berries. I should start a list of all the things that might kill me or drug me."

"Don't touch anything once we reach the forest. There, the more beautiful a thing is, the more likely it is to be dangerous."

"Got it."

After they ate and packed up, they headed into the forest. She wasn't prepared for how dark it was under the thick canopy of vine-covered trees.

"I feel like we should be traveling a yellow brick road to find the flying monkeys at the witch's castle."

"What are you babbling about?"

"Nothing." She stared into the swaying branches. "It's too quiet here. There aren't any birds in this forest."

"There are some, but most here are nocturnal. You'll rarely see or hear them."

"I find that... unsettling for some reason." Like she couldn't trust a forest that didn't have birds.

"You'll get used to it."

"So, how long will we be in the forest of nightmares?" She didn't relish experiencing nightfall here.

"It's not that bad, is it?" Griff's half smile slid into place. It was her favorite smile of his.

"It's creepy."

"We will reach the Villandi River before sunset. Vindur Palace is just across the river.

"Is the river like the lake? Should I prepare to fight the urge to dive in?"

"Not at all. The river flows north to Loch Villandi. Whatever phenomenon makes the lake so treacherous is not present in the river waters."

"Good to know. How will we cross the river?"

"There's a bridge, Brea."

"Well, you all aren't very modern, so how could I know if you'd discovered bridge engineering or not?"

"We aren't imbeciles. We just prefer simpler ways of living."

"You should think about getting cell service here. It beats the heck out of relying on messengers to carry your snail mail."

"Oh, I've seen your phones and the way humans depend on them like a drug. It may provide a certain level of convenience, but I prefer to enjoy a well written letter rather than the instant gratification of emoji texts." He smirked as if proud of himself for knowing what an emoji was.

"Whatever. I'd give my right arm for an hour at Dunkin Donuts with a large iced hazelnut latte, a smartphone, and a good pair of earbuds."

"I have no idea what you just said, but I find you utterly fascinating, Brea."

"I'm not all that complicated or deep, Griff."

"I beg to differ."

Sometimes the way he looked at her made her so nervous she couldn't see straight. *Good job, Brea. Crushing on the hot fae dude.*

"So what's expected of a queen's niece? Do I get a title or something?"

Griff frowned. "I'm not sure, actually. Technically you're a princess as the daughter of the queen's brother."

"Oh gosh, I was joking!"

"They'd probably just call you Lady Brea. But as the queen's niece, you'd have certain privileges, and in time, certain duties I imagine. Nothing you can't handle of course."

"And after you deliver me to the queen, where will you go?"

"I will stay for a while, but eventually, I'll return to my cottage where it's quiet. It will be a lot quieter without all your endless questions."

"You'll miss me when I'm gone."

"Indeed I will." Griff picked up the pace, urging Mack into a trot. "Look there." He pointed in the distance where the trees grew taller and wider than anything she'd ever seen. It reminded her of pictures she'd seen of the Redwood forest back home.

The path ahead ran in a straight line for miles and miles. "It's a lot farther than it seems, but you can just see the other side of the forest. We'll reach the river before sunset."

Brea didn't know what she'd expected of her first look at the forest city of Vindur, but she wasn't prepared for how it crept up on her. They'd traveled the whole day and never once saw another living soul. Brea had become so used to their solitude that it took her by surprise when the first fae woman she'd seen since her arrival in Fargelsi seemed to appear from nowhere.

"Why are they just hanging out in the forest?" Brea looked

over her shoulder to see dozens of fae going about their business.

"We're on the outskirts of the city. Open your eyes, Brea. Not everything here is mere forest."

That was when it clicked, and her eyesight shifted. Fae were coming and going from buildings, visiting businesses and returning to their homes—all sitting among the tree tops."

"How?" Brea turned around in time to see a woman leave her home, skipping down the steps wrapping around the massive tree trunk.

"The Fargelsi fae draw their power from nature," Griff reminded her. "They grow their homes this way."

"Amazing." Brea leaned forward in the saddle, and swore she caught a glimpse inside a home with moss carpet.

"Is the palace like this?"

"See for yourself. The palace is just across the bridge." Griff pointed ahead.

Brea's eyes couldn't decide what to look at first. The bridge was made of thick, green vines that grew from a massive tree trunk into a twisting pattern of knots and leaves that extended across the river. The bridge was wide enough for the two lanes of traffic coming and going from the palace. Far below, the crystal waters of the Villandi River made their lazy way across boulders and over rocks, splashing and tinkling like a symphony of sounds.

The palace itself seemed to have grown up from the riverbed. Vine covered stone spires reached for the skies, and pointed archways rose up in tiers from the main gates to the highest point at the center of the structure. Each spire twisted into three points that wrapped around a light source that shone brightly in the fading sunlight.

"It's breathtaking," Brea murmured in awe.

"The beacons are solar powered," Griff explained. "They provide light for the whole palace."

"Beautiful, functional, and safe for the environment."

The entire scene was picturesque, the way a tributary of the river flowed around the castle on either side, cascading in twin waterfalls over the cliffside to the main river below. Stone bridges grew from the palace at dizzying heights to connect to other wings.

"I have no words. It's possible I'm back to thinking I could be hallucinating again."

Griff's laughter brought her out of her fog. "I've never known you to be short on words. And for the last time, this is real, Brea Robinson. You've finally come home."

As soon as they passed through the castle gates, the queen's men-at-arms ushered Brea and Griff into the grand hall to meet the castellan.

"Lady Einin, it's good to see you again." Griff took both of the small woman's hands in his larger ones. "The queen has summoned us. Is she available?"

"She's visiting with a diplomat from the Eldur court. She's asked me to see the Lady Brea settled in her rooms." Lady Einin turned to give Brea a nod. She was stern-faced and didn't seem to bother much with small talk. "You know where your rooms are, now off you go." She shooed Griff toward a different part of the palace.

"You'll be fine." Griff put a hand on her shoulder. "Lady Einin will take good care of you tonight, and I'll see you first thing in the morning."

Brea nodded, trying to shove back the blazing hot panic at

the realization that her security blanket would be too far away to hear her if she needed help.

"This is your home, Brea. You are safe here." He squeezed her shoulder, leaving her with the allegedly capable Lady Einin.

"This way." Einin called, turning toward the massive staircase made of the most vivid green vines.

Brea followed silently as they climbed the great staircase to the third level of the palace. Einin stopped at an ornate doorway with a pointed arch covered in white vines with pink flowers and the palest green leaves streaked with gold.

"This is the queen's quarters. She has requested to have you near. Be on your best behavior, and don't go wandering about. The maids will bring your dinner and draw a hot bath for you."

Einin slipped an intricate bone key into the lock and stood back to let Brea enter the huge room—suite of rooms. It was fit for a princess, which she wasn't.

"Surely the queen would rather put me in a simple guest room."

"Queen Regan does what she likes. Make yourself at home and ring the bell if you need anything. Good night, my Lady." She dropped a slight curtsy that left Brea completely creeped out.

"I can't have people curtsying." She shivered and ran her hands over her arms. "It's too bizarre. And now I'm talking to myself again."

Brea walked around the oval-shaped sitting room, too scared to touch anything. She definitely needed that bath. Everything was so white, it shone like pearls in the moonlight. She was sure to ruin anything she sat on in her travel clothes.

A white settee occupied the center of the room. It seemed to have grown right out of the floor from the same delicate vines that adorned the doorway. The cushions of flower petals beckoned to her after hours in the saddle, but she couldn't resist checking out the rest of her rooms.

Three arched doorways led from the main room. The first led to a bathroom and dressing area with a huge walk-in closet filled with fluffy pink gowns Brea really hoped weren't meant for her.

The second door led to a bedroom. A vine-covered canopy bed stood on a dais at the center of the room. Strands of sheer white flowers grew from the canopy and fluttered in the warm breeze flowing in through the open balcony doors.

The last doorway led to a study. Rows and rows of books filled the shelves from floor to ceiling. A white wooden desk stood in front of a second pair of balcony doors, and a pair of white fur-covered chairs waited by the fireplace.

"Give me Netflix and Uber Eats and I could live here and never leave these rooms," Brea murmured.

A door opened behind her and three maids entered carrying trays and an assortment of clean nightclothes. They were identical triplets, making identical curtsies, staring at her with identical blue eyes.

"Would you like a bath first or food first, my lady?" The lead triplet asked, with another curtsy.

"Bath, please." Brea decided to go with it. She was far too tired to protest their eager little faces. She would explain to Lady Einin tomorrow that she'd rather see to herself. Servants were definitely not something she wanted to get used to.

"My lady, you must get up. The queen is ready to see you." Triplet Two pulled the warm downy covers away, and Brea wanted to scratch her face off. She'd just had the most restful sleep of her life and she wasn't ready to get up yet.

Triplets One and Three were busy pulling fancy dresses from the closet, while Triplet Two shoved a breakfast tray in her face and went to work on her nails.

"I can dress myself." Brea munched on a delicious pastry and sipped hot spiced tea. It wasn't coffee, but it was tasty. This world had to have coffee somewhere, and if they expected her to stay, someone better find it soon.

"Nonsense." Triplet One said... or maybe it was Two.

In no time they had her brushed, curled, and stuffed into a pink gown with a narrow waist and a long train. They left her to wait for Griff to arrive, and as soon as the trio was out of sight, Brea kicked off the tight slippers that pinched her heels and shoved her feet back into her boots. Under the long dress, no one would know. She felt more confident that she could actually walk without falling over her own feet.

Griff didn't give her time to get nervous. He knocked on her door just as she'd started to pace.

"What's with the terrifying triplets?" She shoved an errant curl out of her face, and snatched off the white gloves they insisted she wear. "I swear they snipped, plucked and trimmed me within an inch of my life."

"You're the queen's niece. There are certain expectations." He tried to hide his smile.

"You can say it, I look ridiculous." She tried to flatten the back of her big hair.

"You look beautiful. But the palace styles are a bit much. It's one of the main reasons I don't live here." He gestured at his own attire. A trim cut suit with tailored pants and a jaunty hat.

"Compared to this get up, you look comfortable. Want to switch outfits?"

"No, thank you." He offered his arm. "Ready to meet your aunt?"

She placed her hand in the crook of his elbow and kicked her train behind her. Blowing a dark curl out of her face, she said, "As ready as I'm going to get."

Griff led her to the hall and into the queen's apartments. "You're wearing your boots aren't you?" He chuckled.

"If you expect me to walk like a normal person, then yes, I'm wearing my boots."

"Don't be nervous, Brea. Just be yourself. She already loves you."

"That's not as comforting a thought as you seem to think it is. She has expectations, and I doubt I'll ever live up to them."

"Don't sell yourself short."

Brea gazed around the huge room filled with dainty gilt-edged furniture and breakable things. Sunlight poured in from the balcony.

"There she is!" The breathy genteel voice washed over Brea like a soothing balm. "I'm so happy to finally meet you, Brea, darling."

Queen Regan was not at all like Brea imagined. She was short and plump with soft white-blond hair that fell nearly to her knees. Her kind blue eyes sparkled with excitement.

"You look so like my brother." Her white-gloved hand rested over her heart. "It's so sad he never knew about you before he died. Come, let me get a good look at you." The queen took Brea's hands and held her at arm's length. "Such a lovely girl. Would you like some tea while we get to know each other?"

She dragged Brea out to the wide terrace where a table covered in pastries and tiny sandwiches waited for them.

"Thank you so much for having me... your Majesty."

"Come now, you may call me Auntie Regan. We are family."

"T-thank you, Auntie." The word felt ridiculous on her tongue, but she liked the bubbly little woman. "My rooms are the most beautiful I've ever seen."

"I'm so glad you're pleased." The queen sat on a tiny vine chair that looked like a throne. "Have a seat, dear." She patted the chair next to her. "And where is Griff?"

"Here, your Majesty." Griff stepped onto the balcony, flashing a brilliant smile for his queen.

"Brother, it's good to see you again." The other voice sounded familiar. Brea turned to find a blond man leaning against the terrace railing. "The last time I saw you, you were rather in a hurry."

"Lochlan, don't be such a stick in the mud," the queen chastised. "We simply couldn't allow my niece to end up in the hands of your queen."

Brea looked from Lochlan to the queen and back to Griff.

"Brothers?"

Chapter Eight

Griffin's lips flattened into a thin line, and his brother didn't seem any happier to see him. Brea couldn't wrap her mind around the fact that the two men who'd tried to kidnap her from the human world were related.

"Impersonating a police officer is a crime." The words spilled out of her mouth before she could stop them, and her cheeks flamed at her stupidity. He'd been trying to abduct her and take her into this whacked out world. He didn't care about committing human crimes in a world that wasn't his own.

Neither brother spoke as they stood in a silent stand-off.

When the queen clapped her hands together, they all jumped. "That's right! I forgot you already met my dear niece." She turned to Brea. "Darling, this is Lochlan O'Shea. You may call him Loch."

"She may not," the man in question snapped.

"Oh, don't be such a bore." She rolled her eyes in the universal expression of *men!* "Don't let Lochlan scare you, niece."

"What are you doing here?" Griff spoke like his brother was the only person on the terrace.

Lochlan's jaw clenched. "My queen sent me."

His queen. Griff mentioned Lochlan worked for the fire queen of Eldur.

"Ah, yes." Griff dropped into a chair beside Brea's aunt. "How is Queen Faolan? Still bent on destroying Fargelsi?" He shook his head and turned hard eyes on his queen. "He shouldn't be here. Eldur is no ally of ours."

"Forgive Griffin." Aunt Regan folded her hands in her lap and looked to Lochlan. "Sibling relationships can be difficult." There was a sadness to her eyes Brea wondered about. Did it have to do with her mysterious fae father?

But she couldn't ask.

Lochlan pushed away from the railing, his cold gaze skittering over Brea, sending a shiver down her spine. "I told my queen this mission was a mistake. Our talks have gotten us no closer to a deal today. I will leave you to your..." His expression darkened. "Family reunion." With that, he turned away.

"The queen has not dismissed you," Griff growled. In all the time she'd spent with Griff, she couldn't remember ever seeing him so tense.

Aunt Regan held out a hand toward Griff, palm up. He placed his hand in hers. "It's okay, Griff. Lochlan, you may leave us."

With a grunt, Lochlan stormed past the guards at the door and disappeared. The tense air choking their gathering dissipated, and Griff's shoulders dropped.

"Niece." Her aunt smiled. "Please, take a seat."

Brea lowered herself into a tiny chair she worried would break if she so much as shifted. Yet, it seemed to hold the larger Griff just fine. Servants descended on them, setting silver teacups in front of them and pouring steaming tea that smelled of oranges.

Needing something to do to quell the nervousness inside her, Brea reached for a pastry only to have her hand slapped away by a servant who used silver tongs to place food on each of their white china plates.

"Ana," the queen chastised.

Ana, a slight woman with tanned skin and caramel colored hair bowed her head in apology. "I'm sorry, your Majesty. Truly. Don't... please... I didn't mean to cause offense. You always tell us no lady should serve herself. I just..."

The queen's eyes flashed green. "You may go, Ana. Do not touch my niece again, or we shall have a problem."

Ana scurried away.

Throughout the entire exchange, Griff stared down at his plate, almost as if he were willing himself not to see the cracks in his liege's kind demeanor.

Brea watched the door Ana had disappeared behind. "It's okay, A-auntie. It was my fault."

"Brea, nothing that happens in this palace is ever your fault. As a Lady of the court, you will grow used to that."

"But I'm not a Lady. I'm just a farm girl from Ohio."

The queen smiled. "I thought Griff would have explained your importance by now." There was admonishment in her voice.

"I did," Griff grumbled. "She just refuses to see herself as special."

"That's because I'm not." Brea took an abnormally large bite of her pastry to keep more words from tumbling from her mouth. Instead, crumbs fell onto the bodice of her dress, and the dry scone stuck like glue in her throat. She coughed, spraying bits of scone onto her plate and reached frantically for her cup of tea.

Guzzling it down, she spit it out when it burned her throat, coating the plate of pastries in a thin layer of regurgitated tea. The coughing fit didn't end, and she pounded on her chest, unable to breathe in the tight dress. Once it finally subsided, she built up the courage to look at her aunt—the queen—which still seemed ridiculous to her.

The queen was too slow to cover up her look of horror, and Brea couldn't blame her. It was the moment Regan realized she'd made a huge mistake, that her niece wasn't fit to clean the floors of a palace, let alone live in one.

"I'm sorry, they didn't teach etiquette at the Clarkson Institute," Brea blurted.

Griff shook in silent laughter, the grim expression he'd worn since seeing his brother gone. She had the urge to reach out and punch him, but that would probably be frowned upon —just like spitting her food all over the queen's impeccable table.

A brown stain spread over the white lace tablecloth where tea dripped from the corner of her plate. Brea couldn't take her eyes from the evidence that she didn't belong here.

A slow smile overtook the disgust on the queen's face, and before long, she joined Griff in his laughter, the sound high and vibrant like the tinkling of a waterfall.

Brea clasped and unclasped her hands in her lap, not knowing exactly what to do. She absently picked up her scone again before staring at it in accusation and setting it down. "The scone was dry." She cringed at her words. "I just mean... at Starbucks, they're more like cake. I wasn't expecting a biscuit, and I bit off too much, but then the tea was hot, and—"

Griff cut her off. "We saw it play out, Brea. We don't need another account."

Brea scooted her chair back and stood. "I'm so sorry, Auntie. I wanted to make a good impression, but this is all a little too much. I'll understand if you want to send me back—not like I have much to go back to other than a murder charge for killing my best friend and parents who think I'm insane." She clapped a hand over her mouth. "Please forget I told you about that. I'm not a murderer. I swear. I miss Myles, and it was my fault, but I didn't mean to kill him. I swear."

"Brea." Griff raised a brow. "You're rambling."

"I know!" she burst out before clapping a hand over her mouth again. "I just yelled in front of a queen. It's just, I ramble. I'm clumsy. Sometimes I even talk to myself. I've lived my entire life with people telling me the things I see aren't real. This is who I am, Aunt Regan. I'm totally not calling you Auntie because I'm not a hundred. Do you want me to stay or not?"

The queen's keen eyes didn't stray from her face as she studied her. "Yes, dear. I knew all these things about you already." She stood. "You will stay. But I believe you could do with some rest. I will send my own personal Lady's maid to look after you."

"But I already have maids."

"The triplets are wonderful housemaids, but they can be a bit... over stimulating, and they haven't trained as Lady's maids yet. You will still see them from time to time, but I think Neeve will be a perfect fit for you, dear. Griff, please escort Brea back to her rooms."

Griff stood and bowed at the waist. "Yes, your Majesty."

The queen bustled away in a swish of skirts, her heels sounding against the floor in her retreat.

"She hates me." Brea flopped face first onto the bed, yanking at the bottom of her dress so it stopped pulling on her.

"She doesn't hate you." Griff hesitated in the doorway. "She just doesn't want to overwhelm you."

"Or overwhelm herself." Her parents never let her forget what a burden she'd been to them with her hallucinations and outbursts. "I don't want to be a burden anymore." Tears gathered in her eyes, but she blinked them away.

"Is that really what you think?" Griff stepped into the room and shut the door. His long strides brought him to the edge of the bed. "That you're a burden?"

Brea sat up and shrugged.

Griff's eyes met hers. "Brea, you're wanted here. I don't know everything you've gone through in your life, but that's over." He bent so they were eye-level. "This is your home now."

"Can you sit with me for a little while?" She patted the spot beside her.

"On your... bed?" He jumped back. "I shouldn't even be in here. It's not proper."

"Please?" She didn't care what was proper in this world. As recent as a few months ago, she'd spent the night at Myles' house sharing his double bed. They'd never questioned it. "I'm not asking you to sleep with me, Griff. This place is so different than what I'm used to. At your house, I could imagine I was on some idyllic vacation. But this, here, is real, foreign. I can't do it alone."

"You're not alone." He sat beside her.

She nodded. "Okay, talk to me about anything else to make me forget I spat tea at the queen."

He laughed. "I haven't been that entertained at a tea in... ever." He bumped her shoulder. "Okay... something different. Confession time. Seeing Lochlan here in this palace completely messed with my mind."

She swatted his arm. "I can't believe you didn't tell me he was your brother. I knew you guys were familiar from your fight in the woods over yours truly, but brothers? Talk about whoa." She paused. "Why didn't you tell me?"

He sighed. "Our family is complicated."

"I understand complicated. Try me."

"I lied to you before. Well, I don't think I actually said I'm Fargelsian... maybe just implied."

"You're not from here?"

He shook his head. "Do you remember I told you about the three kingdoms of the fae world?"

She nodded.

"The frozen kingdom is Iskalt. Lochlan and I were born at the ice palace to the king and queen."

"You're a prince?" Her jaw dropped. "A real, honest to god prince?"

"Was. Our parents died when we were children, and our uncle took the throne. He sent us away, me to be raised in the Gelsi court and Lochlan to be raised in Eldur. It was a compromise, a way for the other kingdoms to allow my uncle to remain king. We were supposed to bring the kingdoms together."

"But that didn't happen."

"No, it didn't. Lochlan hates me. Really, he hates everything. I've never been able to get through to him. When I saw him in the human realm with you in his possession, I realized the Eldur queen wanted you as well."

"Why?"

He shrugged. "We don't know. Maybe Loch being here will give us some answers. Whatever the reason, it can't be good. Queen Faolan of Eldur is born of fire. She can't be trusted, and neither can my brother. That is why I didn't tell you." He dropped his voice to a whisper. "I didn't want you to think less of me because of him."

The corner of Brea's lips twitched up. "I couldn't think less of you, Griffin O'Shea." Her eyes found his as she turned her head. "I don't claim to be the authority on genuine people, but I would bet my last horse you're one of the good ones."

His lips curved into a half-smile. "You don't have any horses."

"I just figured it was the kind of thing people say here. I'll amend it. I'd bet every last one of those frilly dresses in my too-large closet."

"You hate those dresses, so I'm not sure that has any meaning."

"How do you know I hate them?"

"Because, even though you look completely breathtaking in that preposterous mountain of tulle, I can read the discomfort on your face."

"You barely know me, Griff. You can't read my face."

He reached up to tuck an errant strand of hair behind her ear. "Now... that is a bet I'd take." His finger skimmed over her cheek. "Your cheeks redden when you think you've said something wrong." His hand moved up over the bridge of her nose. "Your nose crinkles when something annoys you."

"Usually you."

He laughed. "And these eyes... shine the most brilliant shade of blue when you're content."

"They're always blue. Eyes don't change color."

He pulled his hand away. "How can you see all there is to see in the fae world and still keep these human notions?"

"It's a talent."

"Stubbornness?"

"I was going to say idiocy."

He shook his head. "You're no idiot, Brea Robinson."

She couldn't take her eyes away from the boy saying all the right things, things she wanted to believe. There were secrets in his eyes—like the secret about Lochlan—but she shut those out, needing desperately for someone to trust in.

Leaning into him, she wrapped her arm around his waist. For the first time since Myles' death, she felt she wasn't alone after all.

Brea and Griff spent the day playing cards in her room. He'd found a deck she didn't recognize with symbols she'd never seen before. He taught her to play a game called Flash Magic.

It was designed to be used along with a fae's abilities, and Griff encouraged her to try small things like staring at the deck and using her magic to draw a card. When she finally accomplished it without setting anything on fire—don't look at her curtains—she jumped across the game and tackled Griff to the ground.

He hugged her back, only releasing her when someone cleared their throat. Brea pulled back with a grin to find a tall girl staring down at her with beautiful amber eyes. Thick chocolate brown hair was pulled back away from her youthful olive skin.

"I can come back," she squeaked in a voice that revealed her age more than her appearance did.

Brea picked herself up from the ground, wiping her hands down the pair of pants she'd made Griff fetch from his room. Her own closet was stocked with nothing but dresses. She'd have done just about anything for a pair of yoga pants with pockets.

"No, it's cool." Brea smiled, still riding a high from using her magic.

"Cool?" the girl said the word slowly. "Do you need a fire started in your hearth? It's quite warm outside, but if this room isn't to your liking, I can do that."

Brea suppressed a grin. "No, cool means... never mind. It's fine, you can stay if you tell me who you are."

"Oh." The girl's cheeks paled. "I'm Neeve. The queen sent me to wait on you."

"Well, I don't really need waited on. But do you want to play with us?"

Neeve stared down at Griff with wide eyes.

"Brea." He stood. "Neeve doesn't want to play. She's here to do a job."

"Doesn't mean the job can't be fun."

"Actually, it does." He shook his head with a sigh. "I must be on my way. I've been here most of the day, and there's a formal dinner tonight since the Eldurian negotiators are here."

"Does the queen want me to come?"

"No!" His word came so quickly, her shoulders dropped. Of course, her aunt wouldn't want her in public after what happened that morning.

"Oh, okay."

"I just mean... We don't trust Lochlan and his party. The Eldur queen wants you taken to her court, so it's best if we keep you out of sight until they're gone."

Lochlan had already seen her, but she didn't argue because she had no real desire to stuff herself into an awful dress and sit behind a big table taking rabbit bites of food. At least, that was what the movies said one did at a palace meal.

Griff ran a hand down her arm before squeezing her hand. "Neeve will take care of you. I'll see you soon."

When he left, she stared at Neeve for a long moment, unsure of what to say. She'd never been good at meeting new people. "You're tall."

Neeve bowed her head. "Yes, it is a flaw."

"No, I mean, it's cool, I mean sweet. You know what? I'll just say I like it. In the human realm, you'd be considered beautiful with your long legs and all." She smacked a palm against her forehead. "I'm totally not hitting on you. I like boys."

Neeve cocked her head. "Hitting me? That is your choice if it should happen."

"Hitting *on* you." She scoured her mind for a term that might make her understand. "Courting you. Is that right? I only want to court boys."

Her brow scrunched. "Well, that seems rather limiting." She walked past Brea to examine the burnt curtains.

"You like the ladies? That's cool. Sweet. Fine. Ugh!"

To her surprise, Neeve laughed. "Fae do not choose one type of person to love. We don't fall in love with a fae's... genitalia."

"Wait a second." Brea held up a hand. "Are you trying to tell me I've fallen through some pansexual wormhole?" A grin overtook her face. "That's freaking awesome. Has Griff ever..."

"Lady Brea." Chastisement rang in her tone. "I am a servant. We do not gossip."

"Of course you do. I've seen *Downton Abbey*."

"I won't pretend to know what that means."

"Wait, aren't you like not allowed to yell at me?"

Neeve's face paled. "I wasn't yelling. I was merely..."

"Don't stop. Please. Servants here are all Stepfordy. I like you, Neeve. We're going to be friends."

"A servant cannot be friends with a Lady of Her Majesty's Court."

"Sure they can." Brea climbed onto her bed and sat cross-legged.

"The queen would not approve."

She laughed. "The queen will not approve of about ninety-percent of me. We just won't tell her." She lowered her voice. "Please. I'd like to make friends here." She'd never had that urge back in Ohio, but Myles had been all she'd needed. The more people she distracted herself with here, the less time she'd have to miss him, to let herself wallow in guilt.

If it worked like that.

"You do not seem like the kind of lady who'd move into the palace." Neeve picked up the discarded game on the floor.

"That's because I was kidnapped."

Neeve almost dropped the cards. "You're the girl the queen has been searching for?" She stumbled back. "The one wanted by the Eldur queen?"

"Yeah, didn't I say that?" She flopped onto her stomach and kicked her legs up behind her. "Listen, I don't have any plans to leave this room until everyone forgets what an idiot I am. But I'm starving. Who do I call to get some chow around here?"

Neeve set the game on an ornate white table near the hearth. "I'll fetch you something from the kitchen." Something in her changed, and Brea couldn't figure it out. It was like news of her identity shook something within the servant.

After a long stare, she left Brea to her silence.

The Gelsi palace had the best food.

Brea never thought she was the kind of person to like coated duck in some kind of cream sauce she couldn't pronounce. Or that she'd stuff herself with seven courses of a single meal. At home, they were more the bologna and grilled cheese type of people.

She lay on her bed, her stomach almost bursting in protest. Neeve left after bringing the food, despite Brea begging her to stay and eat with her. Fear had entered her eyes at the proposition, and she went on and on about how servants didn't eat food fit for nobles. Brea tried to convince her to take a single bite, and she'd run out of there as if her dress was on fire.

The remnants of Brea's magic trials in the game with Griff were long gone, leaving behind a pristine room once more. She wondered if the people in this palace ever stopped working.

Thoughts of the fire queen entered her mind. She pictured a woman with blazing eyes and a vengeful spirit. As she'd learned from the movies, anything with fire in these fantasy worlds was bad.

That was how she imagined the Eldur queen. Long white hair, a hard expression, and dragons at her disposal. Did this world even have dragons? Griff hadn't mentioned them. He'd have told her, right? Because, seriously, dragons!

The prospect both scared and intrigued her.

She couldn't let herself fall into the hands of a dragon queen.

A scraping on her door had her jolting up in bed. She climbed off the heavenly mattress and crept across the floor on bare feet. Raising a hand, she tried to call on her magic, letting it latch on to her fear.

But when the door opened, it clogged in her veins, unable to break free as her mind went blank. Before her stood the most beautiful man she'd ever seen. It wasn't the first time she'd thought it, but it was the first time since knowing he was evil.

There was a definite family resemblance with Griffin. For one, both he and Lochlan were ridiculously good looking—but she was starting to suspect half of the fae population of the same.

"Brea," his low growl had her stepping forward not of her own accord.

"What are you doing here?" She had to force the words out.

He shut the door behind him. "We need to talk."

She only stared at him.

"You're in danger."

CHAPTER NINE

Brea's breath released in a ragged stream as the angry fae stalked toward her. She backed away until the backs of her thighs hit the bed. "You shouldn't be in here."

"Neither should my brother."

"That's n-none of your business." Her words shook. "What do you want from me?"

He glanced back at the door as footsteps sounded out in the hall. When they passed, he released a breath. "I left the dinner early to seek my bed."

"This isn't your bed."

His eyes bore into hers like he could see through every one of her defenses. The man before her had none of the lightness of his brother. Instead, he replaced joy with a deep intensity, just as entrancing as every one of Griff's smiles.

And also terrifying.

She rounded her bed so it stood between them.

"You don't need to run from me, Brea. I won't hurt you."

"But you would abduct me—again—and take me to your queen."

His silence told her that was exactly what he wanted to do.

"Let me ask again, what the heck do you want from me?"

He studied her for a long moment. "You aren't safe here."

"Of course, I am," she scoffed. "Queen Regan is family."

"That woman..." he pointed to the door, "...is not your family."

"You think you know me because you picked me up off the floor of a jail cell. You think I owe you?"

"Brea—"

"No, you can't pull your intimidating crap on me. I have spent my life in and out of mental institutions for delinquents. You don't scare me." Okay, he kind of did. "Don't barge into my room thinking I'm going to fall at your feet."

"That's not why I—"

"Stop lying to me!"

Lochlan crossed the room, stopping in front of her. His jaw tensed as he looked down into her eyes. "I am not your enemy."

"Any enemy of my aunt's is an enemy of mine."

"You barely know your aunt." He dipped his head to look at her more closely. "My brother is the one you really trust, isn't he?"

"He has given me no reason not to."

"He's lying to you. You're not safe here, Brea."

"I don't believe you." How could a palace like this be unsafe with all its fortifications and guards? "Are you done?"

"I came to deliver a warning. It is up to you what you do with it." He tore his eyes from her with a growl and turned on his heel, pausing before he reached the door. "If you need help, trust Neeve. No one else."

"Neeve?" Was she betraying Brea's aunt? "How do you know I won't betray her?"

He was quiet for a long moment. "Because I have been watching you for a long time, Brea Robinson, and that is not who you are."

"Watching me?" *Creepy much?* "What does that even mean?"

A knock sounded on the door before Griff's voice filtered through. "Brea, you in there?"

She considered calling out, telling him to come save her from the man standing with his back to her, his muscles bunched.

Something held her back.

Lochlan glanced back over his shoulder, his eyes finding hers. "There's one more thing."

"What is it?" Brea sighed, wanting this night to end. The sooner Lochlan was gone, the better.

"Myles."

The name on his lips caused her heart to skip a beat. "Wha—"

"He's alive."

Without another word, he pulled open the door and found Griff leaning against the wall, waiting.

Griff kicked off the wall, anger overtaking his features. "What are you doing with her?" His face reddened.

Lochlan flashed him a tense smile. "Having a chat."

"You have no right."

"And you do?" Lochlan towered over Griff, using his height to intimidate his brother.

Griff didn't back down. "She belongs here."

Brea backed away from them but the vitriol poured from the two beautiful boys. Brothers, yet enemies. And they both wanted her for some reason she couldn't explain.

They continued to argue, but their angry words blurred together as her heart pounded against her ribs. She turned around, pulling at the loose shirt that suddenly felt too tight, too warm.

Alive. Alive.

Was Myles really alive or was it another trick?

Could she trust anything in this world?

Alive.

Flashes of that day she'd tried to suppress ran through her mind. Myles hitting the ground. Waking up to find him gone. What did the paramedic say to her before she was arrested? She pulled at her hair and collapsed back onto her bed, the hammering of her pulse drowning out the angry words ricocheting around the room like ping pong balls.

"I'd be surprised if he made it to the hospital."

Those were the words, and no one had refuted her thought that he was dead. Not the police or her therapist. Not Lochlan when he first abducted her or Griff since.

It didn't mean Lochlan was telling the truth. She knew that, but the hope expanded within her, pulsing like energy beneath her skin. She needed to know, for someone to be honest with her.

The tingling she recognized now as her magic built up.

"Stop!" she yelled. Glass shattered, spraying shards across the room as every window, every piece of china broke into a thousand tiny pieces.

Pain nicked her cheek, and she wiped away a bead of blood, her chest heaving.

Lifting her head, she found Lochlan and Griff on the ground where they'd dropped to avoid the glass. It settled around them like a blanket just as dangerous as they were.

"Lochlan," she growled, darkness in her voice. "Get out of my room."

He stood, examining a shard of glass sticking from his hand. Pulling it free without so much as a wince, he looked to her once more. "Remember what I've told you." Without another word, he turned and left.

Griff picked himself up. Glass crunched underneath his feet as he approached her. "Are you okay?"

"No," she sniffed. "I'm not okay at all."

The hard expression he'd saved for his brother softened. "Are you injured?"

Other than a few small cuts, she'd escaped her magical outburst unharmed. She shook her head.

"Come on. We can go to my rooms while someone cleans this up. I think we need to talk."

He held out his arms and she let herself fall into them. After carrying her across the glass-strewn floor, he set her down and reached for her hand.

Speaking quietly to a servant outside the room, he explained the situation, and within moments, the triplets rushed in to take care of the mess.

Griff didn't speak to her until they reached his rooms, which looked almost identical to hers, save where her furniture was white, his was a deep cherry wood. Aged vines with deep burgundy flowers wrapped up the walls, never once letting them forget they lived in the middle of a magical forest.

Myles would have gotten a kick out of this.

"Griff." She tugged on his hand and forced him to face her.

"What's wrong?" He released her hand and framed her face with his palms.

"Is Myles alive?"

For a moment, everything stood still, until Griff turned away from her and kicked off his boots. "You know the answer to that."

"Do I?"

His back tensed. "Is this what you and Loch were speaking of? Why you let him into your rooms?"

"First of all, I didn't let him into my rooms. Second, you're avoiding the question."

"What do you want me to say, Brea?" He twisted to face her. "Myles Merrick made it to the hospital where they hooked him up to machines we'd never subject our people to here in the fae world. He lived for two days before succumbing to his injuries."

"How do you know?" she whispered.

Griff sighed and pulled her against his firm chest, wrapping protective arms around her. "We have contacts in the human world."

"Did you keep tabs on him for me?"

He nodded, resting his chin on the top of her head. "I hoped to be able to tell you better news. Lochlan is just using your friend to make you doubt me."

Tears broke free of her eyes. She hadn't yet cried for Myles, because doing so made it real. But this... Her arms wound around his back, and she held onto him as if her world would break apart if she let go. Maybe it already had.

"Brea." His breath blew into her hair. "You can't listen to anything Lochlan says. Ever. His motives are never good."

"I'm sorry I doubted you. All you've done is help me since I arrived."

He pulled back and put a hand on each of her shoulders. "Do you trust me?"

"I do."

A smile spread across his lips.

Something still ate at her. "The fire queen—"

"Queen Faolan."

She nodded. "Sure. She wants me."

He dipped his head to look her in the eye. Sliding a finger under her chin, he tilted it up. "I will protect you from her." His eyes blazed violet as he dropped his voice. "I promise."

She couldn't have looked away if she tried. Griff was right. Lochlan wasn't the guy who'd protected her these weeks. He didn't care about her, not like Griff.

Reaching up on her toes, she pressed her lips to his before drawing back quickly, realizing what she'd done. "I'm sorry. I know you're just helping me because of my aunt, but—"

His lips cut off her next words and he drew her against him, consuming her as if she were the air he needed to breath. She slid her arms around his neck, holding on for dear life, because there was no way this made anything less complicated.

Yet, she didn't stop, couldn't stop. Griff tasted like Gelsi berries and honey, and she never wanted it to end. His hands slid down her back before gripping her waist and pulling her tighter against him.

"Griff," she whispered against his lips.

"Hmm?"

"This is a bad decision." She was at the palace to meet her aunt. Who knew what kind of future she had here? A part of her still expected them to shove her back into the human realm the moment they realized she wasn't the kind of girl who fit here.

But she wanted to fit, with her aunt, with Griff.

"Probably." He kissed her again. "So it's a good thing I have a history of bad decisions."

"I don't believe that." As far as she knew, he was the queen's most loyal follower, her ardent supporter. One didn't gain such power with bad decisions. This was the same man who'd imprisoned her for days, but even that faded to the back of her mind. Bad decision or not, she needed this, a morsel of happiness to fill the empty chasm inside her.

"Are you saying you don't want to kiss me again?"

Was she? She considered him for a long moment before fitting her lips to his once more. "Wait... you're not like related to the queen, right? I know you're from Iskalt, but if there's a reason you rose so high in the Gelsi court... I'm no Jaime Lannister."

He grinned as he pressed a kiss to her cheek. "I don't know who those people are, but we aren't related. I promise you that."

"You and your promises."

He trailed his lips over the curve of her ear. "I promise I want to kiss you again."

"Well, go on then. Can't go breaking your word."

As he kissed her fully, thoroughly, the events of the day faded away. She didn't want to stop, because that was when the questions flooded back, the insecurities and sorrow. When she kissed Griff, she didn't have to mourn her best friend or worry about some far-off fire queen who wanted her for some unknown reason.

And best of all? His lips silenced the part of her mind that waited for the perfect veneer to fade from this new life, because if her old life taught her one thing, it was that Brea Robinson didn't get easy, she didn't get a happy ending.

CHAPTER TEN

"Festival? What festival?" Brea stared blankly at her new Lady's maid. Neeve was a thousand times better than the creepy triplets, but she still wasn't sure she'd ever get used to having servants.

"It is Beltaine, my Lady." Neeve stared back at her, equally perplexed.

"What is Beltaine?"

"It's one of our most special holidays. It's a celebration of peace and prosperity for all Faekind. It is why her Majesty invited the delegations from Iskalt and Eldur, my Lady."

"Please, Neeve, I'm begging you, enough with the 'my Lady' this and 'my Lady' that. My name is Brea, when it's just us here in my rooms, it would please me if you would call me Brea."

"Yes my—Brea." Neeve stumbled over the name.

"I think I've read something about Beltaine before." Brea scratched her head. "Isn't that a summer holiday?"

"Summer?" Neeve frowned. "It is always spring here, ma'am."

"Ha!" Brea whirled around with a smile. "Nice try, but no 'ma'ams' either. Isn't Beltaine in May?"

"Yes. It's always the first of what humans call May." Neeve couldn't seem to sit still, bustling about Brea's rooms with a duster, but there wasn't a speck of dust anywhere. Brea had looked on one of her many boring days spent in her rooms over the last week.

"But that's months away."

"It's tonight."

"It can't be." Brea's heart climbed up in her throat. She couldn't have been here four months already. "It was January when I arrived. That was just a few weeks ago."

"Are you quite well, Brea?" Neeve crossed the room to help her sit in one of those vine chairs Brea was always afraid she'd crush.

"I don't know." Brea fanned her face, blaming her too-tight corset for her dizzy spell. If she was going to be here much longer, the fae world was about to discover sports bras and yoga pants. Surely someone around here could grow her a pair with their magic.

"Are the rumors really true?" Neeve leaned close to whisper. "Did you come from the human realm?"

"There are rumors about me?" Brea groaned. That was all she needed.

"Just a few. Our people are very curious about you. I promise... Brea... I will not repeat anything you tell me. You can trust me."

That's what he'd said. Lochlan. *If you need help, trust Neeve. No one else.*

Brea nodded. "Griff brought me here from the human

realm. But I'm fae," she added quickly. "I just didn't know it till recently."

"Of course you are fae. You have the look of royalty, no less. You're the Fargelsi Queen's niece. Which means everyone is curious about you."

"I get it, but I just... how have I been here four months and not noticed the time passing?"

"Oh dear, I'm sorry, I thought you knew, but of course you'd have no reason to know. Our calendars don't exactly line up with the human calendar. You arrived here when it was January where you came from, and it's been three fortnights. So for you, it's not quite March yet. According to our calendar, for you it is only early spring, though we do not adhere to human months."

"So I didn't lose a whole bunch of weeks I don't remember living?" Brea took a deep breath.

"No, of course not." Neeve laughed. "I'm sorry, I don't mean to laugh. You are just quite funny sometimes.

"So I've been told." Brea got back on her feet and crossed the room on shaky legs. Reaching for her teacup, Brea tried to pour hot water over the tea leaves.

"I'll get that for you, my Lady." Neeve swooped in and grabbed the cup from her hands.

"I can pour myself a cup of tea." She felt like stomping her foot, but that was childish. She wasn't above it, but she needed to keep her cool and remember Neeve was only trying to do her job.

"Please relax, you have a big night ahead of you."

"And what is expected of the queen's niece tonight?" She sighed. Not looking forward to this first of many formal events.

"You will sit in a place of honor with the queen, where you will meet the delegates from all the fae courts. Beltaine is a celebration of peace, love and fertility. A night where all our differences are set aside and new friendships are formed."

"So, I just have to sit there and look like I belong? I think I can manage that. What do I have to wear?"

"You're going to love it." Neeve smiled, but then she probably remembered who she was talking to. "At least I think you will." A frown marred her face. "Are you ready for the triplets? They'll be assisting me tonight."

"Must they?"

"I couldn't manage to get you ready without help."

"You know." Brea sipped her tea. "In the human world, I managed to dress myself without any help at all. I even made my own breakfast."

"This is different, Brea." A note of annoyance crept into Neeve's voice. "Your human clothes were simple. Your costume for tonight is—"

"Costume? You didn't say anything about a costume."

"Well, yes, it's tradition on the night of Beltaine for the nobility to don costumes for the festival. Everyone will dress like flowers and creatures of the forest."

"So it's like a masked ball?"

"No masks tonight. Would you like to see your gown?"

"Call in the trio if you must." Brea sighed. "Any chance someone has a stash of mood suppressers around here?"

"Is that like... a potion? Tonight won't be that bad, Brea."

"Not for me. For the three little maids on speed."

Brea couldn't walk. Her gown was too heavy. It had to weigh more than she did.

"I've heard people talk about suffering for fashion, but this is a new one." Her knees nearly buckled.

"Just lean on me. If you fall down, at least we'll go together." Griff chuckled, tucking her arm around his. "If it helps, you look stunning. Like the first perfect white rose of spring."

"Ooh that was cheesy." Brea giggled behind her fan—an actual white lacy fan!

"Cheesy usually works for me." He straightened his tie with an arrogant smirk.

"You know they built a crazy contraption under all this tulle, you wouldn't believe it if I told you. I've got pillows stuffed around my hipbones to keep the dress foundation from stabbing me. The scaffolding under here weighs a ton and that's before they decorated me like a cake with all these fresh roses. They actually made the roses grow around the dress."

The ball gown was stunning on the dress form with its yards of white silk and the palest pink tulle, but when Brea finally got a chance to see herself in it, she thought she looked more like a marshmallow Peep.

"The triplets spent hours sewing beaded rosebuds all along the bodice and the hem. I've never seen anything like it."

"I take it you are not pleased with the weight of the gown?" Griff escorted her down the grand staircase, gripping her carefully so she wouldn't fall in her ridiculous heels.

"Ya think?"

"Maybe this will help." Warmth from his hand running along her arm spread through her body, and his green eyes shimmered violet for a moment.

"Oh," Brea almost toppled over as the massive weight of the dress lifted and she felt as light as air.

"It seems someone forgot to do that for you."

"And you let me walk down ten flights of stairs before you decided to help me out with that little trick?"

"I find your complaining amusing this evening. And it wasn't ten flights of stairs. It was two."

She studied his 'costume.' A trim cut white suit with a white fur hat shaped like a wolf's head.

"You seem to be missing a tail."

"There's only so far I'm willing to go for a costume party."

"That's what I said, so why can't I opt for the easy suit and hat *costume*?"

"I grew up as the queen's ward, but I'm not deemed part of her family. You are. And most of the people here would give anything to be in your shoes tonight."

Brea took the last few steps at his side. "It's hard for me to think of myself as anything other than plain old Brea Robinson."

"There is nothing plain or old about you, Brea." Griff laid his free hand on top of hers still clutching his arm. "Ready for a night you'll never forget?"

"As ready as I'll ever be." Brea followed him to the rear of the palace, frowning as she realized she hadn't come down from the queen's quarters since she arrived, and she hadn't even visited this part of the palace yet. "Where are we going?"

"To the park just across the queen's gardens. It's magical at Beltaine. You're going to love it." Griff pulled her through the massive rear doors of the palace and Brea gasped at the wonderland before her. Sweeping lawns with pathways and fountains, and every kind of flower she could imagine—in full bloom at night!

"It's beautiful." She breathed.

Brea and Griff followed a line of nobles along the pathways leading to the festivities at the center of the park beyond the high brick walls.

"You will enter with the queen." He whispered in her ear, his breath warm against her skin. "This way." He tugged Brea away from the crowd, skirting the garden walls to a separate gate just for the queen's use.

"Can you stay with me?" She clutched her dress to keep the hem from dragging across the wet grass.

"I will be right behind you and the queen." He squeezed her hand. "I know this is all overwhelming for you, but the people will love you if their queen does. And it's pretty clear Regan already adores you."

"She thinks my clumsy behavior is a riot." Brea laughed. "But I think she's kind of amazing," she admitted. "And so kind. I don't know what I expected, but she's just so delightfully... perfect." Brea couldn't imagine how her aunt could ever have anything resembling an enemy. But there was beef between her and the Eldur queen. Brea might be the Gelsi queen's niece, but she already knew she had no desire to get into fae politics.

"Oh my darlings, you look beautiful." Queen Regan beckoned them to join her at the east gate. "Look at us, we're just a pair of delicate roses tonight."

Where Brea's dress was all white with pale pinks, adorned with dozens of white roses in perfect bloom, Regan's was blood red, covered in red rose petals from the hem of her gown to her bodice, where it flared into a stiff high collar the shape of a rose. With her white blond hair piled on top of her head, she looked just like a fairytale queen.

"You look so beautiful, Aunt Regan." Brea responded to Regan's air kisses with her own. She was getting used to her aunt's larger than life personality.

"Come with me, dear, I want to introduce you to all the nobles of my realm. I hope you've rested because tonight is going to be... oh what do the human kids call it these days? I do love their marvelous expressions."

"Epic?" Brea supplied.

"No, tonight's going to be amaz... no that's not it either."

"Amazeballs?" Brea grinned. For the past few days, Regan had Brea teaching her all the slang from the human world.

They always ended up laughing hysterically by the end of their afternoon tea.

"That's it. Tonight is going to be *amazeballs*, just you wait. Your Auntie Regan has stopped at nothing to make your first Festival of Beltaine a night to remember."

"Thank you, Aunt Regan, I can't wait." And to Brea's surprise, it was true. She felt more relaxed with her aunt now and with Griff right behind her, she thought she just might get through this party unscathed.

Brea fell in step with her aunt as they strolled through the gates; the queen never hurried anywhere she went. Brea could hear the gasp and roar of the crowd, but it had no effect on Regan.

"The Festival of Beltaine is all about expressing love and putting peaceful thoughts out into the world for the coming season," Regan began, lifting her hand to wave at the crowd. "It's no secret that relationships between the fae courts have seen better days. I've invited delegates from both Iskalt and Eldur to celebrate with us tonight with the hope it will foster more positive communication among the leaders of our world. You will help me charm them, won't you, dear?"

"Oh, Aunt Regan, I seriously doubt you need my help charming anyone, but I will give it my best."

"You flatter me, dear. Come sit with your auntie while we watch the festivities." Regan made her way to the raised dais where a throne waited for her. A miniature version of that throne sat to the right of the queen's chair and just slightly back. Regan made herself comfortable and gestured for Brea to take her seat beside the queen.

Brea felt like a piece of fine jewelry on display. The crowd had grown quiet at the queen's entrance, waiting for her permission for the merriment to continue.

"Ladies and gentlemen, I present my niece, daughter of my

late brother, Brandon, Breanna Louise O'Rourke. You may call her Lady Brea."

"But, that's not my name," Brea tried to say, but the queen didn't seem to hear her. She felt Griff standing behind her and wished he could sit at her side.

When he leaned in to explain, his presence calmed her, and she could breathe again.

"Relax. It's just a formality. She hasn't taken your name away. She's just given you a proper title—giving you her last name, no less. This is a good thing, Brea."

"Thank you, Aunt Regan," she managed to murmur, smiling shyly for the crowd.

"Please continue the festivities," the queen said with a wave of her red-gloved hand.

Brea took a deep breath, gazing around the park at the hundreds of fae celebrating the holiday. Bonfires roared in every corner, lively music played, and people danced under the stars. Gymnasts on stilts took great lumbering steps through the crowd, wowing the children from their great height. Fire-eaters and jugglers performed, each trying to outdo the other. Beautiful women wrapped in yards of silk hung suspended from the trees, performing amazing feats high above the crowd.

The evening was perfect. The weather was beautiful, as if Regan ordered a balmy night with cool breezes just for her guests. Servants buzzed around the park offering drinks and the most sumptuous finger foods. Brea and the queen sampled their fair share of the food and wine while they gossiped about the lords and ladies of her court.

"Your Majesty, you do us a great honor introducing your beautiful niece to Fargelsi on this lovely Beltaine evening." Brea had heard a version of this speech throughout the night. This time the nobleman was young and quite handsome, if a bit stuffy.

"Lord Tadleigh Bainebridge, always lovely to see you." Reagan turned her charms on the smitten young man. "Lord Bainebridge oversees one of the largest estates in Fargelsi," the queen explained.

"At the queen's pleasure, of course." The man offered a curt bow to Brea. "It would be my honor, Lady Brea, to escort you this evening." He took her hand, placing a kiss there like all the gentlemen before him.

"Thank you, sir," Brea stuttered.

"I'm keeping her all to myself this evening, Tad." The queen batted her eyes at him. "Another time." Her tone was one of dismissal.

His expression fell, disappointment in his gaze. "Of course, your Majesty." With that, he turned on his heel and walked toward a gaggle of ladies nearby.

Regan's fan unfurled in front of her face. "He may be handsome, but he's older than he looks, that one. I'm told he uses a tonic to keep his hair like that. And he's such an incredible bore."

"With a bit of a brown nose, too." Brea giggled.

"Brown nose? What an odd phrase." The queen took a sip of her wine.

Oh crap. How was Brea going to explain such a saying? She needed to start watching what she said. "Um, well he's rather good at kissing your ... royal ... bum." Brea's cheeks flushed in the firelight. She turned begging eyes to Griff who leaned into the queen's ear and explained.

"Brown nose indeed!" The queen roared, and Brea relaxed. "Don't be so shy, Brea, dear. You can say anything to me. I don't offend easily."

"Perhaps Lady Brea would like to see the sights, your Majesty?" Griff suggested. "It is her first festival with us."

"Oh very well, Beltaine is a night for the young, you two go have fun. Just come back to watch the fireworks with me."

"Of course, I wouldn't miss it." Brea leaned down to kiss her aunt's cheek.

She took Griff's hand and followed him through the crowd, laughing and relishing the moment of freedom from the endless parade of noblemen.

"She's introduced you to every eligible Fargelsian in her inner circle."

"Eligible?" Brea giggled. "For what, like marriage?"

"Yes. It was quite irritating to watch."

"Is she mad?" Brea's mind swirled with too much wine. "I'm not getting married. I'm way too young."

"I'll talk to her." Griff smiled, looking like he might have also taken too much wine. "I'll explain how it is in the human world. She's just excited to show you off. You're all the family she has, you know. Having you here makes her happy."

"And I'm happy to be here." Brea whirled around, making her dress lift in the breeze. "It's so beautiful here, Griff. I just still can't believe this is my real home. It's like a dream come true."

For once, Brea didn't let her cautious thoughts weigh her down. Maybe it was the wine talking, but she was starting to see a future here. A future she wanted. Maybe even a future with Griff.

"A flower for your Beltaine lady?" A wizened old woman offered Griff a perfect blush-stained rose from her basket. He paid the lady for the flower and turned to Brea, tapping the rosebud against her nose.

"This rose reminds me of your blushes." He trailed the soft petals down her cheek. "The way your cheeks flush with the faintest pink when you're embarrassed about something silly and utterly human. It's one of my top ten things I love about Brea Robinson." He pressed the rose into her hands.

"Top ten?" Her voice came out breathless and shaky. "What are the other nine?" She pressed her nose against the bloom to inhale its fresh fragrance. She couldn't remember ever smelling a rose like this in the human realm. They'd always seemed overly fragrant and cloyingly sweet.

"I can't spill all my secrets now. You'll have to wait for the other nine."

She closed the distance between them to kiss him, but he moved away. "We can't here, Brea. It would cause a scandal for the queen's niece to show affection so openly. But please know, I am dying to taste those lips again." He tugged on her hand, guiding her to the tents where the courtiers feasted and drank copious amounts of wine.

They ate roasted venison, spiced vegetables and other things Brea couldn't even identify.

"I need some fresh air." Brea tried to take a deep breath, but the confines of her corset and the contents of her stomach wouldn't allow it.

"I'll meet you by the fountains in a moment, and then we will join the queen for the fireworks."

Brea didn't want to be the girl who needed a buffer, but panic slowly ebbed its way into her heart the moment he left her. She went to wait by the fountains, worried she might make a fool of herself if anyone stopped to speak with her. She watched the crowd come and go, but no one even noticed her. Something was weird about that.

Several young girls skipping around a maypole caught her attention. Their ribbons fluttered in the breeze as they wrapped them around the pole. They skipped and laughed like young girls should, but there was something forced about their merriment. They did and said all the right things, but that sincerity didn't reach their eyes.

The same with a group of young men, dancing with girls about the same age. They were everything carefree teens should be ... but somehow not quite. They lacked a certain joy.

As Brea took in all the queen's guests, a cold sense of dread lodged in her stomach. They were all just going through the motions. Like they only wanted to do what the queen expected of them. But there was a lackluster dullness in their eyes. It gave her the creeps.

"Lady Brea." The cold voice sounded behind her. She knew it was him before she turned. "I should escort you back to your queen. It isn't safe for you to wander around the festival alone." Lochlan gazed down at her, his perfect mouth drawn into a thin line.

Her wine-addled brain wondered what it might do to his features if he truly smiled. He hadn't bothered with a costume, though it didn't surprise her he'd refused to play along. Dressed in dark leathers and a long black cloak, he would blend easily with the night if it weren't for his silvery blond hair. Her wore the top half swept back from his face and secured with a black leather band. The hair just above his pointed ears was tightly braided, but the rest fell down his back just past his shoulders. His midnight blue eyes smoldered under dark blond brows.

"I'm sorry, what?" Brea swayed on her feet, feeling a little dizzy from staring up for so long.

"You're drunk."

"No, you're just stupid-tall." She turned to leave him, but he grabbed her arm.

"I'll escort you."

"I don't need an escort. I'm perfectly capable of walking these two little feet back to my aunt, thank you very much."

She moved to pull her arm away from him and managed to

trip over her own feet. She knew she was going down the moment she lost her balance. Clutching at Lochlan, she tried to stop the inevitable, but the edge of the fountain hit the back of her calves and wet hands *grabbed* her legs. Brea toppled over, dragging Lochlan down with her.

Cold water closed over her head and pulled her dress down into the depths of the pool. Immediately sober, Brea scrambled for the surface. Why was this fountain so deep? Dark things under the surface clamored for her attention, clawing at her hands and feet, pulling her down. Strong arms wrapped around her middle, dragging her up to the surface. Just as stars danced in her vision, Brea thought she saw a sea of angry creatures staring back at her.

Then she was spewing water out of her lungs, coughing and sputtering like a fool in front of her aunt's court. Something hard thudded against her back.

"This damned fool dress almost killed you." Lochlan's hand pounded on her back once more.

"Stop." She tried to wiggle out of his arms to swim to the edge of the fountain, but he stood up with her in his arms. The water barely came up to his knees. The flowers from her dress floated around his feet.

What the hell just happened?

"Are you okay, my darling?" Queen Regan rushed to the edge of the fountain.

"I'd be fine if this brute would put me down." Brea's face flamed with heat.

"Lady Brea, are you okay?" Concerned voices rang out around her.

Oh great, I'm a spectacle now.

"I'll see to the lady," Lochlan said, stepping over the edge of the fountain and back on solid ground. Brea looked over his shoulder for any signs of the creatures she'd just seen, but the shiny bottom of the fountain winked back at her.

"Griffin will see to her," the queen insisted. "Please see to yourself, Lochlan, dear, and come join me with your delegation to enjoy the fireworks."

Reluctantly, Lochlan set her down, but not before he whispered another warning in her ear. "Heed me now, silly girl. You are not safe among this court. There is only darkness here."

Back on her feet, the weight of her dress and half the water from the fountain weighed her down. Griffin pulled her into his strong arms, and she clung to him in relief.

"Our Lady Brea is a delightful klutz, is she not?" His laughter inspired the crowd to respond in kind. "Show them you're not embarrassed, Brea. Laugh with them."

Brea bent into a curtsy, flashing them her most charming smile and shrugged as if to say, I'm a lovable goof—which she'd like to think she was. She'd just rather not make a habit of falling into fountains. And she'd grown quite tired of needing to be rescued.

CHAPTER ELEVEN

It took Brea forever to get warm once she'd changed out of her sopping dress into a still-not-her but more comfortable sleeping gown. Her aunt told her she didn't need to rejoin the festival after the fountain mishap because the night was winding down, and soon only those bent on debauchery would remain.

Debauchery. Brea grinned into the dark. That was her aunt's fancy speak for the drunks. Though, most of the people at the festival had been pretty far into their cups already by the time she left.

As if she'd never seen drunk people before.

It would probably horrify her aunt to hear about her mom's frequent nights out or the way her dad crushed entire cases of beer sitting in front of the TV for college football Saturdays.

No, she was no stranger to debauchery.

Rolling onto her side, she stared out the window. Six weeks. That was how long Neeve told her she'd been in the fae world.

Six weeks since she set foot on the dilapidated farm she'd called home.

Six weeks since Myles walked the earth.

Her life went from psych wards and high school to adventure and romance in record time. Maybe that was why it still didn't feel real. She waited for the day the other shoe dropped. Nothing could be this perfect.

No one.

Not even Griff.

She smiled as she thought of the way he'd escorted her through the festival, past performers and scurrying children. Other than the nobles, no one looked directly at her.

Well, except the delegates from Iskalt and Eldur.

The men and women representing the frozen kingdom sat apart from the rest of the crowd, their icy eyes finding her wherever she walked.

And Eldur... She'd tried desperately to free herself from whatever danger lurked in the waters of the fountain, but only found relief in the strong hands of a man she should hate. Lochlan O'Shea couldn't be trusted. Griff told her as much. But she couldn't shake the protective look in his eyes, or the way he'd refused to let her go until the queen stepped in.

Why did he care what happened to her?

His queen wanted her, she knew that, but this was... different... more.

She strained to hear wolves howling in the woods, reminding her she was far from home.

But maybe this could be home in a way the little farmhouse in Ohio never was.

A sigh rattled through her chest as she sat up, finding sleep impossible. There were too many questions on her mind, and only one person who might give her any sort of answers.

Crawling from the bed, she slipped her feet into woolen slippers and pulled open her door, cringing when the hinges creaked. She waited for a moment to make sure no one was around. It was ridiculous she had to worry about this when she'd spent the last ten years of her life sneaking out and running across the fields to Myles' house. But she didn't want to cause any kind of scandal for the aunt who'd been nothing but kind.

She wound her way through the dark halls until she reached a room she'd been to only once before, hoping the door wouldn't be locked. Only the queen, Brea, and Griff lived in the royal residence wing at present.

Pulling on the handle, she smiled when she heard it click and slipped into the room before a wandering guard or servant found her out of bed.

Griff lay on his stomach with the sheet bunched around his waist. To her disappointment, a loose white linen shirt covered his torso. Ear-length auburn hair stuck up against the feather pillow.

He looked so different from his brother it made it hard to see how they were related. Where Lochlan was light, Griff was dark. At least in appearance. When it came to personality, they were the exact opposite. Lochlan had none of Griff's joy, only intensity.

His hard blue gaze would forever be stuck in her mind.

But he didn't matter right now.

"Are you going to just stand there or come over here?" Griff opened one eye.

Brea shrugged. "I don't know. I just figured I'd watch you like a creeper."

He lifted his head. "I have no idea what a creeper is, but I don't approve."

"Oh yeah?" One corner of her mouth curved up.

"When the most beautiful woman in all the fae realms is in my room at night, I'd much rather have her close."

"Oh, okay." She turned to the door. "I'll go find her then."

"Get over here," he growled.

"Well, if you insist." She slipped out of her shoes and launched herself onto the bed, landing on top of Griff.

"That's one way to wake me up." He gripped her waist and flipped her so her back hit the bed. "But I like this better." Hovering over her, he lowered himself onto his elbows.

"Are you going to kiss me?" she whispered.

"Was that a request?"

She shook her head. "A demand."

"You ask so much of me." He pressed his lips to hers in a slow, sweet kiss. Griff wasn't an intense man, not a passionate man. He didn't devour her or steal her breath away.

Instead, he cherished her.

He rolled off her, landing on his side and propped his head up. "Not that I'm not happy to see you, but what are you doing here?"

"I couldn't sleep."

"And that's enough reason for you to sneak into a man's room in the dead of night?"

She lifted her eyes to the canopy overhead. "I didn't really think anything of it. I've been doing this my entire life."

He reeled back, his eyes widening.

"I didn't mean this," she blurted, gesturing between them. "I used to climb out my bedroom window to get to Myles whenever my parents sent me to my room... which was often and usually after a lot of yelling."

"Have I told you yet how sorry I am about your friend?"

She went quiet for a long moment, not wanting to talk about Myles. She didn't know if it was still too fresh, or if she just wanted to keep her best friend to herself a little longer.

Resting her head on Griff's shoulder, she hesitated before asking the question on the tip of her tongue. "Were you and Lochlan ever friends?"

"He's my brother."

"Yes, but was he your friend?"

His voice went cold. "We were young when my uncle separated us." When he didn't say anything else right away, Brea thought he was done. Finally, he went on. "But before that... I have memories, small ones. Lochlan is two years older than me, and I remember the day we learned our parents had died, or at least bits of it. The only person I wanted was him." He sighed. "The court loved my parents. Everyone sank into mourning. Servants. Guards. Nobles. It was like Iskalt lost its soul. But so did we, me and my brother. We lost so much more than our souls."

"Did you find him that day?"

"I did. I sat next to him, and he wrapped an arm around me." Griff scratched his face and blew out a breath. "I've never told anyone about that day. I don't know why I'm telling you. I don't even know if these memories are true or a child's twisted fantasies."

Guilt gnawed at her for not talking to him about Myles, but she wasn't ready for that. She turned onto her side and stretched an arm across his chest. "You don't have to tell me. But you can... you know... if you want to."

"I've seen too much of Lochlan in the past few weeks. Before I found him in the human realm, it had been four years since our last encounter. It's easier not to think of him when I'm not staring him in the face."

"Maybe thinking of him isn't a bad thing. Do you think you could make up?"

"You mean reconcile?" He shook his head. "Not while he stands at the Eldur queen's side."

"What did he say to you the day your parents died? Do you remember?"

Griff didn't answer at first, and only the sound of their breathing filled the room. "He said it was up to us to make them proud now. That we only had each other, but that he promised it would be enough."

"Your promises," she whispered. It made sense now. Griff obsessed over making promises, and it was because he believed Lochlan broke his.

He rested his chin on the top of her head. "At the time, we thought he would rule over Iskalt with my parents' advisors to help him. He was a kid, but it wasn't unheard of. My uncle had other plans. Within a fortnight those advisors were either dead or disappeared, and Lochlan and I were sent to be raised and educated in other courts under the guise of creating worldly leaders."

"Will your uncle ever abdicate?"

He shrugged. "I'm not sure it matters to me. Lochlan is the rightful king."

Brea wanted to shake him. As an only child, she always dreamed of having a sibling to go through life with, someone to share the struggles. Sure, she didn't know how the fae world worked, but Iskalt didn't only belong to Lochlan. It had been Griff's parents' realm, their people.

How could he forsake that?

"Brea," he whispered.

"Yeah?"

"Say something funny so I can forget about all of this."

"I'm not a funny person, Griff. The sooner you realize that the better."

He pressed a kiss to her temple. "Okay, say something human because that's always funny."

"We're pretty boring. Only elves think humans are funny."

"I'm not a—" He paused. "You're making fun of me."

"Yes siree, Bob."

"There it is." His laugh shook his entire body. "I don't understand half your odd phrases, but they sure are entertaining."

"I live to please." She sat up. "Want to play a game?"

He pushed himself up so his back rested against the cherry headboard. "In the dark? Should I retrieve a lantern?"

"Nope." She popped her p and grinned. "Just give me your hand. We're going to have a thumb war."

"Brea." He frowned. "There's no such thing as a war with thumbs."

"Sure there is. I'll show you."

"I don't want to hurt you."

She laughed. "You won't."

"But it's a war."

"Shut your yap already and give me your hand." When he didn't, she reached out and grabbed his hand, locking it into the thumb war position. Scooting closer to him, she relaxed. "Okay, follow my lead. We count to eight, tapping our thumbs on opposite sides from each other. When we reach eight, try to pin my thumb."

"Brea, I'm stronger than you. How do you think you can win such a game?"

She grinned. He had no idea. She'd spent many nights having thumb wars with Myles when neither of them could sleep and they couldn't turn on the light in case his mom saw.

"Just go with it." She tapped her thumb, showing him how to do it. "One, two, three, four, I declare a thumb war. Five, six, seven, eight, try to keep your thumbs straight." She straightened her thumb, grappling with Griff's before pinning it in two seconds flat.

Griff only stared at their still-interlocked hands. "That's not how war works."

"That's why it's a game, Griff, not a battle."

"Can we try again?"

She nodded and started the count. This time, Griff lasted a bit longer before succumbing to her pin.

"Again," he demanded.

"Oh my, I've created a monster." She raised a brow.

Griff smirked. "You'd have to master your magic to create monsters."

Her jaw fell open. "You can actually make a monster?"

"No." He laughed. "I just wanted to see if you'd believe me."

"I hate you so much."

"No, you don't."

No, she didn't. She pulled her hand away and scooted up beside Griff, tucking herself into his side. Since entering this different world, he'd kept her safe and helped her navigate her new reality. She'd never be able to repay that.

"Can I sleep in here?" she asked.

"That would cause quite a stir with the servants."

"Honestly, Griff, I don't really care."

He wrapped his arm around her and kissed the side of her head. "A lot is going to change, Brea. I don't know what's going to happen now that you've been introduced to Gelsian society. Suitors will present themselves to the queen, no doubt."

She coughed out a laugh. "Griff, there is zero chance I'm ready for marriage. I'm not even eighteen." No matter who her aunt paraded in front of her, marriage was the last thing she wanted. She had enough to get used to.

Griff sighed. "I guess I'm just saying I want to enjoy having you here while I can. Just know... no matter what happens... I'm always here for you."

That sounded suspiciously like a breakup speech, and they weren't even officially courting or whatever people called it here. She didn't know what she felt for Griff. All her emotions were tangled up in the safety he represented, the trust she had in him.

Was it more than that? Maybe. Or maybe not.

All she knew was she wanted to keep kissing him, to feel his arms around her and know she wasn't alone. Because loneliness was the most dangerous thing in the world. It bred misplaced trust and a belief in things that weren't what they seemed to be.

Brea groaned into the damp pillow beneath her face. Gross, she'd drooled in Griff's bed. Sunlight streamed across the room in strips of warm light. Footsteps echoed off the stone floor coming closer and closer.

"There better be coffee on whatever tray you're carrying." She lifted her head with a scowl, deciding right then she was never drinking wine again.

Griff lowered the silver platter to the table beside the bed, a quizzical look on his face. "What is coffee?"

"You have got to be kidding me." She pulled a pillow free and buried her head beneath it.

Griff plucked the pillow out of her grasp, an annoying grin on his face.

"Traitor." She grimaced.

"I had breakfast brought up from the kitchens. Hotcakes—"

"Smothered in coffee?"

He ignored her. "Eggs—"

"Using coffee grounds instead of pepper?"

"And fried pork."

"Fried in coffee grease." She grinned this time.

"Okay." Griff crossed his arms. "I thought I could guess what coffee is—some sort of drink—but now I'm not so sure."

"I was joking about the grease thing, but seriously, how have the fae not discovered the life-giving beverage? You have magic, and they're basically the same thing."

"First of all—" He poured tea into two way-too-small white china cups and handed her one. "If there's truly a beverage that gives life, we must take this knowledge to the queen."

She hid her grin by taking a sip of tea. "And the next thing?"

"What?"

"You said, "first thing" and that implies there's a second."

"Ah." He set his cup down and sat beside her on the bed. "You continue to refer to this world as ours. I know it'll take a while for it to truly sink in—as you humans say. But you are one of us. The magic... it belongs to you as well. This world is your home."

She set her cup on the tray and turned, pulling her feet up under her on the bed. "I forgive you."

"For what?"

She met his gaze, letting his kindness soothe her aching head. "For pulling me into a world where coffee doesn't exist." She pressed a kiss to his lips, smiling against him.

"You're ridiculous."

"That's one of the things people used to say about me when they thought I was crazy."

He frowned. "I didn't mean it like that."

She reached up, tracing the curve on his lips, letting her fingers flit over his smooth cheek—cleaned up for the festival. "I know." She pulled her hand away and reached for the tray, dragging it onto the bed.

Griff's brow furrowed. "Brea, it's not proper to eat where one sleeps."

"Then what's the point of having breakfast brought to the room?"

He gestured to the sitting area in front of the hearth.

Her brow arched. "So, you're telling me, with all these servants, you've never actually had breakfast in bed?"

He shrugged as if this wasn't one of the greatest things in life.

"Well, Mr. O'Shea, this is what we're doing. If you wish to be all formal stick-up-your-butt dude, then you can leave."

"It's my room."

"So." She shoved a forkful of pancake into her mouth. That's what it was called, she didn't care what the fae told her.

Griff only lasted a moment longer before a smile overcame the doubt on his face. He scooted closer to the tray and tentatively took a puff pastry. Biting into it, he watched in horror as a crumb landed on his shirt.

"Lean over the tray." Brea laughed.

Leaning over the tray had been a rule whenever Myles brought her breakfast in his bed. He made what he called the "Myles special." It was usually three different kinds of cereal mixed in a bowl with just the right amount of milk. Yeah, this breakfast was much different.

They ate in silence for a while, until Brea set her fork down, unable to eat another bite. "So, we have something to clear up, you and I."

He took a sip of tea and set it aside, dabbing a napkin across his lips. "Do we?"

"Last night, you told me there were ten things you loved about me. Do you know how horrible it is to do that to a girl? No one has ever loved anything about me, and you come along with ten, but then refuse to tell me nine of them."

Sadness swirled in his gaze. "Brea, I'm sure plenty of people have loved things about you."

"Don't try to ignore the important part of what I said." Getting up on her knees, she moved the tray from the bed to the small table before inching toward him. "You like that I blush."

"No, I love your blush."

"Okay, that's a super weird thing to love, but whatever floats your boat."

"I don't have a boat. As a kid, I never learned to navigate the waters because they're treacherous in Iskalt with the icebergs."

"That's interesting and all, but stop trying to change the subject. I didn't actually say you had a boat."

"Yes, you did."

"Just tell me." The words exploded out of her, and warmth flooded her cheeks. They stared at each other in tense silence before breaking out in laughter. "Please," she wheezed.

"I can't give away all my secrets."

Gripping his arm, she forced him to look her in the eye. "Just six."

"One."

"Five."

His eyes narrowed. "Four."

She nodded, sticking out her hand. "Deal."

He threaded his fingers through hers, and instead of shaking her hand, he pulled her into his lap. "You challenge me. I've never met anyone who constantly tested everything I thought I knew."

She buried her face in his chest, unable to look him in the eye as he spoke. She'd always had a shy streak that hadn't yet reared its head in the fae world.

"Keep pushing your buttons," she whispered. "Got it."

He shook his head like he'd started doing when he didn't understand her human phrases. "I love your laugh. It's like the sun breaking through in the middle of an Iskalt ice storm. The world is so cold until I hear that sound."

"That's three," she breathed, unable to form any other response as her heart stuttered in her chest.

He nuzzled his nose into her hair. "When I'm with you, I feel like I can be good too."

"You are good, Griff." She reached up and gripped his chin, tilting it down so he met her eyes. "All I see in you is good."

His eyes swirled with some unspoken emotion she couldn't decipher. Indecision, maybe? Confusion? Whatever it was lived at the core of who Griff was.

She almost forgot about the last thing he promised her until he spoke again. "And... you're fearless, Brea Robinson."

"No, I'm not."

He smiled down at her. "I took you from the human world, and now you're in the center of a fae court—and without your precious coffee. I keep waiting for everything to overwhelm you, but you sit here joking and laughing. If that's not fearlessness, I don't know what is."

"Griff, this girl you see... it's not me. I'm not all these things. One day, you're going to wake up and realize you only saw what you wanted to see."

"Impossible." He leaned her back on the bed, holding himself over her.

"If there's one thing falling into a world of fantasy and magic has taught me, it's that nothing is impossible."

The Brea Robinson in his mind didn't exist, yet when he kissed her, she let him. When he brought her closer, she held on tightly. He'd see through his own visions of her soon enough, and then all he'd find would be cracks in a ragged soul.

Griff O'Shea was too perfect, too good for the likes of her. That was how she knew the fantasy they lived in would end. She just had to make sure to get out of it intact.

Chapter Twelve

Brea managed to sneak back into her room without notice well before anyone else had arisen after such a late night of festivities.

"Good, you're up early." Neeve's shoulders relaxed when she stepped into the room.

"And that's a source of relief for you?" Brea liked to tease her maid. It loosened her up so she acted like a normal person.

"Normally, you're like trying to wake the dead, and then you're an ill-tempered child until I get some tea in you."

"If you could just send someone out for coffee, we wouldn't have this problem." Brea would give anything for a decent caffeine boost.

"If you could tell me what coffee looks like, it would be much easier to find it." Neeve bustled about the room readying Brea's clothes for the day.

"It's heaven in a cup." Brea threw her head back against her pillow and stretched.

"That still doesn't tell me what it looks or tastes like." Neeve set a stack of fabric at the foot of Brea's bed.

"It's dark like coffee, it tastes like coffee, and it smells like coffee." Brea groaned as she moved to sit on the edge of the bed. "What's this?" She eyed the soft looking fabric Neeve brought with her.

"A few Beltaine gifts for you. I don't know what yoga pants and t-shirts are, but you seem to prefer men's clothing and soft things so I had these made for you."

Brea snatched the pile of fuzzy woolen clothes and squealed in delight. The pants were very yoga-like leggings, and the shirt was a long tunic in a dark blue fabric. A belt, a pair of sturdy trousers, and a jacket completed the ensemble. There was even a descent attempt at duplicating the sports bra she'd worn when she arrived at the cottage with Griff. "This is perfect, Neeve, thank you!" She gave the tiny woman a hug. "I'm sorry, I didn't get you anything."

"And you shouldn't." She gently shoved Brea back down on the bed. "It wouldn't be proper."

"Proper-schmoper."

"You say the silliest things." Neeve shook her head, a smile tugging at the corners of her mouth.

"At least I seem to be entertaining everyone. So what's on my agenda today?"

"Brunch with the queen."

"Is she mad?" Brea winced. She didn't mention she'd just eaten in Griff's room.

"Mad? Why on earth would she be upset with you?"

"For taking a dive with a delegate in the fountain?"

Neeve stood with her back turned, brushing imaginary wrinkles from Brea's dress for the day. Her shoulders shook with silent laughter.

"It's okay, you can laugh it up." Brea rolled her eyes. "It was pretty epic."

"Only you could manage to fall into a fountain at the queen's Beltaine festival." Neeve's laughter was infectious.

Brea shrugged. "Like I said, at least I'm entertaining."

"Better get ready, Brea. The queen will expect you soon." Neeve offered her a stack of fresh undergarments and shooed her behind the screen in the corner of the room. Brea had insisted she could at least put her own undergarments on without assistance. It was a compromise Neeve finally agreed with.

"Is this a fancy brunch with all the delegates?"

"Just you and the queen."

Brea breathed a sigh of relief. She loved her aunt and looked forward to the times they spent together. It was when other people were involved that she tended to stress out.

"Good morning, dear." The queen was all smiles today. Not a hint of a hangover or lack of sleep marred her beautiful face. She'd never seen her aunt *not* dressed like the fae Marie Antionette. Regan really liked to wear pink.

"Good morning, Aunt Regan." Brea bobbed a quick curtsy before she took her seat opposite the queen. "You're looking lovely this morning."

"Too much wine last night, darling. Far too much wine." Her laughter echoed across the terrace where they normally had their afternoon tea.

"Tell me about it." Brea winced.

"I just did." The queen blinked in confusion.

"Oh, that just means I'm commiserating with you." Brea laughed. "Way too much wine. But last night was wonderful."

"Was it amazeballs?" Regan leaned forward in earnest.

Brea thought about the late night spent with Griff in his rooms. "It was definitely amazeballs. But I'm so sorry about the incident with the fountain." Her face flushed with fresh humiliation.

Regan's laughter sounded like bells. "I'm just glad you're okay, dear. Don't ever apologize for your clumsy behavior. It's endearing. Don't change on my account."

"Thank you, Aunt Regan." That might have been the first time a family member ever told her to just be herself. Without thinking, Brea stood and approached the queen.

"What's this, my darling?" The queen's sweet face stared up at Brea just before she wrapped her arms around her aunt.

"Thank you, auntie."

"For what, sweet girl?" Regan awkwardly patted Brea on the back.

Brea wondered how long it had been since anyone hugged Regan. "For loving me just as I am."

"What's not to love?" Regan took Brea's hands in hers. "We have much to discuss this morning."

"Shoot." Brea returned to her seat only to realize she'd said something confusing again. "Sorry, it seems we need a translator." Brea laughed. "That just means, go on, I'm listening."

"All right then, I'll shoot."

Brea stifled a giggle behind her hand.

"I said it wrong, didn't I? Oh well, we have plenty of time for human silliness later. Did you ever wonder why I brought you here, Brea? I mean besides the obvious that I wanted to meet my only niece."

"Of course, I wondered." Brea nodded for Neeve to stop hovering and pour her tea.

"Some of my nobles thought I intended to make you my heir so they feared your arrival. I would claim you as my own if not for your human side. I love you dearly, child, but Fargelsi needs a strong fae ruler when I am gone."

"I understand," Brea rushed to say. There was nothing she wanted less than to be Regan's heir to the throne. "It wouldn't do for a half-human-half-fae klutz to take your place."

"I'm so glad you see it that way too." Regan gave a curt nod to Neeve to finish serving their brunch. "Before all of this uncertainty about what your arrival might mean, the Fargelsi court feared I would make Griffin my heir, which has always been my greatest desire. I've raised him as my own, and a more loyal son couldn't possibly exist. But he is an Iskalt prince, and many would like to see him return to his uncle, the king."

"So, it would be dangerous for him if you publicly named him your heir?"

"It would. Unless..." Regan paused to sip her tea. "Unless he was betrothed to a Gelsian royal."

Brea's mouth went dry. Her aunt couldn't possibly be thinking about marrying her off like some kind of pawn on a chessboard? "What now?" Brea squeaked.

"You and Griff fancy each other, do you not?" Regan asked bluntly. "I saw your flirtations last night. You suit each other quite well."

"Um, well. I... um..."

Neeve saved her by sliding a plate with a slice of quiche and a side of fruit drizzled in caramel sauce in front of her. The caramel sauce danced on her plate like magic until it formed the words '*everything she says is a lie.*' Brea choked on her tea as the caramel sauce blurred and the words disappeared. She glanced at Neeve, taking a moment to breathe.

Neeve's grave look was warning enough. Brea needed to tread carefully here. But could her aunt really be lying to her? She'd gone to great lengths to make Brea feel welcomed and loved. She couldn't imagine any of that was fake.

"I do. Um. Like him, that is. Griff is a charming young man. Whom I just met and we're, ah... still getting to know each other."

"Strong marriages have been built on far less." Aunt Regan nibbled on her quiche like she hadn't just scared the pants off her niece. "We will announce your betrothal to Griffin in a fortnight. After your marriage the following month, I will name Griffin heir in the event of my death. Any children of yours shall become my blood heirs. They will continue my line. This way you will be a queen of Fargelsi one day. That would make me very proud."

"Children? Queen? A month?" Brea sputtered. She was about to tell the queen she was a lunatic when Neeve interjected.

"Perhaps Lady Brea needs some time to think, your Majesty?"

"She has time."

"May I remind your Majesty, she has also grown up in the human world where these things are quite different. By their standards Lady Brea is still a child who wouldn't be ready for marriage for several more years."

"Is that so?" The queen frowned. "This proposal seems strange to you, dear?"

Brea only nodded. She couldn't get the words out that the queen was off her rocker if she thought she was going to marry a cute boy she just met.

"Too fast." Brea finally managed to string two words together.

"Yes, that's right," Neeve continued. "Even adult humans much older than Lady Brea will court a young woman for a year or more before proposing marriage."

"I see. I suppose we could announce the betrothal in a month, and then give her a few more months to prepare for the big day. How does that sound, my darling girl?"

It sounded like it was time for Brea to get the hell out of Fargelsi.

Back in her room, Brea clawed at her clothes. She couldn't breathe under so many layers. "Get this thing off of me."

Neeve worked quickly to remove her dress and unlaced her corset with nimble fingers. "Just breathe, Brea. It will be okay. Lord Griffin is a good man."

"Yep, yeah, he's a great guy." Brea gulped air into her lungs, kicking the dress across the room. "I just don't want to marry him when I'm not even old enough to buy beer without a fake ID."

The other shoe had just dropped, and it crushed Brea.

"Was any of it real?" she asked, fanning herself. "I need air." She stumbled for the balcony.

"Brea, you can't go out there in your under clothes." Neeve rushed to wrap a silk robe around her. Brea let Neeve fuss about her clothes as she breathed in the lavender-scented air.

"I knew it was all too good to be true." They just wanted her for her bloodline so they could make Griff a king. Did he even care for her at all? Was his *top ten things I love about Brea Robinson* just a line she'd fallen for like the stupid girl she was?

For that matter, did she mean anything to Regan but a means to an end? Tears burned her eyes. She'd cried more tears in her lifetime than was remotely fair. After years of believing she was insane, she finally found where she belonged, and that was a lie too.

"It's all a lie. Just like you said."

"What, my Lady?" Neeve patted her back.

"In the caramel sauce. You said it was all a lie."

"I don't know what you're talking about." Neeve's hesitant smile stopped her tears. "It's treason to spell out dire warnings in caramel sauce."

"He said I could trust you."

"You can, Brea. Of that, you should never doubt."

"I have to talk to Griff before I do anything stupid." Like trust something Lochlan O'Shea said. "I have to know if Griff had any part in this."

Chapter Thirteen

Brea stumbled through the palace, forcing her way past guards wearing her aunt's colors. She sprinted down a spiral stone staircase, thankful not to have a dress tripping her up. The clothes Neeve procured for her gave her some sense of normalcy. Sure, they weren't exactly the styles she'd have worn on the farm, but close enough.

Her breath rattled in her lungs as she kept running down the long hallway. Servants scurried out of her way as she rushed out the double doors that stood open to the long bridge crossing the river to the rest of the palace grounds. The waterfall crashed to her right, sending a spray of water into the air.

The forest closed in on her as she crossed the bridge, careful not to look over the sides into the depths below. The horse stables stood shrouded in vines at the far edge of the property with a paddock out front. Riders came and went while stable boys led horses from their stalls.

It looked nothing like Myles' farm, but the smell—of horses and hay—allowed her to imagine she was back there where she'd felt safe. Any moment Captain America would walk into the paddock with her new colt by her side. She'd give Brea a look in that understanding way of hers that made her want to spill all her secrets.

Entering the bustle of the long stables, Brea inhaled deeply, her fingers twitching as if she could feel Myles' hand in hers. A familiar head appeared, snorting when it saw her.

Maisie, the sweet horse she'd ridden from Griff's house. The house she never should have left.

Everything she says is a lie.

That had to have been a message from Neeve, but then why would she deny it? And what did it mean? The kind and welcoming aunt she'd come to love was lying to her? About what?

That same aunt wanted to marry her to Griff to make him king. It was the reason she'd been brought from the human realm. Could she trust nothing that had happened since her arrival?

"Hey Maisie." She reached the stall and unlatched it before slipping inside and shutting the door.

Fresh hay was spread over the ground. "Nice digs, Mais." She approached the horse, running her hand along her smooth neck. "Looks like they're taking good care of you."

Just like her. That was the problem. She'd been well taken care of, having everything given to her on a silver platter—literally. But now she wondered if she was in a cage just like Maisie with no say in her future.

"What would Myles say about all of this?" she whispered, not sure if she was talking to the horse or herself. He'd probably tell her to do whatever it took to be free. That she didn't owe these people anything just because they took her away from a bad situation in the human realm.

But still, she felt she owed them everything. Her love. Her

loyalty. Her life?

Sliding down the wall, she sat in the hay and looked up at the beautiful beast, the only thing here that could possibly remind her of home. Tears built in her eyes and a wind whipped through the stall, pulled by the magic she now knew was tied to her emotions. Would it ever go away?

She didn't want power.

The wind intensified.

She just wanted control of her own body again. Was that so much to ask?

Sniffling, she held in the tears.

"Brea?" Griff's voice sounded far off as the magic buzzed in her ears. "Brea!"

Strong hands shook her, and she looked up into Griff's worried face, a face she'd kissed only hours before. Now, she wanted him to leave her alone.

"Pull the magic back in!" he shouted.

It was only then she realized Maisie was cowered in the corner of the stall. Seeing fear in the horse, the string pulling her magic snapped and the wind died.

Brea slumped back against the wall.

Griff crouched in front of her, his arms resting on his knees. "I've been looking everywhere for you."

"Why?"

"What?"

"What do you want from me, Griff?" There was no strength to her voice, only resignation.

"Brea." He scratched the back of his head. "I—"

"Need me? Yeah, I've been told." She pushed away from the wall and got to her feet.

"Where are you going?"

"Away." She shoved open the stall door and stomped from the barn, anger burning along her skin. But if she let this magic out, she feared she wouldn't be able to pull it back in.

Griff ran after her. "Talk to me."

She reached the bridge and turned on her heel to face him. "I don't think you want to hear what I have to say!" She had to shout to be heard over the waterfall.

"What's going on? This morning, we—"

"This morning was a lie. Everything is a lie. Me. You. My aunt."

"Okay, slow down. What happened between when you left me this morning and now?"

So, he hadn't spoken to her aunt. With a grunt, she turned and stomped across the bridge. She entered the palace, the noise from the falls dying down as she walked deeper inside. This wasn't a conversation she wanted to have where they could be overheard.

By the time they reached her rooms, her anger had lessened, leaving her with the sinking feeling of being alone in a world that was not her own. She'd have given anything to have Myles with her.

Griff shut the door and approached her, his arms crossed over his chest. "Number six. When you get angry, your lip juts out stubbornly, and all I want to do is kiss the frown away." He leaned in, but Brea sidestepped him.

"Do you really want to kiss me, Griff, or is that what you're supposed to make me believe?"

"Why would you say something like that?"

She turned to the window, looking out on the realm she'd marveled at only a day before. Now, Fargelsi had lost its shine for her. She'd longed to belong here, but she wondered if she ever truly would.

Griff put a hand on her shoulder and she let him, having no more energy to push him away. She turned into his embrace, burying her face in his shirt. "Tell me the truth," she whispered. "There's no prophecy about me."

"Brea—"

"Why did you really come to the human realm for me?"

When he didn't respond, she lifted her eyes to his. "It was so you could become king, right? You needed someone with my aunt's bloodline to make you a legitimate contender."

He released her and stepped away. "You don't understand."

"I think I do."

"Regan is my queen. She has been a mother to me. That throne is rightfully mine."

"And what of me, Griff?"

"I lo—"

"Don't say it!" Her hands vibrated in anger. "I swear to God, Griffin O'Shea. If you tell me you love me right now, I'm going to punch that pretty face of yours."

"I never expected to feel this way about you."

A harsh laugh pushed past her lips. "Oh, that's rich. You don't get to be this guy. The one who says everything he did was for my own good."

"You were being arrested when I found you." He scrubbed a hand across his face.

"No." She shook her head. "I was in jail when your brother found me, not you. Was I just a game to the two of you? Some competition?" She calmed her breathing and jolts of magic leaked from her fingertips, sending sparks across the floor. "I know why you came for me, but Loch? How does he play into all of this?"

"I don't know."

Her eyes narrowed. "And I don't believe you."

"It's the truth."

"Do you even know what that is?"

A knock sounded on the door and a gruff voice filtered through. "Lord Griffin, are you okay in there?"

"Yes," Griff called back.

Brea pressed herself back against the cool window. "How did they know you were in here?"

Or that they were arguing? She thought of Neeve's odd behavior when she brought up the message or the fact that she'd resorted to covert methods instead of speaking to Brea in the ample private time they had. Lifting her eyes to the vines creeping along the ceiling, she looked for any kind of listening devices. But this wasn't like back home where they'd use cameras and recording devices.

No, here, magic could be anywhere.

She stepped toward Griff, forcing him back.

"My aunt is listening to me." Her jaw clenched.

"That's not possible."

"Yes, it is. Anything is possible here." She could see it in his expression, in the tightening of his eyes, the flattening of his lips. The truth. He'd known. "I need to be alone." If she didn't step away from him, she'd lose her minimal control over the power inside her.

"Brea—"

"Go!" The word roared out of her, a command more than a request.

Griff's shoulders dropped, and he stared at her for a moment longer. "Not everything was a lie." The words were so quiet she almost missed them.

When he was gone, she slumped onto her bed, the tension leaving her body as she sucked in a few deep breaths.

Nothing could be as perfect as this new life seemed. She

should have known they didn't want her around for her. It was all a scheme.

As a little girl, she'd never dreamed of being a princess or living in a palace. She'd only wanted to be as normal as everyone else, to have a family who loved her.

But that had been too good to be true.

How much of what Griff told her was a lie? She sat up, an impossible thought coming to her. Would he really lie to her about that? Loch's words came back to her, and she had to know.

Wiping tears from her face, she left her room, holding her head high as she made her way down the now familiar hall. Only this morning she'd been so happy making her way back from Griff's rooms.

It took no time at all for that bubble to shatter.

She rapped her knuckles against his door and leaned back on her heels.

He took his time opening the door. His eyes widened in surprise when he saw her. "I thought you didn't want to see me." Hope tinged his voice.

She pushed past him into his room. "Is my aunt listening to what happens in this room too?"

Griff shut the door. "No. We can talk freely here."

Relief washed over her. It creeped her out to think of her aunt listening to everything that had gone on in this room. She hugged her arms across her chest, afraid of the question she'd come to ask.

Griff clasped his hands behind his back, nerves flitting across his face.

"I will marry you," Brea said.

A smile spread across his lips. "You will? Truly?"

"Yes, but I have one condition. There is a question I need you to answer honestly. You owe me this after all the lies.

That is my bargain. A marriage for an answer. Do you agree?"

"Of course. I don't want to lie to you anymore. I want you by my side as we rule this kingdom."

"I never wanted to rule a kingdom—or get married at seventeen for that matter. You'd have known that if you bothered to ask. Instead, you plotted with my aunt to get what you want. But I'm starting to see that's how this world works. You fae are worse than humans, and I never thought that was possible."

His smile fell, replaced by a look of sorrow. Some part of her wanted to comfort him, but the fondness she'd felt only hours ago was gone, replaced with wariness.

"Ask me your question, and I will answer honestly." He reached for her, but she stepped away to gather herself.

"Is..." She closed her eyes. "Is Myles alive?"

She opened her eyes when he didn't answer right away. His jaw tensed and he took a step back, widening the space between them. "Lochlan put this notion into your head."

"Yes." She wouldn't sugar coat it for him. "But he was right, wasn't he?"

Griff sighed, his shoulders tense. "I don't know."

"What do you mean you don't know?"

He ran a hand through his auburn hair. "When we left the human world, he'd been taken to the hospital. I do not know what happened to him after that."

She couldn't breathe. Her lungs cried out for air, and she bent over clutching her chest. Angry tears washed down her face. "You... you told me he died, and you didn't even check?"

But Lochlan had. The grumpy Eldur delegate must have gone back to the human realm to find out what happened to her best friend, the only person who'd ever truly loved her.

"Myles is alive." But could she trust Lochlan's words?

She wiped a hand across her damp cheek. Griff didn't

deserve her tears, but they weren't for him anyway. Myles' smile flashed through her mind. What if she hadn't killed him?

He had to still be alive.

Straightening, she hardened her expression. "You and I are not friends, Griffin O'Shea. I will marry you and give you legitimacy, but that is all. I could have forgiven the lies about your motive in bringing me here or even the eavesdropping in my rooms. But Myles... that lie is not one I will ever move past." She walked to the door.

"Brea," Griff called, his voice thick. "Please."

She paused before opening the door. "I am not some fae girl who will fall at your feet and beg to be queen. I don't care if half my blood is of this world. I am human, and we make decisions for ourselves."

Calling on the magic she still didn't understand and still couldn't control, she blasted through the door, sending wood splintering against the wall in the hallway.

As she stepped across the broken frame, she looked back over her shoulder. "You will never control me."

The day after her fight with Griff, Brea woke with little energy. The triplets brought in her breakfast, setting it on her bed as they'd learned she liked. Their shared looks told her they must have heard what happened the day before.

They didn't dare bring it up in a room where privacy was only an illusion.

"Where is Neeve?" She pushed the food around on her plate, having no real appetite.

"The queen wanted her to help down in the kitchens," Triplet One said, her voice way too high this early in the morning. She leaned in. "She's the only servant Queen Regan really trusts, and with the farewell dinner for the Iskalt delegation tonight, she wanted Neeve overseeing preparations."

It surprised Brea that the delegation from Iskalt was still there when the Eldur people left right after the festival. They'd been meeting behind closed doors with her aunt, but Brea knew so little about the fae world relations she couldn't begin to guess why.

Triplet Two bounced on her toes as she twisted a long lock of blond hair around her finger. "There's a rumor around the palace that you're to marry Lord Griffin."

"He's perfect," the third girl sighed.

Sure, perfect if one wanted a lying, manipulative, power seeker. But she couldn't tell them he only wanted her as a means to get the crown. "We haven't announced the engagement yet."

"Don't wait too long." Brea lost track of which triplet said what. "There are plenty of noblewomen who'd gladly take your place."

Brea would happily let them. If she had her way, she'd never have to see Griff again.

Unable to take more of this inane chatter, Brea got out of bed and rummaged through her armoire. "I must go see my fiancé."

"Fiancé," one of the girls giggled. "That's a funny word."

"Oh, um, I mean betrothed."

"You won't find him at the palace." One of the girls pursed her lips. "I heard from one of the guards who heard from a servant of Lord Griffin's that he left early this morning on a mission for the crown. He won't be back for a week at least."

"He... left?" She agreed to be his wife, and he left without a word the next morning?

"Yes, the guard said it was a matter of utmost importance, but a secret mission nonetheless."

She couldn't imagine what would take Griff away from the palace. He'd told her since they arrived that one day he'd have to return to his cottage because palace life wasn't for him. But that had only been another lie.

"No matter." She abandoned the dress she'd planned to wear to speak with Griff in favor of the outfit Neeve brought for her the day before. Turning back to the triplets, she raised a brow. "I'm going to change."

They didn't budge.

"Erm... please go. If I need you later on, I'll call. I mean, I'll send someone to fetch you."

"Yes, your Highness." They each curtsied before skittering from the room.

Brea stared after them, their "your Highnesses" ringing in her ears. She wasn't meant for such a title, and if she had a say, she would never hear them utter it again.

It was time to stop lamenting her situation and act on it.

Changing into the comfortable clothes quickly, she hurried from the room and took the winding path through the palace, across an open-air bridge, and down a spiral staircase into the palace kitchens.

A cook looked up when she entered, a scowl on her plump face. "This isn't the place for you, my Lady."

"I'm sorry. I'm just looking for someone."

"Well, look elsewhere. We're quite busy this morning." She went back to her task.

Others paid her no mind as she skirted the outer edge of the grand network of rooms where cooks and bakers plied their trade. Servants rushed through with trays laden with fruits, pastries, and pots of tea, no doubt attending to the many nobles currently residing at the palace.

"The queen isn't going to like that." Neeve's strong voice cut through the bustle as she chastised one of the cooks in front of a boiling pot of sauce. "She'll want more Gelsi berries in the sauce."

Gelsi berries? The same fruit that dampens magic?

Neeve's gaze found Brea and her eyes widened. She wiped her hands on the white apron tied to her waist and rushed toward Brea. "My Lady, you should not be down here."

"I needed to talk to you, and it couldn't wait."

Neeve looked back over her shoulder at the cooks before gesturing for Brea to follow her around the corner into a storage room. She shut the door, sending them into semi-darkness.

"Are they putting Gelsi berries in the food?" It was the first question to escape her lips.

Neeve nodded, glancing at the door. "Queen Regan dampens the powers of all those staying within her walls. It is how she keeps such tight control—especially when foreign delegations are present."

Was that why Brea had only had a few outbursts here in the palace? Back in the human realm, she'd constantly felt on the brink of losing control.

"But then..."

Neeve must have sensed what she meant to ask, because she answered. "Your magic must be quite powerful with the few times you've been able to use it."

Brea shook her head to clear it. This wasn't why she'd come. "Tell me the truth. The warning in the caramel sauce was you."

Neeve nodded.

"Lochlan said I could trust you, but I don't know if I can believe what he says. Everyone is lying to me."

Neeve met her gaze. "Lochlan O'Shea does not lie. He's a lot of things, but when he speaks, you can believe him."

"And his brother?"

"That's more complicated."

"I'm supposed to marry him."

"You can't," Neeve whispered before collecting herself. "There's so much you don't know, but I can't be the one to tell you when I only know bits."

"I can't stay here, can I?" Not when they'd lied to her and tried to trap her. Her aunt seemed kind and caring, but now Brea realized she didn't know her at all.

Neeve shook her head. "It's not safe for you."

"I have nowhere else to go." She wanted to go back to Myles, but a jail cell waited for her in the human world.

"You do." Neeve gripped her arms. "There is one place in this world you'll be safe." She implored Brea to believe her with her eyes. "You need to get to Eldur."

Brea backed away from her. Eldur. The fire kingdom with an evil queen and most-probably dragons. "I can't go to Eldur."

"You must. Do not believe what you have been told. The beauty of Fargelsi is a trick meant to make the beholder trust in their safety. There is no safety to be had here for anyone. We are all trapped, but you have a chance to be free. You must take it. For all of us."

"What do you mean you're trapped? Can't you come with me?"

She shook her head, her eyes shining. "We don't have time to explain. There is a pathway through the marshes of the Southern Vatlands. I can take you only part of the way before I must return to the palace. The marshes lead across the border into Eldur where a contingent of the Fire Queen's soldiers stand guard."

"Why are they in the Vatlands? I thought those were neutral zones."

"They're there for the rare occasion I can get people out of Gelsi. Only those without full Fargelsi blood can cross the borders and the Eldurians protect them. You must navigate the marshes until you reach their camp. With them, you will be safe."

"When do we leave?"

Neeve offered her a sad smile. "Tonight. You will leave the farewell dinner for Iskalt early, claiming you are ill. I'll attend to you. Lord Griffin is away from the palace at present, so this gives us an opportunity. I'll put together some food for you and procure a horse to get you to the Vatlands. You cannot pack anything else."

Brea breathed heavily as she tried to calm her racing heart. "I'm scared, Neeve."

Neeve's expression softened, and she put a hand on each of Brea's shoulders. "You are a human girl traversing these strange fae times. If you were not scared, I would think Fargelsi is where you truly belonged."

"What does that mean?"

"That being scared will keep you safe. Here in this court of never-ending spring and beauty, we live in a perpetually emotionless state. Everything is for show. You aren't one of them, Brea. I knew that the moment I first met you."

"That doesn't make me feel any better, you know." Not on the eve of fleeing from the place she'd wanted to call home.

Neeve smiled. "Just remember—at dinner, don't eat any of the sauces. No matter how untaught your power is, you will need the full strength of it in the marshes." She opened the door, gave Brea one final encouraging look, and slipped out.

Brea leaned her head back against the wall. How had everything gotten so messed up in such a short period of time?

Oh right... the man she'd thought she was falling in love with lied to her about the death of the only true friend she'd ever had.

She glanced at the door Neeve disappeared through.

Until now.

The maid would probably deny it, but no one risked themselves for someone else unless they cared.

Lifting her eyes to the dark stone ceiling of the cool storage room, she sighed. "I will find out what happened to you, Myles," she whispered. "If it's the last thing I do."

Chapter Fourteen

"You look lovely, darling. If a bit morose." Queen Regan looped her arm through Brea's as they made their way down to the banquet hall for the big Iskalt send off.

"Griff left without saying goodbye." Brea had decided to play the part of a lovesick teen. She'd seen enough of the girls' theatrics back home to pull it off here.

"Don't worry yourself, dear. I sent him on an important errand that just couldn't wait. He had little time to prepare, much less make time for a romantic farewell. He'll be back soon, and we can talk about wedding plans. I'm so pleased you've agreed to his proposal."

She made it all sound so normal and romantic, like he'd actually gotten down on one knee and popped the question. In the back of Brea's mind all she heard was *what would Myles say about all of this?* First, he would be stoked to find the fae realm exists, and he'd want to explore it with her. Second, he would do that side-splitting laugh thing he did at the news of her impending *betrothal.* Just the thought of his laughter brought a smile to her face.

"That's better." Regan smiled as they approached the banquet hall. "Smile for the delegates, dear. They'll be on their way back to their frozen tundra by morning, and we'll have the place to ourselves for a while."

By then, Brea would be neck deep in the marshes, if she even made it that far. She wasn't looking forward to the next few hours.

"Do you entertain often, Aunt Regan?" Brea needed to play the part of the dutiful niece.

"One of the many perks of being queen. You get to throw parties as often as you like. Don't worry, we have your betrothal and wedding celebrations to look forward to. There will be plenty more parties where you'll be the guest of honor. We'll have to start planning your wardrobe right away."

This woman didn't know Brea at all if she thought more parties and uncomfortable dresses was the way to cheer her up.

Brea followed her aunt into the banquet hall after the herald announced her and a footman guided her to the high table where she sat beside the queen. She smiled and nodded and engaged in the conversation as best she could, but her mind was elsewhere.

"None for me, thank you," Brea murmured, covering her goblet with her hand. The servers had been plying her and the queen with wine all night.

"Are you feeling well, dear?" The queen asked, eyeing her plate.

Brea had done a good job making it look like she'd eaten, but she didn't want to accidentally eat one of her aunt's magic-stifling sauces by accident.

"Actually, I am feeling a little under the weather," Brea

admitted with feigned reluctance. "Just tired and a bit off from too much wine lately. I'm not used to it."

"And missing a certain handsome young man?" her aunt teased.

Anger caused her face to flush, and Brea hoped the queen would take it for a lover's blush.

"Very much," she murmured.

"Very well, dear, you may retire. Come to my rooms for a late brunch tomorrow morning and we'll get started on wedding plans."

"Thank you, Aunt Regan." Brea rose from her chair, intending to rush from the room, but every delegate at the table rose with her.

"Er, um. Excuse me, ladies and gentlemen." She bobbed her head.

"My niece is a bit tired this evening," the queen explained. "And missing a certain gentleman," she whisper-shouted behind her enormous peacock-feathered fan. Her laughter sent the Iskalt delegates into a tittering fit.

Stumbling over her train, Brea made for the door as quickly as she could and still look like the refined lady she was supposed to be. Once she hit the empty grand hallway, Brea hiked up her skirts and ran up the stairs to the queen's quarters.

"Psst, my Lady," Neeve's voice drifted down the hallway leading to Brea's rooms. "In here."

Brea turned toward the sound of her voice and found her waiting in a small servant's room. "Is this yours?" Brea looked around at the tidy room. It was nice. Nothing like her luxurious suite, but it was homey and comfortable in a way Brea's wasn't.

"The queen likes to keep me close, so I don't sleep in the servants' quarters like most palace maids. It will be safer for you to change in here. No one bothers to spy on me."

"You thought of everything." Brea kicked off her heels and

turned her back so Neeve could help her out of the fancy dress. Neeve was already dressed for their trip to the Vatlands. Brea just hoped her friend wouldn't get caught helping her escape the palace.

"Relax, I've done this before. We won't get caught."

"You a mind reader?" Brea wiggled out of her bodice and tossed it on the floor with a none too gentle kick. She hoped she never had to wear such stifling clothes again.

"You're a kind young woman, Brea. In another time and place we might have been the best of friends. You care about the people around you. It doesn't take a mind reader to see that." She glanced at Brea's reflection in the mirror above her dresser. "In this world, that's a rare commodity. It would be a shame to see you lose it."

Brea dressed quickly in the sturdy travel clothes Neeve had acquired for her. Dark leather leggings, a linen tunic layered under a leather vest and jacket and a belt with a knife she didn't know how to use. Tying her long ebony hair back into a messy bun, Brea retrieved her pack.

"There's a change of clothes, food, and water in there for you. In a moment, we'll take the servants' stairs down to the kitchens. If anyone stops us, you're a new house maid. I'm giving you a tour of the palace before I take you to your new quarters."

"Got it." Brea hefted the pack up on her shoulder. "So, we'll just slip across the bridge to the stables then?"

Neeve shook her head. "The queen has eyes everywhere, Brea. We have to be smart about this. I need you to stay close and keep moving no matter what happens to me. Trust no one."

"Okay, serious faces on." Neeve's grave look shook Brea. "This is a big deal, escaping."

"A very big deal." Neeve hefted a pack onto her shoulder. "I don't know if the queen simply wants you to give Lord

Griffin legitimacy through his marriage to you, or if she has something far worse up her sleeve. I only know it's important to get you out of here as soon as possible. Once we get to the kitchens, there's another stairway we'll take down to the dungeon."

"Dungeon? This place has a dungeon?"

"It will lead us out to the riverbed behind the falls where we'll make our way into the forest. A friend will meet us there with horses. From there we'll head south toward the Vatlands marshes. If we get separated, you're to head southeast and keep going until you find the Eldur camp just over the border. There's a map in your pack in case you need it."

"Thank you, Neeve. I'll never be able to repay your kindness."

Neeve peeked into the hallway, waving for Brea to follow.

Sneaking down the stairwell, they arrived in the kitchens unhindered.

"What are you doing, Neeve?" The head cook bellowed. "Shouldn't you be prepping the nobles' rooms for the evening?"

"Mistress O'Sullivan." Neeve rounded on the woman. "Just showing the new maid around. She starts in the queen's quarters tomorrow."

"What's your name, girl?"

"Ygritte," Brea blurted. "Of the Free Folk. North of the wall."

"Well, Ygritte, we don't know nothing about no free folk here. Best you finish your tour and get to bed early with you. Big day tomorrow cleaning up this mess of a palace."

"Yes ma'am." Brea and Neeve bobbed their heads and turned for the dreary halls leading to the servants' quarters.

"North of the wall?" Neeve rolled her eyes. "What human nonsense was that?"

"It just came out. I don't actually think about these things before I say them."

"If you want to survive in this world, you'd better start thinking ten steps ahead of everyone else, Brea."

"You're right." Brea followed her down the long hall but was unprepared when Neeve took a sharp left behind a bookcase in the wall. "Secret passages?" Brea stepped through the opening. Darkness engulfed them as the bookshelf slid back into place.

"This palace is a labyrinth of secrets and lies."

Neeve whispered a few unintelligible words before a fire blazed, lighting a torch she'd procured from her pack.

"Was that magic? Like a spell? Griff said our magic didn't work like that."

"Lord Griffin has been liberal with his lies, I'm afraid. He is a good man... deep down. But the queen has had him in her clutches far too long. This way."

Brea followed silently, taking the slimy stone steps carefully. They seemed to wind down into the depths of the earth with no end in sight.

"Those born of Fargelsi draw our power from nature," Neeve explained. "But we do rely on spoken spells and words of power for much of what we do. It is different in the other realms."

"So, Griff lied about that too?" Brea frowned. *Was there no end to the lies?* The musty smells and constant dripping grated on her nerves.

"I do not know his motives."

Brea followed in silence, her thoughts a tumble of chaos. It didn't matter if Griff cared for her. He'd told her Myles was dead when that might not be true. That was unforgivable.

White noise rushed to fill Brea's ears.

"The waterfalls," Neeve called over the roaring din. "We're

nearly to the river." Neeve's skirts dragged across the damp stones and muck as they began to climb.

Finally, moonlight illuminated their path as they crossed under the falls. Brea carefully followed Neeve's footsteps to avoid the deluge. Hopping from stone to boulder, they made their way past the waterfall to the river's edge just below the great palace. Sounds of the party—in full swing now—floated down to them.

"They won't notice you're gone until late morning." Neeve spoke a few odd words, and the flame of her torch died.

"You have to teach me that trick someday." Brea rushed to keep up with her friend's pace. "But something tells me it's a little more complicated than *Lumos* and *Nox*."

"There you go with your silly words." Neeve chuckled. "I will miss that."

"Then come with me," Brea begged. Truth be told she was terrified of traveling a strange land alone—through miles of swamp no less.

"I can do more good here than I can out there, Brea. I'm nobody here. The small things I do to fight the injustices in Gelsi matter to my people. In some ways, I'm all they have."

"I want to be you when I grow up." Brea huffed and puffed behind the small woman. Weeks of rich foods, wine, and too little exercise had sapped Brea's stamina.

"Hurry, we're nearly to the meeting place."

"This friend of yours is trustworthy?" Brea jogged along the rocky riverbank to catch up."

"Moira? I trust her with my life."

"Is she your girlfriend?"

"My intended you mean?"

"Why can't a woman just have a passing flirtation with a pretty girl or a cute guy and it *not* end in a walk down the aisle?" Brea muttered under her breath.

"Moira might be my wife someday. When we are free."

"Neeve?" a feminine voice called from the darkness.

"Here, Moira." She picked up her skirts and ran to the woman who'd risked a great deal to meet them in the dead of night.

Brea held back to give the two lovers a moment of reunion. She imagined they didn't get to see each other often.

"Come, Brea. We must hurry," Neeve called a moment later.

"My Lady." Moira gave a curt bow and offered her a dark cloak. "This will help shield your face and keep you warm. It can get cold in the swamps."

"Thank you, and please call me Brea." She slipped the cloak over her shoulders and lifted the hood over her head. "Thank you for the horses. I know you took a great risk in coming here."

"Anything for Neeve." Moira gave her intended a devilish wink. "She's a tough one, my girl. You're safe with her, and you'd do well to follow her instructions to the letter. She's always right. It's frustrating." She grinned, dipping into an awkward curtsy for Brea.

Brea watched them. The way they respected each other it was clear this couple was on an even footing in their relationship. Moira didn't coddle Neeve or insist she needed protecting. She was confident in her ability to help Brea flee Fargelsi.

I want that kind of relationship someday. She lifted herself into the saddle, grateful for the cloak.

"Keep to the back southern roads. Travel well, and may you return to me quickly, my love." Moira waved as Neeve and Brea charged into the night.

They rode hard for several silent hours before Neeve took the east road toward the marshes. Brea could smell a hint of brine in the air. It reminded her of the ocean she'd once visited with her family. In the years before her *sanity* issues became a big problem, her family used to take a rare vacation every few years. Some of her fondest memories with her family were from that vacation to the beach.

Neeve slowed to a stop when the road ran out. "This is where I leave you." She slipped down from her horse. "I have to get back to the palace before sunrise, so I must hurry."

Brea stared into the darkness ahead. Fear gripped her as she dismounted her horse. She would have to travel the rest of the way on foot. The marsh was too dangerous for a horse.

"I'm afraid, Neeve," Brea whispered.

Neeve took both of her hands in hers. "Look at me."

Brea lifted her chin, meeting Neeve's cool gaze.

"You are strong, Brea Robinson. You haven't come of age yet, so I don't think you realize how strong you really are. Regan fears that kind of inner strength. She wanted to stifle it. To put you in a position with no power. As her heir's wife, you would be nothing more than a pretty face. Just another prisoner. You can do this, Brea. You have to."

"What if I get lost?"

"You won't." Neeve searched through her pack, coming up with a bottle of oil. "Keep heading east, and if you should lose your compass, look for the brightest star in the sky and keep it directly overhead." Neeve flicked the contents of the bottle, spritzing Brea from head to toe in the foul-smelling stuff.

"Ugh, what is that awful smell?"

"It will keep the creatures at bay."

"Creatures?"

"Go, Brea." She pressed a lantern into her hands, speaking the words of power to light it and gave her a gentle shove.

"Head east until you reach the Eldur camps. Don't stop. Don't sleep. Keep going. You should make it there by morning."

Brea nodded, taking a deep breath before she flung herself into Neeve's arms. "Thank you. I've never had many friends, but you are one of them. I hope to see you again someday."

With that, Brea lifted her lantern and headed into the grim forest of creepy cypress trees, hanging moss, and lots of mud. It squelched under her feet as she walked. Glancing back over her shoulder, Neeve had already gone.

"It's just me and the marsh." Brea checked her compass and set her path for east.

The first mile was easy. The second mile was pretty bad, but the third mile was the stuff of nightmares. Brea stood in mud up to her knees, searching for semi-solid ground in the dim glow of the lantern. Her arm ached from holding it in front of her, but she was terrified of the dark.

Mosquito-like creatures buzzed around her face. They continued to dive-bomb her, drinking her blood until she slapped them against her skin, crushing their vile little bodies, covering her in mushed bug goo and blood.

"Oh my gosh." Brea stumbled back, putting as much distance between herself and the slithering creature she'd just encountered. "I hate snakes!" She shouted into the darkness. "Fairy land should have no snakes. That's like a rule somewhere."

Lifting her foot out of the squelching mud, she took a step forward, her knees screaming in protest from the push and pull on her joints. Her left foot found firmer ground, and she nearly sobbed in relief.

Brea pulled herself up onto the mossy bit of ground, tempted to take a rest, but she'd promised Neeve she'd keep moving, and she'd barely begun. Taking just a moment to rub some life back into her knees, Brea stood, her body protesting.

"Maybe I could sit here long enough to eat something." She reached for her pack, taking a sip of water from her canteen. Something moved in the deep water near her somewhat-dry perch. Something large. Brea fumbled to put her canteen back in her pack and searched her surroundings for the quickest path.

A snapping turtle struggled out of the water, and she sighed, slumping against the tree at her back.

"That was—" Brea's heart stopped as a pair of massive jaws appeared out of the water and closed around the turtle.

The second creature chomped on its crunchy meal and slithered out of the water. It looked like a huge lizard and an alligator had a really ugly dragon-baby. Brea stood rooted to the spot as the creature's tail stretched out behind it. It had to be twenty feet long. She almost peed herself when it lifted its head toward her, flicking its long tongue as if to taste the air around her.

"Please be full from your turtle snack," she whispered, unable to move. She had nowhere to go anyway. She eyed the trees around her, wondering if she could climb if it came to that. Not a tree branch in sight low enough for her to reach.

The creature hissed a warning, showing its massive razor sharp teeth before it ambled away. She swore it wrinkled its nose in disgust.

"Thank you, Neeve, for making me stink." Brea wasn't sure her heartbeat would ever return to normal. She stared at the creature until she couldn't see it anymore. "Get it together, Robinson." She reached for the lantern at her feet. Her hands shaking as she wondered how many of those things were out there.

Her body said, "I live here now," but her mind disagreed. Taking a careful step off the mossy perch, the tension in Brea's shoulders eased some. Solid ground.

With her compass guiding her way east, Brea moved as quickly as her feet would allow her, ever mindful of what she might step on. Nocturnal creatures were out and about, making a ruckus all around her. Insects and small furry creatures she could handle. Even the orange salamanders that scurried about didn't bother her.

Owls hooted and fish splashed in the ponds. She even heard the distant growl of a very large cat she hoped she wouldn't encounter. As the ground grew soft again, Brea searched for an alternate path. She didn't want to end up in mud up to her knees again.

Her stomach growled, and she thought of the food Neeve packed for her. Setting her lamp down, Brea rushed to retrieve the bacon sandwiches from her pack. Just a quick bite, and she'd be on her way again. Resting against a cypress tree, she ate quickly. Feeling better with something in her stomach, Brea leaned her head back against the tree, sipping from her canteen.

"No crazy swamp dragons here." She shoved off the tree and hauled her pack up on her shoulder. Leaning down for her lantern, something heavy and scaly landed on her back.

Brea screamed, throwing the huge snake across the swamp. The slithering, hissing black snake landed with a thud. It was huge and angry. Brea took a step back and stumbled over her lantern. Darkness fell all around her as her only light source went out.

"No!" Brea nearly wept.

Hissing sounded nearby, and she wasn't waiting around for the snake to find her or call his buddies in for a group attack. Clutching her compass, Brea followed the path of semi-solid ground until it ran out.

Within moments, the mud reached her calves, but she kept

moving East. Without the lantern, the bugs had finally left her alone.

Thunder rumbled in the distance, and Brea laughed. "Of course it's going to rain." She threw her hands up toward the sky. "It's certainly not wet enough around here."

She trudged forward, avoiding the nocturnal growls that sounded far too close for comfort. The larger creatures seemed to want to check her out until they got close enough to smell Neeve's concoction on her, and then they probably decided she didn't smell like food.

"Thank you, Neeve. I smell so bad not even the dragon monsters want anything to do with me."

To make the time pass and to keep her mind off the creepy crawlies, Brea kept her eyes glued to a grove of trees in the distance. When she reached it, she found a long branch to use as a walking stick. Checking her compass to ensure she was heading in the right direction, she selected a new landmark to focus on. This time it was an outcropping of rocks rising from the swamp.

She was on her fifth landmark when it started to rain. Her seventh when it started to pour. By the tenth landmark, Brea was in mud up to her thighs with no solid ground in sight.

She was exhausted and scared out of her wits. The area around her was more water than mud, and Brea's heart raced with the fear of what monsters might lurk nearby. She clutched her walking stick, using it to keep her balance in the swamp.

The magic she didn't understand thundered through her body. She had no knowledge of how to control it, only that it responded to her emotions. Griff claimed he was going to teach her how to harness her emotions so she wouldn't lose control, but that had never happened. The evidence against him continued to mount, and Brea wondered why it had taken her so long to see it.

She could feel it sizzling under her skin, begging for release. The longer she struggled to move through the swampy waters, the more the magic gathered inside her, latching on to her fear and anger like a blazing fire consuming oxygen.

Brea took another step forward, and she was up to her chest in muddy water as the rain continued to beat down on her. Lightning flashed, and something slithered against her thigh

Struggling to move faster, Brea's exhaustion overwhelmed her. Her tears mixed with the rain. "I just want to go home."

She'd gladly face the assault charges that awaited her back in the human world if it meant she could put this nightmare behind her. If she could see Myles again. Even her parents would be a welcome sight right now.

Splashing through the water, the ground began to rise, and Brea lurched forward until her knees were above water for the first time in hours. Checking her compass, she was still on the right path and the land ahead of her seemed rather solid in the moonlight.

As she moved forward, the magic pooling just under her skin seemed to reach a critical point. Stumbling, Brea's heart rattled in her chest, and her lungs seized. She clutched her walking stick like a lifeline, but she couldn't stay upright. She could feel the magic like a welling pressure in her body. With a scream of anguish, Brea tumbled forward, and a yellow light rushed from her open mouth, clashing with the lightning overhead. Sparks rained down around her illuminating the expanse of marshlands she still had to traverse.

Brea fell headfirst into the putrid mud. Rolling to her side, she tried to stand, but her vision went blurry.

I'm going to die out here all alone, and no one will even care.

CHAPTER FIFTEEN

Thunder ripped through Brea's mind, and she jolted up in bed.

Bed?

Her chest rose and fell with rapid succession as she tried to see her surroundings, hidden by the dark.

The marsh. Creepy alligator-lizard-dragons.

She released a sigh as she gripped the thin wool blanket pooled in her lap. Had it all been a dream?

Or had her magic really almost killed her?

Her eyes darted from the bed to the sliver of moonlight appearing through a crack in the... tent door? Yeah, she was in a tent. How? Who?

A flash of lightning illuminated the sparse surroundings for just long enough to take in the small bed roll beneath her and little else. Her pack rested in the corner next to a set of saddle bags.

Brea's stomach ached with hunger, and she couldn't take her eyes off the familiar bag Neeve had given her. It took her a moment to realize the steady drumming on the canvas overhead wasn't in her mind. The rain kept coming like it had no intention of letting up.

Scrambling from the bedroll, she crawled across the mossy ground to her pack and ripped it open. Yanking every one of the few belongings she had out, she searched for the remaining food that should be there.

Nothing.

Turning her attention to the unknown saddle bags, she pulled them into her lap and dug through the stranger's provisions. Still, no food.

Warm, briny air blew into the tent, bringing with it the rain. She scooted back from the opening, dragging her bag with her. Going through it more slowly this time, she found the small knife Neeve had given her. Whoever found her must have taken it off her body.

Tucking it into the waist of pants she didn't recognize, she pulled her legs up to her chest. Weariness invaded her mind. Her limbs tingled with weakness, and it took her a moment to realize what she felt... or what she didn't feel.

No magic pooled underneath her skin. It didn't churn with her emotions and lend her strength in her greatest moment of need.

"It's gone," she whispered.

She should have felt relief. Her entire life, she'd stood on the edge of a precipice, her volatility threatening to send her into the abyss—or get her locked up in the Clarkson Institute. She now knew it had been the magic, her fae heritage, expanding everything she felt.

But now, in the absence of that, with the prospect of being just a normal human, there was an emptiness inside her, a void in her heart.

She had to figure out where she was. If whoever found her

was taking her back to Gelsi, she may as well have stayed with the lizard things. A shiver wracked her body and she couldn't make it stop. Wherever they were was warmer than Gelsi, but even that couldn't still her body's shaking.

Her teeth clattered, and she pulled her tangled mass of hair over one shoulder, running her hands through it as if that could provide her the comfort she needed.

"You are Brea Robinson," she said. "You survived being pulled into a different world and living in a palace of lies. A manipulative aunt, a man who betrayed you, and... snakes." She closed her eyes, trying to make herself believe the words. "You can survive whoever is outside this tent."

A crash of thunder made her jump, sounding like it split the sky in two. If the fae world cracked open, would it let her return to the safety of Ohio corn fields, where the biggest danger was psychiatrists overanalyzing everything and mean kids at school?

At least none of them had swords.

She fingered the hilt of the knife, wondering what any of the kids she'd known would think if they saw her now.

"I need you, Myles," she whispered. She pulled the blanket around her as if it could protect her from this world. "I really hope you're alive."

And if he was, she'd see him again. In all of Griff's stupid promises, he'd never been able to give her that hope. How could he even keep all of his promises and lies straight?

She couldn't go back to Griff, not after everything.

Kicking the blanket away, she stood and crept to the tent opening, peering out into the storm.

Two guards stood nearby, seemingly impervious to the rain in their leather armor. Tents sat haphazardly around the small clearing with cypress trees looming as shadows overhead. Were they still in the marshes?

Voices came from the guards. "We can't stay here forever," one of them said.

The other didn't respond right away. "We have our orders. The girl must be awake for the journey. And we cannot leave until given the order to march."

"What if she doesn't wake up? We don't know what happened to her out there."

The second guard shrugged. "We will deliver her to the palace whether she lives or not."

Lives or not. There words were so cold, Brea realized they must mean to bring her back to her aunt. After everything, she refused to go back there. What would they do to her after she ran?

She'd made it this far. Neeve's words came back to her. "*Don't stop until you reach Eldur.*"

She couldn't give up now.

Sparing one more glance for the tent flap and the guards beyond, she pulled her knife free and scooted across the bed to the back of the tent. Gripping the thick material in her shaking fingers, she stabbed the tip of the blade into it and sawed, cutting a line down the tent.

When the slit was big enough, she stuck her head through. Water wicked into her eyes as it streamed down her hair into her face. She glanced up at the stormy sky, hoping the deluge would hide her escape.

She couldn't make out her surroundings and didn't know which way to go, but she'd figure that out once she was away from these Fargelsian soldiers. Gripping her knife tightly, she slipped through the opening and jumped to her feet. Pumping her legs, she sprinted as fast as she could for the trees.

Shouting erupted behind her, but she didn't stop no matter how much her burning legs ached for it. Weakness vibrated through her, but she didn't give into it. She couldn't.

Solid ground turned to mud underneath her feet. As more soldiers shouted for her to stop, she had to keep going, wading into the swirling goo. It rose up around her legs the deeper she got, refusing to let her go. By the time the mud reached her thighs, she couldn't move.

A cry left her lips as she tried to free herself, only managing to get deeper into the mud. A snake slithered by her legs, and she stabbed at it with her knife, flicking it away from her. It hissed and left her alone. This was it. She was going to die stuck in mud in a foreign world as soldiers chased after her during a storm.

She lifted her face to the rain as it broke through the tree cover. "I'm sorry, okay? Whatever I did to deserve this, I didn't mean it." She slapped her arm. "Brea Robinson, if there was ever a time to wake up, this is it." Some small part of her still hoped this was a nightmare, a horrid and all-too-real nightmare.

"Don't move!" a voice boomed out of the dark.

"Good thing I can't, then!" she yelled back. "You're lucky I'm stuck in mud or you'd have never caught me."

In reality, her escape was doomed from the start. She was a half-human girl who only ran when being chased, not for any sort of exercise. Yeah, she was screwed.

"Stay there."

"Already told you I have no choice." Rain pounded into the mud harder and harder as her heart rate kicked up. Whatever Gelsi held for her was better than dying right here.

"Reach out," the voice commanded. "As far as you can."

She grappled in the dark, trying to find something to hold onto as she bent toward the voice. Her hand touched flesh, and she reached her other one out, gripping the man's hand with both of hers, their fingers slick against each other.

"I'm going to pull you out."

He tugged on her hands, and another set of hands clamped

down underneath her armpits, lifting her as the other man pulled.

"Don't let go!" someone yelled.

"Not planning on it." Relief flushed through her as her legs came free little by little.

An arm wrapped around her waist and hauled her the rest of the way. She almost cried when her feet hit solid ground.

"I could kiss you right now!" she yelled at one of the soldiers over the rain.

"My Lady." He jumped away from her, thoroughly scandalized.

Brea didn't have the energy to laugh. She rolled onto her stomach and pushed herself to her knees as she tried to catch her breath.

Without waiting for permission, one of the soldiers lifted her into his arms and walked back through the trees. He didn't speak until they reached the tent she'd escaped from.

He set her down, his aged face marred by a scowl. "Stay here."

Turning on his heel, he marched away.

Brea looked around the tent, thankful for its semi-safe surroundings. She sat down on the bedroll, her entire body shaking with cold. Water streamed down her back, but it didn't matter because the bed was already soaked from the rain entering through the slit she'd cut. She closed her eyes, trying to calm herself, until commotion sounded outside her tent.

A man walked in, his lips forming a smile that did not belong in this moment. "Well, my Lady, you have caused quite a stir."

She shrank away from him. "What do you want from me?"

He removed his helmet, revealing a face even younger than she'd thought. He couldn't have been much older than her. "I believe I should be the one asking questions. My men found you unconscious in the middle of the marshy Vatlands. No one travels the Vatlands alone except for one reason."

"What's that reason?"

"Tell you what, I will give you some answers, if you do the same. Let's start with a name."

"Breanne of Tarth," she blurted before she could stop herself. Something prevented her from giving her real name.

He nodded as if that was a perfectly plausible name. "Tarth, is that a Gelsi province?"

She nodded.

"Well, Breanne, you're safe here." This time, his smile reached his eyes. He had a face one wanted to trust, but then, so had Griff. "My name is Finn. The only brave souls who traverse the Vatlands on their own are those who manage to escape the Fargelsian queen."

"You're not..." She sucked in a breath. "You aren't taking me back there?"

He reeled back as if she'd slapped him. "No. Why would we do that? These men are stationed near the border to intercept those fleeing tyranny just like you. I am only here because my traveling companion has been waiting for someone." He eyed her carefully. "How did you escape Gelsi?"

"I had help." She didn't want to reveal Neeve's identity.

Finn rubbed his jaw. "Yes, well, even still... do you know of the border spell?"

He didn't wait for her to respond. "Those with full Fargelsi blood are forbidden from crossing the border by the queen. Her magic keeps them there unless she releases them."

Neeve had explained all this before, but it hadn't really hit Brea then. That was why Neeve couldn't come. Everything Brea knew about her aunt flashed through her mind. She'd known she was manipulative, but would she really go to such lengths to keep her power? To keep her people imprisoned?

Did Griff know? She wanted to believe he was just naive in all this, but she didn't know him, not like she'd thought she did.

"I'm not..." What had she meant to say? She wasn't a full Fargelsian fae? She wasn't fae at all? No matter who her father was, she didn't belong in that world.

An angry voice entered the relative calm of the tent as someone barged their way in, shaking sopping wet blond hair out of his face. Brea looked from Finn to the new intruder.

Lochlan.

He pushed his hair back, allowing her to see his blazing eyes.

"Ah, Loch." Finn grinned as he turned to the other man. "Meet our newest Gelsi escapee, Breanne of Tarth."

Lochlan's dark eyes met hers. "If this is Breanne of Tarth, then I'm Jon Snow."

Brea's jaw fell open. "How... what... I mean, what?"

Lochlan's jaw twitched, but he didn't explain how he knew about a human TV series. Instead, he turned to Finn. "This is her." He turned on his heel and marched away.

Brea scrambled from the bed, but Finn blocked her path, his face red with embarrassment. "You fooled me, Brea Robinson, but it is a pleasure to meet the woman who can vex the unshakeable Lochlan O'Shea."

"Yeah, yeah." She shoved him out of the way. "You can thank me for my service later. I need to talk to him."

Darting out into the rain, she caught sight of Lochlan's retreating back and ran toward him. "You can't just walk away from me."

He whirled to face her. "I can do whatever I please. I am the ranking officer here. These men follow my orders. I would appreciate if you no longer ran from them."

"I make no promises."

He approached her with the eyes of a predator, dark and

dangerous. Griff hadn't had a lot of the traits of the fae from stories she'd seen. He was beautiful, sure, but also smiley and seemingly kind. Lochlan on the other hand fit everything from human fiction novels. Cunning. Cruel.

Achingly attractive.

"How do you know about *Game of Thrones*?" she asked.

Lochlan shook his head in exasperation and gripped her arm, pulling her into a nearby tent. "It's a deluge out there."

"I noticed." She crossed her arms over her soaking shirt. "Are you going to answer my question?"

"No." He stepped around her and stripped the blanket from his bed. Holding it out to her, he met her gaze. "Wrap this around your body so you don't catch a chill."

"I'm fine."

Lochlan's scowl deepened. "Do you know how much risk you took tonight? We are in the middle of the Vatlands. Traveling at night is nearly impossible because of the mud pits that only get deeper and deeper. They've claimed many lives. You could have died."

"But I didn't."

"Because of my men."

He was right. She'd made a rash decision trying to escape and almost paid for it with her life. "I'm sorry."

His expression softened for a beat before hardening into another scowl. "You are not to do it again. Since you so gratefully destroyed the tent we gave you, you will sleep in here tonight where I can keep an eye on you."

"How will you keep an eye on me if you need to sleep? I could slit your throat with my knife." She wouldn't, but she could.

"What knife?"

She pulled the blade free and held it up.

Lochlan reached her in a flash, knocking the blade from her hand and retrieving it off the ground. "Not anymore."

"Hey," she protested. "That's mine."

"Let me be clear, Lady Robinson. I do not trust you. I have instructed my men not to trust you. We will deliver you to the palace unharmed, but should you try to injure any of them again, you will arrive tied to the back of my saddle. Do you understand?"

Her eyes narrowed. "The palace? Which palace?" He was a prince of Iskalt but a delegate of Eldur. She wasn't sure which realm she feared more.

"Eldur."

"With the dragons?"

He turned to the door. "Don't worry, Lady Robinson. The dragons don't eat things that smell like you."

She would have sworn there was laughter in his voice as he sauntered from the tent.

She sniffed the shirt she wore and grimaced. Neeve's smelly stuff had mostly worn off, leaving behind a faint rancid scent mixed with the smell of travel.

She just hoped Lochlan was right about the dragons.

"How long was I out?" Brea asked Finn as he sat in front of her, taking the first watch. He'd brought with him a canteen of water, stale bread, and dried meat. It wasn't the gourmet meals she'd grown used to in Gelsi, but as hungry as she was, it tasted like five-star cuisine.

Finn sipped water from a tin cup, studying her over the rim. Finally, he lowered it and wiped his mouth. "Two days."

Her eyes widened. So, they definitely knew she was

missing from Gelsi by now. Had Griff returned and found her gone? Were Neeve and Moira okay?

"You should get some sleep." Finn used his knife to slice through the bread and popped a piece in his mouth.

"Apparently, I've been sleeping for two days." She couldn't have relaxed if she tried.

Neeve told her she'd be safe once she reached the Eldur camp. Well, here she was, and she didn't feel any safer.

"Why is Lochlan such a jerk?" she blurted.

Finn choked on his food, wheezing for breath. "I'm going to need you to say that again when he's within earshot."

She raised a brow. She'd only just met Finn, but she felt she knew Lochlan by now. From abducting her from a human prison to warning her in Gelsi, they'd already been through a lot together. "He's your friend? You seem like nothing bothers you, yet he is kind of a douche."

Finn sighed and ran a hand through his chestnut brown hair. "Appearances can be deceiving, Lady Robinson."

"Can you stop with all the lady nonsense?"

"It's what you are."

"Because the Gelsi queen is my aunt? I'll gladly relinquish that distinction."

"No. Not because of that." He didn't elaborate, instead focusing on the meat in front of him. He offered her a piece.

She bit down. It tasted similar to beef jerky, only better. Myles used to make her gorge on Slim Jims and barbecue jerky his dad made in their smoker. She'd never liked it, but he did, so she went along with it.

"Why does the Eldur queen want me?" she asked.

Finn kept his eyes trained on his hands, but it was another voice that responded.

"That is not our business." Lochlan stood in the opening of the tent with rivulets of water dripping off his powerful frame.

"We do not question our queen. We follow her orders." He gave Finn a pointed look that told Brea the two of them totally knew what the Eldur queen wanted with her. "I will take over Lady Robinson's watch."

Finn stood. "She wants to be called Brea."

Lochlan grunted as if what she wanted was of little importance to him. It probably was.

Finn offered her an encouraging smile before leaving her be.

Brea crossed her arms over the dry shirt Finn had provided her with. "I'm surprised you want to sit in here with me considering I smell too bad even for dragons."

He eyed her warily and took Finn's spot on the floor. Ripping a piece of bread, he took a bite and chewed slowly. "You can bathe once we reach the palace."

"And when will that be?"

He shrugged. "Four days? Five? Depends on this storm."

"You know what she wants with me."

"Yes." He kept eating, not looking her way.

Her eyes narrowed, and she leaned back on the bed, refusing to look at him. Rustling sounded to her right, and when she turned onto her side, she caught sight of a very naked Lochlan pulling on dry clothes.

Her face heated as she rolled back over, trying to forget the image of his corded back and firm… She shook her head. Griff drew her in with his looks and his charm, she wouldn't let that happen again. At least Lochlan had no charm to speak of.

"I trusted Neeve," she whispered. When he didn't respond, she kept talking. "Like you told me to. So… thanks."

His sigh filled the tent, and when she turned to look at him once more, he sat back in his spot with his head bowed. "I wish we could get her out of there."

So, he did care about something.

"Lochlan?"

He lifted his eyes.

She needed to know the answer to the question that could crush her. "Is he really alive?"

His eyes met hers, never wavering. "Yes."

She didn't know how, but she knew he told her the truth.

Tears built in her eyes. She blinked them away before more took their place. Shifting so Lochlan couldn't see her face, she let the tears trail over her cheeks. Myles was truly alive. Her chest expanded like she could breathe for the first time since that awful day at school when she'd thought she'd killed him.

"Lochlan?" she whispered, her voice shaking.

"Yes?"

"Thank you." When she got control of her voice, she spoke again. "Can I ask another question?"

"I'm coming to realize there's no way to stop you short of a gag."

She smiled at that. "Why do you hate me?"

As soon as she said the words, he tensed, revealing she wasn't wrong. He'd been gruff with her since the first day in the human realm.

"I don't—"

"Please, just be straight with me, I don't think I can take any more lies or half-truths."

He rubbed a hand over his face. "People have died for you, Brea. People I loved. I helped you at the request of my queen, but do not mistake anything that has happened as anything other than me following orders. You're right, I don't like you. I don't want to sit here staring into the face of the girl who has taken so much from me."

"I don't understand." What had she taken from him? Who'd died because of her? Her pulse hammered in her temples, sending waves of pain through her head. Her tears continued to fall.

"I wouldn't expect you to. You may have fae blood running through those veins, but you're just a human girl who has cost our world too much."

"I—"

"Go to sleep, Lady Robinson. Our conversation is through, and tomorrow will be a long day." He leaned his head back, closing his eyes.

Brea curled her legs up to her chest, trying to still the shaking of her body. She never thought she'd long for the solitude of the Clarkson Institute.

Maybe being delusional would have been better than being right.

The fae existed as she'd always seen, but their world wasn't meant for a girl raised on a simple human farm.

Chapter Sixteen

"You can let me have my horse back. I won't run again." Brea slumped in the saddle in front of Lochlan. She'd banked on being better on a horse than Lochlan's men when she made a run for it. She hadn't had a plan beyond not going to the Eldur palace.

She also hadn't banked on Lochlan being the one to catch her. Of course he came crashing down on her like a blond fae-god riding Secretariat.

"You've proven I can't trust you. So, you will ride with me to the Eldur palace. You will sleep in my tent, eat my food, and remain in my sight at all times until I hand you over to the queen."

"Would you like me to wipe your butt while I'm at it?"

"That won't be necessary, unless you try to escape again. You would do well not to push me human-girl."

"The Loch-to-Brea translation there, is he will likely pop that vein in his forehead if you try to run again." Finn rode beside them, offering helpful tidbits to the conversation, much to Lochlan's irritation. He didn't seem to like that his friend enjoyed Brea's company.

"At least let me ride with Finn so it's not like riding with a boulder at my back."

"I think the lady just called you soft." Lochlan jeered at his friend.

"The lady meant the boulder comment in terms of personality." She shifted in the saddle. While that was partially true, Lochlan's bulk was like leaning against a stone wall. A cold stone wall.

"You're just jealous that the pretty lady likes me more. Honestly, it's the story of his life." Finn grinned. "Poor guy never gets the girl when I'm around."

"Why don't you go check on the rear and let them know we'll make camp soon?" Lochlan dismissed his cocky right-hand man.

"Right away, sir. Catch you later, Breanne of Tarth." Finn winked at Brea before he turned his mount and left them in an uncomfortable silence.

Lochlan snorted at his retreat. "Preening peacock."

"You're just jealous because he's charming and you aren't."

"My brother is charming. How did that work out for you?"

"I think I like you better when you don't speak."

"Hashtag same."

Brea turned in the saddle to meet his gaze. "How do you know all the human lingo?"

"I've spent a lot of time there over the years."

"Doing what?"

"Keeping you alive. Now, I've had enough of your questions, girl."

Despite her desire to continue needling him, Brea let the matter drop. She sat quietly until she couldn't take his stony silence for another second.

"So... who's your favorite *GOT* character? Tyrion Lannister was my favorite. *That's what I do. I drink and I know things.*"

"Of course you would like the talker."

"So. Who's your favorite?"

"Davos Seaworth. A quiet, loyal man."

"What season was he in?"

"I do not watch television. I read."

"Oh, you're like Myles..." Her voice caught on his name. "He was always trying to get me to read the books." With her thoughts on Myles, she didn't care about the silence anymore.

As the day wore on, Brea started to sweat. It was really hot in Eldur compared to the relative perfection of Fargelsi.

"We make camp here," Lochlan called to his men. It surprised her that he would stop when it was still light out.

"We still have hours of daylight left, sir," a young soldier gave voice to Brea's observations.

"The oasis is the last source of fresh water we will encounter before we reach the palace. We will rest here and stock up on water before we set out early tomorrow morning," Finn explained.

Lochlan lifted Brea down from the horse—like she couldn't possibly dismount a horse on her own—and instead of setting her on the ground he carried her to a small wooded area offering the only shade she'd seen all day. A small lake shimmered in the sunlight.

"What are you doing?" She gasped as he tied her hands together and wrapped the rope around a tree. "Are you even serious right now?" She kicked him hard in the shins.

"Did you just kick me?" A brow arched over his dark blue eyes.

"Come here so I can do it again," Brea growled.

"Do not ever kick me again or you will regret it." He turned to address his men.

"Lochlan, don't you dare leave me tethered to a tree like a dog!" Brea stomped her foot, itching to kick him where it really hurt. He ignored her, directing his men to make camp around her as he walked away to help.

Once the tents were ready, Lochlan finally returned.

"You're a jerk." Brea shoved her wrists in his face.

"And you stink." He tossed her pack and a cake of soap at her feet. "If I have to ride with you for the next two days, you will at least smell better." He released the knot around the tree, giving her a longer tether before he secured her to the tree again and moved her restraints from her wrists to her waist.

"Release me. Now." Brea slapped him hard across the face and immediately regretted it.

His eyes flashed with carefully controlled anger. "Go clean the swamp stink off." He pointed toward the lake, just in reach of her leash.

"I won't escape." Brea's face flamed with fury—the lack of her magic more obvious than before. "But I will not bathe in front of you and your men."

"Trust me, no one will be looking. Fae do not get caught up in the idiocy of human modesty. It's time you abandon your human tendencies."

"I'm part human, you jerk." She kicked a clot of dirt at his face. "And I'm a really good swimmer." She yanked at the knot around her waist.

"You couldn't escape even if you wanted to." Lochlan gave her an arrogant smirk. "We're surrounded by desert. You'd die of exposure before you could find help. And that knot isn't going anywhere."

"Well, if there's nothing but desert around us, then why bother tying me up at all?" Brea lifted her chin in defiance.

"To teach you a lesson in humility. Now go before I throw

you in the lake and bathe you myself." He turned his back on her.

Brea snatched up her pack and the soap and stomped to the edge of the water. He was right, she couldn't even get her fingers around the magical knot at her waist. If she wasn't so incredibly dirty, she'd refuse to take a bath, but she also didn't want to see if Loch would follow through with his threat to bathe her himself.

Her face flaming with humiliation, she cast a glance over her shoulder to find not one soldier looking her way. She quickly shed her clothes and slipped into the cool, refreshing water until she was up to her neck. The water was crystal clear, and for once she didn't fear what evils might lurk beneath the surface.

Brea frowned as she worked the soap up into a lather. Everything in Fargelsi was beautiful on the surface with vile and all manner of evil things lying in wait just out of sight. Loch Villandi. The fountain. Magic-blocking Gelsi berries. Beautiful but poisonous flowers, and a vicious queen who spouted lies and played with lives. So far, Eldur seemed to be exactly what it appeared. A hot, dry desert kingdom without the first dragon sighting. Maybe they lived with the queen and guarded the palace? One could hope.

Just as she was rinsing the last of the caked mud from her hair, something tugged at her waist and she went slicing through the water like a fish on a line.

"What is your problem?" Brea sputtered, trying to shield herself in the shallow water.

"Bath time's over." Lochlan dropped a linen blanket on the ground and turned his back.

"You know, you could learn a thing or two from your brother." Brea snatched the blanket and wrapped it around herself several times. "He may have lied to me—and that is unforgivable—but at least he's a decent person."

"Griffin is many things, but decent isn't one of them." He tugged on her leash, nearly dragging her into his tent. "Get dressed."

Brea stumbled into the larger tent, grasping for her anger and the magic that normally came with it, but it was gone. And just when she really wanted to use it.

"Stupid handsome blond jerk-face." Brea let out a string of curses that would have gotten her grounded at home.

"I heard that," Lochlan called just outside the tent.

Brea stuck her head through the flaps. "I meant for you to!" She called him a few more names.

"Lady Brea!" Finn sounded shocked. "I've never heard a noble woman curse like that."

"You meant to call me handsome, Lady Brea?" Lochlan and a few of his soldiers laughed.

Brea shoved her arms through the soft tunic Neeve had made for her, grateful someone took the time to wash her things after her trip through the swamp. Slipping on her leggings and shoving her feet into her boots, Brea stomped through the tent flaps.

"Let's get one thing straight, Lochlan. Stay away from me. Don't talk to me. Don't even look at me."

"If you'll be quiet, you've got yourself a deal, my Lady." Lochlan smirked up at her from where he lounged in the shade.

"Hungry?" Finn offered her a bowl of stew and a chunk of dry bread.

"Starving." Brea accepted the meal and returned to the tent.

"It's going to be hot in there, Brea," Lochlan called. "I'd hate for you to have to take another bath."

Brea kicked the tent flaps aside and sat down under the

shade beside Finn. "What did I *just* say?" She shot a glare at Lochlan before she turned away, determined to pretend he didn't exist.

Brea could feel Lochlan moving around the tent in the early hours just before dawn. She hadn't slept at all in the muggy hot space. Rolling over to face him, she regretted it instantly. Naked once again with his back to her, beads of water rolled down his lean body after a dip in the lake.

"Jeeze, Loch, put some clothes on." She rolled away.

"That is what I'm doing." She heard the rustle of his clothes as he dressed. "Most ladies find my form appealing. Do you not?"

"Does it matter?"

"Not at all. I am simply trying to understand your odd human behavior."

"I am seventeen years old, Lochlan. In the human world you could get arrested for exposing yourself to someone my age."

"I am only a few years older than you." He sounded like he didn't think any of this was odd.

"You'll have to excuse me if I find it odd to wake up to a naked fae butt in my face first thing in the morning."

"But you will be of age soon. How does a few weeks make a difference in your world?"

"It just does. And how do you know I'm almost eighteen?" She had no idea what the date was, and with the weird fae calendar added into the mix, she didn't know when her birthday was, only that it was soon.

Lochlan crouched beside her bedroll, still shirtless, his long blond hair dripping from his early morning swim, but at least he'd put on pants. "Your magic is erratic, yes?"

Brea nodded. If you could call absent erratic, then hers was a mess.

"All fae magic is tied to our emotions. Surely my brother taught you that much?"

"Yes. He was going to help me learn how to control my Fargelsi magic." Brea sat up, clutching her blanket to her chest. "But we never got around to it."

"There is a reason I goaded you all day yesterday, Brea. You magic has slipped out of your reach since your difficult journey through the Vatlands. You don't know how to use your magic, much less control it. I was trying to push it out of you through your temper, but that isn't working. When you come of age, it will return in full force, but you need to be prepared to deal with it when that happens. The last time the magic built up within you, you knocked yourself out. You can't let that happen again."

"Then what do I do?"

"I will help you." Lochlan stood up, reaching for his shirt. "Get dressed and eat something. We leave in an hour."

"Seriously? We're doing this again?" Brea stared up as Lochlan mounted on his horse, reaching down to lift her up.

"Seriously." The muscle in his jaw ticked.

"You've still got me on your leash, so just let me ride my own horse. It's not like I can go anywhere." She fumbled with the rope around her waist, but it wouldn't budge.

"Get on the damn horse, Brea." Lochlan jerked her forward by her tether.

"Rude." She climbed up in front of him, dreading another hot day riding far too close to her least favorite person.

"Take this." He handed her a thick piece of rough-cut glass.

"What is it?"

"Crystalized sand. You're going to practice while we ride today."

"Magic? How?"

"Your magic is inside you. You need to find it and funnel it into the crystal. It will glow with the color of your magic when you do it right. This exercise will help you learn to sense your magic when it is close."

"So, I just *find* my magic and use it to light up the crystal?" She turned to look up at him. "You do realize you've failed to explain *how* I'm supposed to accomplish that."

"Focus on your emotions and feelings, and you will find it. This is an internal battle no one can do for you, Brea."

"You're just trying to keep me quiet," Brea muttered.

"That is simply an added benefit of the exercise." Lochlan nudged his horse forward across the rocky desert terrain.

Brea stared at the piece of crystalized sand for the first few miles, wondering how she was supposed to find her magic when she didn't know where to look for it.

"You're not trying, Brea," Lochlan pressed.

"I'm trying to decide the best approach." Brea closed her eyes, letting her thoughts drift over the frustrating events of the past weeks. She had good memories of her time in Gelsi, but that it was all a lie just made her angry, and anger didn't seem to help her connect with her magic.

Instead, Brea focused on happier memories of Myles before all of this happened. But that just made her sad. Sadness didn't seem to be a strong enough emotion to stir her magic.

"I feel like I'm trying to cast a patronus, and I don't have enough happy memories to pull it off."

"You're not Harry Potter, Brea. This isn't make-believe nonsense. Now, focus." Lochlan pressed the glass into her hand and wrapped her fingers around it.

"Of course you've seen *Harry Potter*."

"I have *read Harry Potter*. Human books fascinate me. You should try reading sometime. It's a far better use of your time than mindless movies that never tell the whole story."

"Myles used to say the same thing."

It was the only thing they ever argued about. A smile came to Brea's lips at the memory of all their stupid fights about nothing. Just knowing he was still out there living his life made her happy. She just wondered if he hated her. A surge of fear rose up inside her at that thought. She couldn't bear it if he hated her for what she'd done to him.

"Brea, look." Lochlan nudged her. She looked down at the crystal pulsing with a vivid yellow light before it winked out.

"I did it!" A grin spread across her face. "Myles is my patronus."

"You didn't do anything because you let it go before you took control."

"That wasn't just nothing. You don't get to poop all over my success."

Finn's laughter rang out behind them. Lochlan-the-jerk-face had made him ride behind them today so he wouldn't distract her.

"I don't get to what?" Lochlan stilled behind her.

"You don't get to poop on her success," Finn supplied—for Lochlan and any of the soldiers who'd missed it the first time.

"That was not a success."

"It was," Brea insisted. "Now we know my magic is yellow."

"Yes, we do." Lochlan sighed. "What emotion filled you when the magic pulsed in the crystal?"

Brea didn't want to tell him it was fear. She could only imagine how many ways he'd try to torture the magic out of her. "Happiness," she finally said.

"Do not lie to me, Brea."

"I'm not lying."

"Yes, you are."

"So, what do I do next time when the light pulses in the crystal?"

"Take control."

"How?"

"Use your instincts, Brea."

"What if I have no instincts?"

"Just try it again. And keep your eyes open this time."

"Fine." Brea stared down at the crystal in her lap and revisited some of the scariest moments of her trip through the swamp. The image of the alligator-dragon beast filled her mind. She conjured up every last harrowing detail she could recall right down to its creepy forked tongue.

The crystal glowed with a faint yellow light, and Brea focused harder, urging the light to shine brighter. Sweat beaded on her forehead and rolled down her face. Her hands shook with the effort to keep the yellow light from winking out. When she lost it, Brea cursed and chucked the crystal as far as she could throw it.

"Brea. Don't be a child." Lochlan raised his hand and somehow summoned the crystal, catching it in his outstretched hand and stuffing it back in hers.

"Why don't you show me how to do that?"

"Because you haven't mastered the most basic mechanics of magic that even our youngest children learn through instinct alone."

"How about we do the not-talking thing again for a while?" Brea felt like crushing the stupid crystal in her bare hands.

She spent the next hour running the gamut of her emotions, searching for the right thought or feeling that would stimulate her magic. But the darn thing refused to light up again.

Looking up, Brea saw stunted trees and cactus replacing the barren desert sands they'd traversed. "Where are we?" Brea yawned, reaching for her canteen.

Lochlan pulled her back against his chest, his arms tense. "Quiet, Brea." That was when she realized he gripped his sword in his free hand.

"What's going on?" she whispered, not liking the way Lochlan's soldiers had fanned out around them. Before he could answer, a crossbow bolt slammed into a boulder just feet from Brea and Lochlan. She nearly jumped out of her seat, but Lochlan's arm was like a vise around her waist.

Several more bolts whizzed past them, and a battle cry echoed through the sparse forest as men and women charged toward them. Brea's heart lodged somewhere in her chest as Lochlan and his men entered the fray.

"Take this." Lochlan shoved a huge round shield in front of her. Brea clutched it tight and huddled behind the barrier. His arm slid around her again, but his free sword hand hacked away at the nearby soldiers.

"My uncle's men." Lochlan snarled in her ear. "None of them leave this place alive!" He shouted to his men.

Brea had never experienced a battle up close before, and she had no desire to experience this one. Ducking her head behind the shield, she just managed to avoid an arrow to her face. The shaft stuck in the shield, and as she reached to snap it off, three others replaced it.

Adrenaline and fear shot through her system. Still clutching the crystalized sand, it blazed with the yellow light of her magic now.

Lochlan struggled with a fierce warrior Brea thought she recognized from the Iskalt delegation party in Fargelsi. Their swords clashed, and Brea screamed, clutching the shield, grateful for Lochlan's hold on her.

"You can tell Callum O'Shea he'll have to do far better than an ambush in the desert. I'm coming for him and everyone who serves him," Lochlan snarled, sending the man flying from his horse. Lochlan turned his horse around to meet another attack.

"Loch!" Brea screamed, and her magic exploded from her body in a useless wave of yellow light.

The soldiers kept coming, and Lochlan slashed his way through them with his soldiers at his sides. He was ruthless in his rage. The icy blue light of his magic tipped his sword, dropping his enemies one by one.

"There's another one." Brea pointed at a woman charging past Finn with a determined set to her jaw.

She was so focused on the woman she didn't see the man riding toward them until it was almost too late.

Lifting the heavy shield, Brea deflected his sword, saving Lochlan from a grievous injury.

"Stupid girl." The man spat, his blade coming down on her.

Brea felt the tug and rip of fabric first as the sword bit deep into her shoulder. The shock of his cold magic lit up her insides as the soldier sliced down her arm. She screamed in agony as her arm went limp, and she dropped the shield.

"Brea!" Lochlan shouted over the din of battle.

Magic churned under Brea's skin, latching onto her fear. Without a thought to what she was doing, Brea grasped hold of her magic and sent it soaring toward the man who'd tried to kill Lochlan. The last thing she saw was the horrific sight of the man's head parting ways with his body before her magic rebounded on her and darkness won.

CHAPTER SEVENTEEN

Pain seared through Brea, and she woke screaming as someone bent over her with a burning blade pressed to her shoulder. "Stop! Stop!" But he didn't. Her eyes found Lochlan over the man's shoulder, and she grit her teeth. "I hate you so much right now. What is this guy doing to me?"

Her fingers dug into the blanket beneath her as she bucked off the bed.

Hands gripped her shoulders, holding her down, and she looked up into the face of Finn. "You were supposed to be the nice one." Her body jerked again as heat flooded her.

"Relax, Brea." Lochlan's hard eyes landed on her. "It'll be over soon."

"Relax?" she screamed as another jolt of pain struck her. "Relax! You relax!" A tear slipped from her eye, and she squeezed her eyelids shut, picturing something, anything other than the crowded tent where the Eldur soldiers tortured her.

The heat abated, but the pain remained.

"Lady Brea," a hard voice said.

She shook her head, unwilling to look at the men and women surrounding her.

"Brea," Finn called, his voice softer than Lochlan's. "You can open your eyes. We're through."

Her eyes slid open, and she viewed the soldiers crowding her bed. The man with the hot blade sat back on his heels. Two women hung back, blood splattered across their armor.

Finn withdrew his hands from her shoulders.

Lochlan crossed his arms, looking as uncomfortable as he should feel.

"Why were you torturing me?" She could barely muster the energy to speak.

Finn and Lochlan shared a look before Lochlan spoke. "We do not torture. You were injured and dying. Now you're not." He turned on his heel and pushed through the tent flap without another word. The rest of the soldiers followed him, save for Finn who moved to sit beside her.

"I really need to stop losing consciousness and waking up in strange places." She lifted her head, trying to see her shoulder. They'd cut her shirt away from the wound, but she couldn't get a look.

Finn grinned at her. "I don't know, Brea. It probably makes the travel easier if you're unconscious for much of it."

She laughed, wincing at the pain it caused. "What did they do to me?"

"Lewis is our unit's unofficial healer. He's quite adept at cauterization."

"Cauterization?" She gulped.

Finn nodded. "There was no way for us to stitch up your wound before returning to the palace, and by then you may have been as dead as those Iskalt warriors we fought. So, Lewis used his magic to heat the blade and sear your wound."

The odor of burnt flesh hung in the air, and nausea welled up in Brea. She tried to roll onto her side as her chest heaved.

Finn jumped forward, helping her up.

"Get me out of this tent," she wheezed.

He lifted her into his arms and ran out into the fresh desert air.

"Down," she pleaded.

As soon as Finn set her feet on the rocky ground, she fell to her knees and the meager contents of her stomach exploded from her mouth. Her entire body shook as it emptied itself.

She lifted her arm to try to wipe her mouth, but pain paralyzed her at the movement. "Other arm, you doofus," she whispered to herself, as she lifted the arm attached to her non-injured shoulder to wipe the remaining vomit from her face.

"Feel better?" Finn asked.

She'd forgotten he was there, but she was in too much pain to feel embarrassed. Imploring him with her eyes, she begged for assistance to stand so she didn't make a bigger fool of herself than she already had.

He wrapped an arm around her waist and lent her his strength.

"No," she protested when he tried to lead her back into the tent. She couldn't stand the thought of the rancid smell for one minute longer. "Not there."

Finn pursed his lips. "You mean you're going to make me sleep in there all alone tonight?"

She gaped at him. "That's your tent? What happened to Lochlan claiming he wouldn't let me out of his sight?"

"Our dear Loch wanted some peace after that battle, and you, my dear, give him very little peace." He helped her down onto the ground outside the tent, and she leaned back against a smooth boulder.

"He's angry at me for getting injured, isn't he?"

"No." Finn chuckled as he sat beside her. "He's angry at himself that you got injured at all."

"But if I hadn't stepped in, he'd be dead."

"That would be preferable to him than having to tell Queen Faolan that you died under his watch."

She eyed the stoic man across camp. "And probably that he had to be saved by little old Lady Brea."

"Brea, you are an odd one."

"How is it that Lochlan knows *Game of Thrones* and *Harry Potter*, yet no one in this fracking world understands anything I say?"

"Fracking?" He grinned. "Is that a human world for f—"

"Stop! I have delicate ears."

He laughed. "There is nothing delicate about you. We all just watched Lewis burn your shoulder purposefully, and now you lay here under the desert sun making jokes."

She grimaced as she lifted her head, trying to avoid the pain. "Fracking is from another TV show. TV is—"

"Yes, Lochlan has explained the odd instrument that provides entertainment to small human minds."

She was about to protest his characterization of TV nerds when a shadow crossed over them. An irritating shadow. "What do you want?"

Lochlan scowled down at her, his face never softening. "Your shoulder needs tended to."

"Wasn't that what the torture was for?" She narrowed her eyes.

"It wasn't torture." He looked away. "Finn, help her up and bring her to my tent."

He stalked back the way he'd come.

Finn's body shook with silent laughter.

"What?" Brea snapped.

"I just… Lochlan never gets perturbed. He controls every emotion, every impulse."

"Are you saying I perturb him?" She almost laughed at the funny word.

Finn stood and dusted off his butt before bending and sliding his arms under her. "I'm not quite sure yet."

She let out a squeal of surprise as he hoisted her into his arms, jostling her shoulder and sending sparks of agony curling through her. He carried her into Lochlan's tent without waiting for Lochlan to enter.

A single thin bedroll occupied the far corner next to a bucket of water and a stack of cloth strips.

Finn set her on the bed and backed away. "Well, I'll leave you to Lochlan's care."

"Traitor," she called after him. Her words died off as Lochlan entered, taking Finn's place.

He didn't speak to her as he pulled leather shoulder plates over his head and set them aside. Crimson blood coated his shirt, making it stick to the ridges of his stomach. The sight of the remnants of battle stole any remaining biting words from her.

"How many soldiers did you lose?" She pictured the Iskalt warriors and the way they overwhelmed Lochlan and his people. There was no way they came through unscathed.

His shoulders dropped just the slightest bit, and he turned away from her to view their small camp through the tent opening. "Four."

"I'm sorry." She'd never seen battle before, but they were no strangers to the cost of war in the human realm. Many young men from their small Ohio town joined the military after high school. Some never returned.

He rubbed a hand across his face and looked back over his

shoulder at her. "They knew the risks of this mission. My queen is not the only ruler who wants you."

She'd spent her entire life wanted by no one, and now, suddenly three realms fought for her. It was surreal, and she didn't understand it. Which one of them was good? Could she trust any of them, or was she just a pawn to all?

With a shake of his head, Lochlan turned and lowered himself to his knees beside where she lay. His long fingers reached for the bucket of water and pulled free a small sponge.

"We must keep the area around your wound clean." With surprisingly gentle fingers, he dabbed the sponge along her skin. They'd cauterized the gash in her shoulder from the sword, but tiny cuts still stretched out from the wound. Each time the sponge made contact with a wound, her breath hissed between her teeth.

Lochlan refused to even meet her eyes as he cleaned the area.

"Are you mad at me?" She knew what Finn had said, but she still sensed a new irritation in Lochlan.

He only grunted.

"Is it because you had to be saved by a woman?"

He pulled the sponge away and dropped it back in the bucket with a splash. "Brea, we fae are not like the humans you've lived around—or even the fae of Regan's court. One's gender is of no import."

She remembered what Neeve told her about them not falling in love with a gender, but surely the army was different. "You can't tell me you value the women in your unit as much as the men."

He finally met her eyes. "Why would I not? They are as skilled as any other. You forget we have one thing humans do not. Magic. It is the great equalizer. Our fights rely little on brute strength, allowing us to put aside any human biases. Fae do not stoop to such levels."

He wrung the sponge out and cleaned the remaining blood from her wound, his touch flitting across her skin with a care she'd never imagined from him.

"You're trying to tell me this is some feminist dream world?"

His brow creased. "I know not what a feminist is."

A laugh burst out of her. "You know human fantasy books but not basic principles of human life?"

"I have been to the human realm many times, but you would be mistaken if you think your people are of any interest to me. I find humans to be cruel... vindictive. But they're also fantastic writers."

She snorted. "Yes, well, I just escaped from a fae realm where everything was a dangerous lie. Don't get up on your high horse about fae morality."

He dried her shoulder before unrolling a long strip of fabric. "I do not understand you, Lady Brea."

"Ditto, Douchey Loch. See, I can call people things they'd rather I didn't too."

"Douchey." He paused for a moment. "I like the sound of that. What does it mean?"

She choked on a laugh. "Erm... noble."

He nodded. "Then you may call me by that name if you wish."

Winding the fabric tightly around her shoulder, Lochlan looked on with honest-to-God sympathy in his eyes as she winced in pain. Who would have thought he could feel anything other than irritation?

His fingers worked nimbly to bandage her shoulder and the upper half of her arm.

"If Lewis is the healer, why isn't he doing this?" she asked, trying to distract herself from the pain.

Lochlan looked away under the pretense of trying to find something, but nothing was there. "You are my responsibility."

"But why? Your queen wants me. I get that. But everyone keeps mentioning your trips to the human realm that supposedly had to do with me. We didn't meet until that day you stole me from the police."

"They were going to send you to one of those human prisons, and I can guarantee they're not like our prison realm."

She'd ask later about there being an entire realm for a prison. That sounded... extreme. "Because I almost killed my best friend. What do you have to do with any of this?"

He sat back, not looking at her. "I cannot give you the answers you seek."

"Well, that's just peachy, isn't it? I'm stuck in this creepy world. Someone stabbed a sword through my shoulder. I have no clue what's going on or why I'm some special snowflake everyone seems to want a piece of. And you... the most frustrating man I have ever met... Just leave me alone. Please. Send Finn to watch me or something. He's much better company."

Lochlan stared at her for a long moment, his eyes icing over. "No." He seemed to shake off whatever had come over him and pushed to his feet. "There is a shirt for you on the end of the bed. I will step outside for your human modesty."

"What about you?" She gestured to his blood-stained clothes.

"I do not have another garment, but it will only be a couple days until we reach the palace." His eyes flicked from her to the remaining strips of fabric before he turned to walk out.

"Wait," she called.

He didn't stop. She felt the bandage on her shoulder, knowing where the fabric came from. Lochlan cut up his only spare shirt for bandages, leaving him with memories of the battle caked into his clothes.

He'd said many things that altered how she saw this world, but maybe it was what he didn't say that mattered more.

Lochlan O'Shea was a man of secrets and hidden thoughts. She laid her head back, staring up at the canvas ceiling. How did a man she barely knew, one who spoke in grunts and scowls, make her feel safer than his brother ever had?

Griff had been a fantasy, one that crashed down around her when she learned none of it was real. Lochlan... he didn't put on faces, he didn't lie or connive.

But just like in Fargelsi, she was still his prisoner, and she couldn't forget that one simple fact.

CHAPTER EIGHTEEN

After another day in the saddle in the dry desert heat, Brea's arm throbbed beneath the cauterized flesh. It felt tight and hot, and she was restless.

"I thought I perturbed you," Brea muttered when Lochlan carried her into his tent.

"You do that quite well, Lady Brea. I've asked Lewis to make you something to help you sleep."

"Can you ask him to make an AC unit for the window?"

"We don't have windows in tents. You're such an odd girl." She thought she heard laughter as he laid her on a bedroll for the night.

"No blanket." She shoved his hand away. "Too hot."

"Today was a hot day. It will get cooler as we approach the palace."

"She still awake?" Finn ducked into the tent.

"Unfortunately." Brea groaned at the pounding in her head.

"I have some medicine for you from Lewis." Finn crouched

beside her and helped her sit up. The simple wooden cup frothed with smoke and smelled like a dead moose's butt.

"Ugh, I'm not drinking that."

"Pour it down her throat," Lochlan ordered.

"Ignore him." Finn shot him a glare. "It will make you feel better, I promise. And it doesn't taste as bad as it smells."

Brea held the cup up to her lips and winced.

"It's best if you chug it," Finn said.

Brea took a tentative sip and gagged. "Ugh, that's worse than it smells, Finn!"

"That's why I told you to chug it." He rolled his eyes. "Just pretend it's wine and don't stop till you see the bottom of the cup."

"Fine. But this better make me feel better." Brea tipped the cup back and choked down the brown smoky concoction. "That was vile."

Brea burped and smoke flew out of her mouth. She'd normally be embarrassed but a warm fuzzy cloud settled over her.

"Oh, that's nice."

Finn helped ease her back onto her bedroll. She stroked his smooth face with her good hand.

"You're a nice person, Finn. Not like Mr. Grumpy Pants over there with his grunts and scowls."

Finn chuckled, brushing the sweaty strands of hair from her face. "I know I shouldn't laugh, but this girl is hilarious."

"She's a menace," Lochlan said.

Brea hummed in satisfaction. "My complements to Mr. Lewis. He should p-put that stuff on t-ap." She yawned, belched, and fell asleep.

"No! Myles!" Brea cried out, trying to reach her friend but the police officer refused to let her near him.

"The boy probably won't survive the ride to the hospital."

Those words gutted Brea all over again.

"She's burning up," Finn's voice reached her through the fog of her fever.

"Cut her bandages off," Lochlan ordered.

"Ouch," Brea muttered as the fabric peeled away from the crusty burned flesh on her arm.

"The wound is infected," Finn announced. "The medicine should have prevented this."

"I don't think my human half liked that stuff," Brea managed.

She screamed when Lochlan came at her with a knife. He held her down as he slipped the tip under the massive scab on her arm. Infection oozed out, and her stomach churned.

"We have to cool her down." Lochlan gathered her up in his arms.

"We're in the middle of the desert, Loch. How are you going to get her temperature down?" Finn followed them out of the tent.

Lochlan handed Brea to Finn and mounted his horse. Reaching down, he took her back into his arms.

"Ugh, no more riding. Take me to see Myles. He's in the hospital. They can give me a shot of antibiotics."

"What is she saying?"

"More human nonsense," Lochlan said. "I'll ride for Loch Langt. Meet us there."

"Will she make it that far?" Finn asked.

"What?" Brea struggled to fight through the fog of her mind.

"Shh, Lady Brea," Lochlan said in a soothing voice. "You'll be better soon. The cool waters of Langt is our best chance."

He gathered the reins in his hands and took off, galloping across the dusty desert plains.

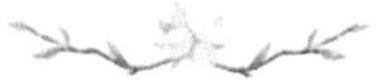

"Stay with me, Brea," Lochlan refused to let her sleep. "Tell me about your favorite *Harry Potter* movie."

"*Goblet of Fire*," she groaned. "Shoulda been two movies."

"That was a great book."

"I don't feel good, Loch." She curled against him, her skin on fire.

"We're almost there. I can see the lake just over the next rise. Once we get you cooled off, we'll have to work on that infection."

"Promise you won't cut off my arm." Brea blacked out before she heard his promise.

Cool water splashed against her legs as Lochlan rode his horse straight into Loch Langt.

"That's freezing," she complained.

"It's about to get a lot colder." He slid off the horse and carried her into the deep cold waters of Langt.

"Too cold." She squirmed against him, her teeth chattering.

"Take a deep breath, Brea." Loch held her against his chest, plunging them under the surface.

The water stabbed like a thousand tiny needles. But that wasn't good enough for Lochlan. Brea gasped for breath when they broke the surface, but he only stripped away her tunic and trousers until she was down to her undergarments in the icy water.

"Why are you doing this to me?" Tears slipped down her cheeks.

"To save your life. The water is freezing because your

temperature is too high. You'll die if we don't get it down. Now, take another deep breath for me."

She barely got a breath in before they plunged beneath the surface again. Brea thrashed around until Lochlan pressed his palm against her chest, right above her heart. Everything slowed with the blue glow of his magic. They sank to the bottom of the lake as she shivered in his arms.

His blond hair swirled around them like a cloud, tangling with her dark tresses. Hers black as ebony and his pale as fine silver. Her lungs were about to burst when Lochlan propelled them back to the surface.

Brea gasped for air, her mind clearer than it had been all day.

"I can't take it much longer, Loch." She shook with tremors, and her lips turned blue.

"Let's get you warm and dry and see how you feel." He carried her out of the lake and wrapped a warm dry blanket around her. "We don't have much in the way of supplies, but I'll make a fire. Sit here and drink as much water as you can stomach. Sip slowly." He handed her his water skin.

Brea shivered under the hot sun and knew she was in trouble if the fever didn't break soon.

Sweat rolled down Lochlan's face as he built a roaring fire. He even gathered a pile of huge palm leaves to build a quick shade for her to lounge under.

"I'm afraid this is going to hurt, Brea." Lochlan pulled his knife from the pot of boiling water over the fire. "But I have to clean the infection out."

Brea nodded. "Do what you have to."

"Put this between your teeth and bite down." He slipped a piece of leather between her lips. "I'll try to hurry, but if you can pass out, don't fight it."

Brea screamed as the hot knife sliced through the

remaining scab over her arm. Putrid infection seeped from the wound. Lochlan wiped it away with a strip of fabric he'd boiled with the knife. Strips from his only shirt.

When he squeezed her arm, stars danced in her eyes, and she mercifully passed out.

When she woke next, she floated in Lochlan's arms in the shallow water. It was pleasantly cool this time. Her back against his chest, she glanced at her shoulder under the water. Bright red blood seeped from the fresh opening, but the cool water numbed her flesh.

"Your fever broke about an hour ago. I think the worst of it is over."

"Thank you," she murmured, weak as a kitten. She couldn't manage more than that.

"My men will be here soon, and Lewis will make you another tonic for the pain. I've made a poultice that will help with the infection. It should be ready now."

Brea nodded, draping her arms around his neck as he lifted her from the water. "I am sorry to be such a burden." Her head lolled against his shoulder.

"It is not your fault. You were hurt in battle trying to save my life. I will be here to see you through this injury, no matter what you need. I am only sorry it will likely leave a scar."

Brea shrugged her good shoulder. "Scars are badass." She eyed the few she could see marking his chest and back.

Lochlan settled Brea under the makeshift shelter, though the sun was setting along the horizon now. A vivid green poultice warmed by the fire. "That smells awful."

"I made this while you were asleep. It is similar to the human Aloe Vera plant but with more advanced healing properties. It will pull the poison of inflammation from your arm. I should have sent someone out to find the herbs when you were first injured."

"It's okay, Loch. You couldn't have known about the infection."

His jaw muscles ticked as he painted a thick layer of the green goo over her arm, layering pieces of fabric over it to hold it in place.

"Lie still and try to sleep if you can. I'll work on finding some food." Lochlan draped the blanket over her and left her to rest on her own. They'd come a long way in the few days since he'd taken to leading her around on a leash. Then again, she couldn't run even if she wanted to.

The men arrived at dusk, and Brea ate two bowls of stew before Lewis approached with a new tonic he promised would help her heal and give her a good night's rest.

She woke again later that evening, feeling like a new woman after a dip in the lake to rinse off the remains of Lochlan's life-saving poultice.

"Feeling better?" Finn crouched beside the water's edge as she emerged, wrapping herself in a dry blanket.

"Weak, but I'm feeling clear headed now and much better."

"Want to see something you'll never forget?"

"Sure." She changed back into her clothes after making him turn around.

"This is a special place for the men," Finn explained as they walked back toward camp. "But it's a bit of walk to the next ridge. We'll ride if you don't mind."

"Okay." Honestly, she'd rather go back to sleep, but Finn really wanted her to see whatever he was so excited about.

"Have you ever seen a snúa aftur?"

"Bless you." Brea chuckled. "I have no idea what you just said."

"Look just there." Finn pointed up to the sky. Swirls of green, purple, and yellow lights illuminated the night.

"An Aurora Borealis."

"Bless you." Finn cracked a smile.

"That's what we call the Northern Lights in the human realm."

"Here it's the Southern Lights called snúa aftur. To the soldiers it means we're almost home. This will be our last night at camp."

"We'll reach the palace tomorrow?" Her nerves immediately spiraled into panic mode. "What does the Eldur queen want with me, Finn?"

"I don't know, Brea, but I know you can trust her with your life. She's a good woman and a fair ruler."

"Thank you for bringing me here." She settled onto the ground to watch the lights with the soldiers. "It's beautiful."

The cluster of soldiers were all silent as they watched the colors dance across the night sky. Brea leaned against Finn's shoulder, cradling her injured arm. It was such a soothing sight. The tension in her body relaxed as she watched a riot of colors shoot across the sky.

Each of the soldiers sent a spark of color into the sky to join the phenomenon.

"What are they doing?"

"It's their magic," Finn explained. "They're making wishes. It's an Eldur tradition."

"It's beautiful." Brea wished she could send up a streak of yellow, but she barely had the energy to keep her eyes open. "What do the colors mean?"

"It's like a signature." A tiny ball of orange left his fingertips. "Each Fae's magic has a distinct color that connects their magic back to them. Families sometimes share a similar color, but not always. It depends on the strength of their magic and their heritage from both sides."

Brea wondered if the mystery of her own heritage would ever be so clear.

CHAPTER NINETEEN

"The Fargelsi palace is nice, I suppose, if you're into trees and flowers everywhere." Finn chomped on a piece of desert fruit that was somewhere between a pear and a peach. "But the Eldurian palace is really something special."

"Have you always lived at the palace?" Brea had gathered Finnegan Donovan was the son of soldier and had grown up with Lochlan. She appreciated his chatter. It kept her from thinking about the pain in her arm and the unpleasant experience that waited for her when they arrived at the palace.

"We have a family house in town, but we spend most of our time in the palace when I'm home."

"Finn made himself at home so often when we were boys, the queen gave him his own apartment so he'd stop sneaking into mine and Princess Alona's rooms." Lochlan rolled his eyes at his lifelong friend.

"Who is Alona?" Brea asked.

"Queen Faolan's daughter and the Princess of Eldur," Finn explained.

"Her mother must have had a time chasing after two young boys and a girl."

"Mothers." Finn corrected. "Alona has two mothers. Queen Faolan Cahill is the ruler of Eldur and gave birth to Alona. Queen Tierney Cahill is Faolan's wife."

"Cool." She was impressed with how they never seemed to fret about sexuality like humans did. But at the moment, Brea wouldn't care if they were queens of a dung heap if she could just get off this horse and sleep in a real bed and get some real painkillers for her arm. She was much better than she was two days ago, but the fever had left her exhausted and in need of rest.

"Look there," Lochlan murmured in her ear, pointing in the distance. "Your first look at the palace."

"Oh, it's so green." Brea hadn't expected that. After days of dry desert heat and miles and miles of red dirt and sand with the occasional sparse forest of stunted trees, the Eldurian palace sat like a jewel along the horizon.

"The Dalur River flows through the south eastern corner of Eldur, creating a fertile valley, much cooler than the desert."

"It's beautiful." Brea squinted to see the many-tiered structure that rose from the green valley like a pyramid. Rich green plant life sprouted from each tier where vines crept down the walls. "It looks like the Hanging Gardens of Babylon."

"Very good assessment, Brea." Lochlan sounded impressed. "It's not the Hanging Gardens of the ancient human world, but it's close enough to make you wonder if the legend of the Babylonian gardens might have been rooted in fae lore."

Other structures rose behind the gardens. Tall towers with bulbous domes covered in brightly colored mosaic tiles.

"Where are we going?" Brea frowned when they turned away from the palace.

"There is a river and a canyon between us and the palace,"

Finn explained. "We'll ride up through the canyon where you'll see the great city of Raudur."

"The scenic route. Great." Any other day she would be pleased to see all the exotic city had to offer.

"We will be there soon, and you can rest. This is the most direct path home," Lochlan murmured for her benefit. "The palace entrance lies under the gardens and towers. It's a sight you won't want to miss."

Even as weary as she was, Brea couldn't help getting caught up in their excitement of homecoming. She just hoped she could truly trust Finn and Lochlan when they said she had nothing to fear from the Eldur queen.

The road began to climb and narrow as they headed into the canyon.

"Your roads could use some guardrails." Brea eyed the lazy Dalur River hundreds of feet below them. She shrank against Lochlan, suddenly grateful he insisted she ride with him. Stone bridges arched across the narrow canyon at different intervals. They were like highways, guiding the city dwellers to different parts of the city carved into the sheer sides of the canyon.

Brea gawked at the archways and partial domes emerging from the desert rock on either side of the river. Brightly painted doorways and arches broke up the monotony of the dusty red stone.

They made their way along the winding roads leading through the city to the palace gates. Exotic flowers bloomed in gardens and pots, and spicy aromas filled the marketplace, making Brea's mouth water and her stomach rumble. It was the most exciting city she'd ever seen.

As they neared the largest bridge, Brea spotted the palace entrance. Tall arched doors stood wide open, welcoming all citizens to the home of their queen. The tiered gardens sat atop the gates like the crowning jewel of Eldur's greatest city.

"What does your queen want with me?" Brea asked the question for the last time.

"I truly do not know, Lady Brea," Finn said. "But I promise she has nothing nefarious in mind. I believe she simply wanted to save you from Queen Regan's grip. To give you a chance to understand what is at stake before you make any lasting decisions."

"If that is the case, then I am grateful for the meddling. I just wish I understood why all these queens seem to think I'm so important."

"Perhaps Queen Faolan will have the answers you seek."

"Let's hope." Brea held her breath as they crossed the arched bridge—apparently the crazy Eldurians were daredevils who didn't see the sense in safety railings.

Beyond the palace gates stood an exotic courtyard complete with splashing fountains and brightly colored flowers and plants. Brea swore she saw several parrots hanging out in the trees.

Lochlan dismounted and tossed the reins to a servant before he helped Brea down. "Can you walk, or do you need help."

Brea closed her eyes, feeling a little dizzy. "I'm okay. I'd like to walk on my own if I'm about to meet any queens."

"I'm sure we'll have a chance to rest and change before she summons us."

"Lochlan? Is he here?" A beautiful raven-haired woman stood on a balcony overlooking the courtyard.

"Or not." Lochlan shrugged. "Yes, my queen."

Lochlan crossed the bricked courtyard to meet Queen Faolan as she rushed down the carved stone stairs. She was a petite woman with dark eyes and a tanned complexion. Next to Lochlan she looked like a doll. A terrified doll.

"They've taken Alona." She took his hands in hers. Her sad eyes drank him in like a long-lost son.

"Taken?" He stared at the queen, then something snapped inside him as a heartbroken look swept across his face.

"Where?" Finn rushed to the queen's side, an equal look of heartbreak on his face as well.

"More than a week ago. She was on her way to Sandur to visit Lady Driscoll when your uncle's men attacked her camp at Loch Sol. They've taken her to Fargelsi."

"We will leave at once." Lochlan released her hands.

"Eamon Donovan was with her when she was taken. He escaped with most of his men and sent word back. He's trying to get through the Gelsi border as we speak. He loves her like a daughter, he will bring her home."

"I will kill my brother for his part in this," Lochlan snarled.

"A week ago?" Brea's small voice broke the tension between them.

"Do you know something?" Finn came to her side. "Anything that might help us find the princess?"

Brea counted the days since the night she escaped Fargelsi. It felt like a lifetime ago, but it was no more than seven days ago. "Griffin left on an unexpected mission for Regan just before the farewell banquet for the Iskalt delegation. The timing would be about right."

"If he took her, she'll be in the dungeons by now." Lochlan ran a frustrated hand through his hair as he turned toward Brea. She suddenly felt like a dirty and travel-worn sloth. Wrapping her threadbare blanket around her like a shawl to cover her stained clothes she glanced at the distraught queen.

"Brea Robinson. It's lovely to meet you." Faolan took an awkward step forward. "I am sorry for everything you've been through at the Fargelsi court. That was never my intention. I had hoped to bring you here safely and avoid such confusion altogether. I'm sure you have many questions for me, but now is not the time. We must see to my daughter."

"I do." Brea gave a half-hearted curtsy. "Have questions, I mean." She was suddenly feeling lightheaded and a little woozy.

Finn reached out to catch her as she stumbled, and her shawl-blanket fell away from her arm.

"Lochlan, she's hurt." The queen gasped. "What happened?"

"We had a run in with some of my uncle's men. It seems the Fargelsi queen will stop at nothing to get her hands on both women. Brea was injured and suffered an infection."

"Finn, get her inside. I'll call the healers to see to her." Faolan ran back up the steps. "Lochlan, meet me in the throne room in twenty minutes." The tiny queen barked orders as Finn swept Brea up in his arms. "Rowena, see to the girl."

Finn carried her inside the palace residence where a servant woman waited to escort them to what would be Brea's rooms. Inside, the palace was cool and shady with fresh breezes flowing from room to room. Brea heard the splash of fountains and birds chirping throughout the great hall. It was like one big garden with walls and doors open to the outside.

"In here, Sir Finn." The servant woman rushed to open a pair of double doors. "Let's get the Lady Brea settled and comfortable." She bustled about the room, opening windows and fussing with the curtains.

Finn set her on a mahogany settee with a needlepoint cushion. Sweeping the hair back from her face, he crouched before her. "Are you feeling okay?"

She nodded, staring around the room. "Just tired and a bit overwhelmed."

"I need to speak with the queen. Rowena will take good

care of you." She could sense his urgency to get rid of her so he could find out the details of Alona's situation.

"Go, I'll be fine." She hugged the blanket around her shoulders.

He didn't hesitate, and a moment later Brea found herself alone with a new servant.

"Would you like a cool bath, my Lady?"

"Please call me Brea. And yes, a bath sounds wonderful."

"Oh, I couldn't do that, my Lady. It wouldn't be proper." Rowena stared at Brea with tears in her eyes before she darted into an adjoining room to see to Brea's bath.

Suddenly she felt like she was back at square one, and she really missed Neeve. Her rooms were every bit as nice as the ones she'd had in Fargelsi, but the decor was like a different world—which she supposed was fairly accurate. Brea stood to explore her surroundings. Rich dark wood furniture filled the sitting room and silk fabrics billowed in the windows that faced the canyon. A small balcony overlooked the courtyard below. Just off the sitting room was a bedroom with the most enormous bed she'd ever seen. Big windows let the sunlight in to shine on the bed.

A small dark room occupied the back of the suite. Brea peeked into the room and was greeted with a burst of cool air. It was a grotto carved into the canyon walls. This would be the best place to retreat during the hottest part of the day. There was even a daybed there for napping.

"Lady Brea, your bath is ready," Rowena called from the sitting room.

"Thank you." She followed the servant with the round, sweet face into a garden room with open skies and leafy green plants. A sunken bathtub the size of a pool occupied the center of the bathroom. Exotic scented flower petals floated in the water.

"It's beautiful, thank you so much." Brea folded her tattered blanket, eager to sink into the bath for a nice long, quiet soak.

"I'll see to your clothes and bring you something to eat. Enjoy your bath, my Lady." She smiled and backed out of the room. "It really is lovely to meet you, Lady Brea."

Finally alone for the first time in ages, Brea heaved a deep sigh. Shedding her stained and travel-worn clothes, she sank into the deep bath trying not to feel sorry for herself.

Since the moment she escaped the palace in Gelsi, Brea had been running. Running from a bad situation into the unknown. Now that she was here—in the very place she'd once feared the most—she didn't know what to expect next.

After her bath, Brea felt blissfully clean and exhausted beyond belief. She didn't have the energy to contemplate another palace full of secrets and lies. Her arrival here in Eldur reminded her too much of her arrival in Fargelsi when everything was exciting and new and she had no reason to suspect anyone was lying.

Brea found a soft silken sleeping gown and crawled into bed. Thoughts of Myles drifted through her mind, wondering if she'd ever see him again. If he would ever forgive her. If she'd even live through this experience to find out one way or another if their friendship was broken beyond repair.

Tears rolled down Brea's face as she realized she even missed Griff and his ability to make her smile.

Despite all the luxury around her. Despite knowing she was part fae and possessed magic, that her mental illness was just another lie, Brea wanted to go home to her familiar and predictable life with her best friend, Myles.

CHAPTER TWENTY

Dried tears crusted the corner of Brea's eyelids as she tried to pry them open. Footsteps sounded against the stone floor, and she froze. Someone was in her room. She'd never get used to servants constantly being around and having very little time on her own. For once, she wished everyone would just leave her to feel sorry for herself.

She rolled over to see a figure illuminated by the silver glow of the moon. The intruder stood looking out the big windows at the sprawling Eldur palace.

Another palace. A different queen. Still not the human world.

She cleared her throat and the woman turned, revealing the face of the Eldur queen who'd only given Brea a moment of attention when she first arrived.

Brea pushed herself up in bed and scooted back against the headboard. Queen Faolan had the windows open, letting in the warm night air. It blew dark hair away from her face, revealing blazing yellow eyes that cut through the darkness of the night.

"What do you want with me?" The whispered words were the first Brea could think of. For some reason, two queens abducted her, and a king tried to kill her. None of it made any sense. She didn't know if she believed Griff's words about a prophecy any longer, not after finding out they really only wanted her to give him legitimacy.

There had to be a real reason why she—normal girl Brea Robinson—was such a hot commodity to the royals of the fae world. She cringed at the thought.

The queen's eyes swirled before settling into a more natural amber color. "You're not Alona."

Brea's brow creased. "I'm Brea Robinson."

She nodded. "Yes, yes, I know that. But I expected some... feeling that would make me believe I had my daughter back. She's been gone for months now, and we've had no request for ransom. That's why I sent Lochlan into the human realm. I had to protect my daughter no matter what. Everything has been to protect the lineage." She carved a path across the room and back again, her footsteps heavy as she paced.

Nothing she said made any sense.

Her entire body stilled, and she turned back to face Brea. "You're not her!"

Queen Faolan's fiery gaze burned yellow again, and Brea could hardly breathe. *Dragon queen. Dragon queen. Dragon queen.* The words repeated in her mind, stirring fear in Brea's gut. Her magic latched onto the emotion, refusing to let it go away. It built up, begging for release.

She tilted her head to the side, trying to hold it back, knowing blasting the queen with magic wouldn't win her any favors.

The queen's eyes widened. "Your magic... your eyes." Her voice lowered to a whisper. "Yellow."

Brea couldn't handle her scrutiny any longer. "My eyes are

and have always been blue." It was one of the only traits she inherited from her mother. "You're the one with the yellow eyes." *Dragon Queen,* she called her in her head.

Lochlan and Finn trusted this woman, but Brea barely knew them, and she'd been burned before.

Queen Faolan moved closer to the bed. "My eyes turn yellow when I am controlling my magic—which I'm trying very hard to do right now despite the sun not being out at this hour."

"Right, well I won't be your prisoner. Been there, done that." She shoved the fear she felt away. There was nothing to lose anymore because everything had already been taken from her. "I am only here because your dog Lochlan tied me up, took me into battle, and said some very grumpy things. The human world sucks, but it's better than this place, and I expect you to take me back there."

The queen's eyes flashed, and she turned away, crossing her arms over her chest. "I sent Lochlan to bring you here from the human world. Do you know what that cost? My most trusted man wasn't here to protect my daughter when she was taken." She looked back over her shoulder. Tears shone in her eyes, but she blinked them away and strode from the room.

Kicking the thin sheet off her legs, Brea scrambled from the bed, half expecting her door to be locked.

When she pulled, it clicked open, revealing a long, dark hallway, deserted in the dead of night. Starlight spilled across her path under archways leading to the outside. In the still of the night, everything was quiet save for the slow trickling of fountains.

As her feet hit warm bricks, she realized she'd forgotten to put on anything other than the pale pink silk sleeping gown draped over her shoulders. She stared down at her legs peeking past the trim, remembering what Lochlan said about her human modesty. The fae didn't care if she revealed herself here at court because they wouldn't look. A body was not the fascination to them that it was for humans.

Still, she'd have killed for a razor and gigantic bottle of shaving cream so she didn't feel like a woolly mammoth in the short gown.

Archways led from courtyards to doors she hadn't yet seen behind. The Eldur palace was larger than the one in Fargelsi and even more grand. Everything seemed to be centered around the outdoors—something she hadn't expected in a desert kingdom.

Stepping into one of the many courtyards, a grand fountain depicting two male fae in a state of... erm... bliss had her face heating again. She averted her eyes from their naked bodies and lifted them to the clear sky above, wondering if they were the same stars hanging above her home in Ohio.

She expected to see dragons flying overhead, their giant wings silhouetted against the moon. Okay, expected was probably the wrong word. She'd hoped to see them, for them to be real.

"What do you think you'll find in the stars?" Finn's voice startled her out of her dream of dragons.

She looked back over her shoulder to where he stood leaning against the doorway into what looked like a library. "Dragons." It sounded stupid after she said it.

He shrugged. "I'm not sure exactly what a dragon is, but I hope you find it."

She laughed at that. "Well, there's my answer. No dragons. They're these giant winged reptiles that breathe fire and destroy cities."

"Ah, now I remember. Alona was obsessed with such creatures. She read about them in Lochlan's human books he brought back and always said a desert kingdom should have such animals."

Brea crossed the courtyard to him. As she got closer, she could make out the tired expression on his face. His lips drew down into a frown, but it was his eyes that spoke of hidden pain. "Are you okay, Finn?"

"I should be asking you that. You've arrived at yet another palace—injured I might add. Are you feeling okay? I wanted to make sure you don't take anything the queen says personally. She isn't in a good place right now, so she'll come see you soon, I'm sure."

"She already did." She'd never forget the queen's desperate words or incoherent babbling.

Not giving him a chance to respond, she walked past him into the library, her breath rushing out of her lungs at the sight before her.

Finn lifted a hand, illuminated the room, revealing bookshelves as high as she could see. Painted ceilings depicted grand adventures to preside over what must be thousands of books. Leather-bound tomes crowded the shelves in the circular room.

"This was Alona's favorite place in the entire palace." Finn ran a finger along a line of embossed spines. "She and Lochlan spent many hours together sprawled across the benches along the back wall."

He led her through the shelves to where a reading nook sat against a window overlooking a garden. Bench wasn't the right word. It was more like an extra-wide couch carved right into the wall, shielding it from view of the rest of the library. Pillows lined the surface. It was built up over a row of three-shelf bookcases.

Brea bent to examine the books. "*Harry Potter*," she whispered. "*Game of Thrones*." And on it went. *Lord of the Rings*. *His Dark Materials*. The entire collections by Robin Hobb and David Eddings.

Finn sat on the bench. "Every time Lochlan went to the

human realm, he returned with stacks of books. For weeks, he'd spend every spare moment with Alona devouring the words." He picked up a book sitting on the arm of the bench and held it out to Brea. "This was what she was reading right before she left."

"*A Court of Thorns and Roses.*" Brea took the book. "Myles read this, and I had to hear endlessly about it."

"Alona thought it was quite funny the humans were writing about fae as if they knew anything about us except old lore we allowed into story books many generations ago."

She offered the book back, but he shook his head and she set it on one of the shelves.

Finn lay back, his eyes focusing on the beautiful ceiling overhead. "Here in the desert, we don't get a lot of rain, but when it does come, it stays for days, sometimes weeks. In the past, if my training was cancelled, I'd join Alona. We laid here and talked of fantasy futures, so different from the ones we could have."

"You can have any future you choose." It was a stock line humans said to each other, but rarely was it true.

"Come now, Brea, do not start lying to me now. Look around. We are in a palace. Do not for one moment think any of us have a choice in our path."

This wasn't the boisterous happy man she'd traveled with from the Vatlands. "Has something happened, Finn?"

He sighed. "Just being here... Everything reminds me of Alona."

Brea climbed up next to him and lay back. "She's not just the princess to you, is she?" She looked sideways at him and watched a tear curve over his cheek.

"Have you ever loved someone so much it killed you when they were gone?"

She wanted to say no, to ignore that kind of pain. She knew

now she'd never loved Griff. It had been a trick she played on herself in her desperation to not be alone in a foreign world. But Myles? He was her person, her other half. It wasn't a romantic kind of love, but it was just as strong. When she spoke, her voice was no more than a whisper.

"You feel as if you're no longer alive, like your heart refuses to beat until you see them again."

Finn's hand found hers, threading their fingers together. "We wish the pain away, but in the same breath we hold onto it as a reminder of what they were to us."

"Are."

"What?" He rolled his head to look at her.

"What they are to us. Alona was taken, but she might yet be alive." Just like Myles.

"She has to be. If she comes back to us, I'm going to lose her again, but at least she'll be safe."

"Why do you have to lose her?" Brea would never understand a world in which people could love each other and not be together.

"Because, Brea, Alona has no magic."

"I don't know what that means."

His voice shook as he explained. "Fae born without magic cannot remain among the noble or royal classes beyond coming of age. Upon her eighteenth birthday, she must join the servant class, leaving her family behind."

Brea sat up. "But that's not fair! It's cruel." She suddenly felt for this girl she'd never met, the one mourned by both the queen and this soldier beside her.

"It is our way." He sat, turning to face her. "Magic is everything to the fae."

Her respect for the fae dwindled to nothing. "It isn't right. Magic isn't more important than family." She'd never turn her back on Myles no matter what happened to her, and she refused to let this missing princess suffer her fate. "Alona will be found, Finn. And when she is, you and I will find a way to save her from such a stupid fae tradition. Maybe we can even convince douchey Lochlan to help."

One corner of his mouth curved up. "Maybe you are just what our kingdom needs. Someone to challenge what we all think we know."

"If you're telling me to be a pain in the butt, I can totally do that. It's basically my personality. But you listen to me, Finn. You and I are friends now."

He opened his mouth to speak, but she shushed him.

"I don't care if Loch tells you to leave me alone, you will not do that. I'm a bit short on friends at the moment. You can be my fairy whisperer, making sure I don't embarrass myself. And one day, we will get to see our people again—the people we love don't get to just disappear from our lives."

His eyes glistened with unshed tears as he nodded. "I'd very much like us to be friends. I just have one question first."

"Go for it."

"Lochlan told me you're calling him douchey Lochlan because you think him noble, but that isn't what the human word means, is it?"

She flashed him a grin and scooted to the edge of the bench to climb off. "Goodnight, Finn."

She turned to walk around a shelf, colliding with a giant wall of flesh. Gripping her shoulder as pain seared from the contact, she looked up into Lochlan's stormy face.

"Did you love my brother?"

CHAPTER TWENTY-ONE

Lochlan's hazy eyes darted around the room before landing on Brea, a mix of anger and drunken desperation on his face.

"What?" She only breathed the word.

"Were you in love with my brother?" he slurred. "I heard you talking to Finn about loving so much it killed you to lose them." He leaned close, sneering in a very Lochlan-like way. "You didn't lose him, Lady Brea, you ran."

"Loch." Finn appeared behind Brea, resting a hand on her shoulder. "Stop this nonsense."

"I used to love him too, Brea," he went on, stumbling back as if he couldn't control his own steps. "Griff is a master manipulator. He makes you believe you're part of his family before stabbing you in the back. Don't waste your breath missing him."

Anger burned through her, but it didn't latch onto her magic, not the way fear seemed to be able to. As she looked at the pathetic excuse for Lochlan, she wasn't afraid.

He was wrong. She didn't love Griff. But maybe he wasn't

so different from his brother. They both had a cruel streak a mile wide. "I don't have to answer to you." She tried to push past him, but he grabbed her arm.

"Loch," Finn snapped. "Let her go."

"Not until I know why."

"Why what?" Her voice shook with rage. "Why I let him kiss me? Why I sought him out in the dead of night to crawl into his bed?" She narrowed her eyes. "Because I enjoyed it. Do I need more reason than that?"

His grip tightened. "Griff could have killed you."

As she studied his slack expression, she realized why he was so upset. Alona. Whether he was in love with her or not, she didn't know, but Lochlan knew the truth of why his queen wanted Brea. He'd lied to her just like his brother before him. And something about whatever knowledge he possessed made him intensely protective of her.

Finn put a hand on Lochlan's arm. "Stop this."

"Don't you see it, Finn? Brea Robinson is the reason Alona was taken." The queen had said the same thing, but she didn't understand it.

"Why? How are we connected?" What did a fae princess and a half-human girl have in common?

Lochlan released her, turning with a huff. He paced back toward them, his face a storm cloud of emotions. "Griff knew. He knew!"

"Knew what?"

"What our parents died for." He wobbled where he stood before leaning against a bookshelf to stay upright. "He knew kidnapping Queen Faolan's daughter would force the truth into the light. He tried to take you both as proof, but you ran away before he could come back with Alona."

"I still don't understand!" The words exploded out of her. She was tired, so tired, of all the half-truths and semi-lies.

Lochlan turned on her, his jaw clenched. "Alona is like my sister. You... you're nothing."

Tears built in her eyes at his words. "If I'm nothing, why did you go to such lengths to save my life?"

"I had orders." He ran a hand through his hair, tugging wildly at the ends as his breathing grew more erratic. "I can't... control..." He buried his face in his hands as his entire body shook.

"Brea," Finn yelled. "He's losing control of his magic. Get out of—" That was the last word she heard before light encompassed the room, knocking the breath from her lungs as she slammed back into a bookshelf, pain exploding from her shoulder as blackness crept across her vision. Again.

Just another day in the fae world, another time waking up in a strange place after being knocked out.

A groan reverberated from Brea's throat as she flexed her limbs, making sure everything still worked. When she finally opened her eyes, she found a tall broad-shouldered woman with cherry red hair and kind eyes staring down at her.

"Amazonian," she whispered.

"What?" A concerned look flashed across the woman's face.

"Nothing." Brea shut her eyes as pain throbbed in her temple.

"How are you feeling, dear?" Her voice was like a quiet symphony.

"Are you a healer?" She cracked one eye open. "Because if you are, I could totally do with some drugs right now."

"Ah yes, Lochlan did tell me of your strange human speak."

"Lochlan?" Her eyes shot open. "Is he okay?" The last she remembered he'd lost control of his magic.

"Yes, he sat beside your bed with Finn most of the night. He can't forgive himself for hurting you."

"It wasn't his fault. His magic… I saw it take control of him. He couldn't stop it."

"I know that, dear, and so do you. But Lochlan is a stubborn man who likes to believe everything bad is his fault."

"Where is he?" She tried to sit up. "I want to speak with him."

"He left with Finn at daybreak to follow a lead in the search for Alona. In truth, I wanted to be by myself when I met you."

"Who are you?"

"My name is Tierney. I am the queen consort of Eldur."

"You mean—"

Tierney nodded with a smile. "I am Queen Faolan's wife."

Brea already felt more comfortable in this woman's presence than the queen. "It's nice to meet you."

"Darling, I have longed to meet you since I first heard of your existence."

"Why? No one will give me any answers."

She brushed hair away from Brea's forehead. "Oh dear, I have quite the story to spin. My wife would have us wait for the right time, but you have waited long enough. And frankly, Faolan could use something good right now."

"Good?"

"You, Brea. You are good."

For the first time since learning the truth of her aunt in Eldur, Brea believed someone was finally going to be honest with her. "Why am I here?"

"Because, Brea Robinson, you were born in the fae realm."

Brea's heart stopped as her mind tried to grasp that piece of information. "That's impossible. My mom—"

"Is not your mother. You're a changeling, Brea."

"A what-ling?"

"When you were born, your fae mother wanted to protect you. But your father was of the royal line of Fargelsi. That kingdom believed you belonged to them and tried to make it so. They needed an heir after your father died and his sister took the throne. They sent many people to abduct you, but the kingdoms of Eldur and Iskalt protected you. Together, they decided you weren't safe in the fae world."

"Wait, so you're saying I'm not half-fae?"

"No, Brea, this is your world completely. You mother sent her greatest friends to exchange you with a human child. It angered Fargelsi, but they did not know of your whereabouts, and you were safe."

"Then why am I here if I was safe? Why did Lochlan and Griff come for me?"

"Because Queen Regan grows in power, and it was time to bring you home before you gain full use of your magic when you come of age. With Griffin on Regan's side, it was only a matter of time before she found you."

"Home?" Brea's gasp made Rowena come running from across the room, but Tierney waved her away. Brea recalled the bits of information she'd learned before. Princess Alona had no magic. Was she the human girl? Regan tried to keep Brea in Fargelsi through marriage, thus securing the throne.

And Queen Faolan... her rambling... the way she'd stared at Brea as if trying to see something that wasn't there.

"Queen Faolan is my mother." The words felt right, somehow, as if a piece of herself fit into place as soon as she said them. "I belong here, in Eldur," she whispered to herself. For the first time in her life, someone was saying she had a place in the world.

The Robinsons in Ohio with their drinking and cruel words didn't define her. She didn't come from them. They were Alona's parents.

Tears flowed freely down her face as she looked at the only woman brave enough to tell her. Lochlan had known, she was sure of it. Yet, she couldn't muster up the anger for him.

Not when she wanted this truth so badly.

"Can I..." She sucked in a breath. "Can I see her?"

Tierney's shining eyes met hers, and she nodded. "She will be vexed I told you, but you aren't the only one who needs something to hold onto, Brea. Just... be patient with her. Recovering one daughter does not lessen the pain of losing another."

Tierney gestured to Rowena to help Brea from the bed. Her feet hit the stone floor and she no longer felt strange about wandering the palace in a sleeping gown. Rowena helped her into the hall, but Brea shrugged off her hand and started running, having no idea where she needed to go.

Tierney caught up to her, grabbing her hand and running to match Brea's speed. She led her through the labyrinth of half-covered walkways and courtyards. They stopped outside a set of high wooden double doors.

"The throne room," Tierney whispered, gesturing to the guards to open the doors. "She will be alone at this time of day while she waits to receive her people."

The doors opened, revealing a long white carpet meandering through sandstone pillars wrapped in pale pink silks.

Queen Faolan relaxed on a gilded golden throne with purple cushions to keep her in comfort. She leaned her head back, closing her eyes, a troubled expression on her face.

Tierney prodded Brea forward.

Brea's bare feet hit the carpet, leaving indented footprints behind her as if marking this day, showing that she was there.

Her breath rattled in her lungs, drowning out the pounding of her heart. The pain in her shoulder and head seemed to fade into the background as Brea searched the woman before her for the similarities she'd never found in her mother.

"Your eyes," she'd said. Did they blaze yellow with her magic? Was that a family trait?

Full fae. It made sense now. Why her Aunt Regan wanted her. Why they were attacked on the road.

Lochlan's disdain.

One day, she hoped to help him find the woman who'd been like his sister.

She stopped at the bottom of a set of stairs leading to the throne, and only one word came out. "Mom?" She cleared her throat, realizing that must be a human word. "Mother."

Queen's Faolan's eyes snapped open, settling on Brea with an intensity that should have scared her. She flicked them to her wife who stood watching with tears streaming down her face. Brea glanced back over her shoulder before facing her mom again.

"Is it true?"

Her mother covered her mouth with her hand.

Brea stepped closer. "Please, tell me it's true."

The queen, unable to speak, nodded as her eyes glassed over. Brea had longed to go back to the human realm since the moment Griff pulled her through a portal, but as she stood looking at the woman who put her there, who subjected her to a life of being named crazy and insane, she didn't know what she wanted.

"Do you have any idea what my life has been like?" She stumbled back, her emotions breaking free in a cascade of tears. "H-how..."

Her mom scrambled from her throne and ran down the steps, crushing Brea into her arms. "My dear." She wiped tears from Brea's face and looked into her eyes. "It was far better than letting the Fargelsians get their hands on you."

"And what of Alona? You ripped her from the Robinsons."

"She has had a good life here. I promise you."

Until they forced her into the servant class. But Brea didn't have the energy to argue the morals of exchanging a fae child for a human one.

"Mother." She buried her face in her mom's shoulder. "Why didn't you tell me last night?"

"I don't know. My heart is broken, child. Alona is missing, and to think of everything you've been through." She rested her chin on Brea's head. "It's over now for you. You're safe here. This is your home."

The truth in her mother's words didn't hit her until right then. This information broke her open, letting loose a million questions she feared to ask. But she could rest now because she was safe.

Tierney joined them, wrapping both her wife and new daughter in her long arms.

"They'll bring her back," Brea whispered. "Lochlan and Finn will find Alona."

They had to.

Brea finally found a place she was meant to be, a mother—two of them!—and people she cared about—even douchey Loch. But none of them were whole without their missing princess.

Brea's mom cancelled the morning sessions in the throne room and spent hours eating a way-too-large breakfast with Brea and Tierney. They smiled and laughed, but a tension ran beneath every action, a sadness.

By the time Brea finally made it back to her rooms, Rowena

awaited her, chastisement in her eyes at the sight of Brea still in her sleeping gown.

After changing into a loose-fitting dress—much better than what they'd made her wear in Fargelsi—Brea returned to the courtyard with the fountain statue of naked men.

Sunlight glared off shining stones, sending light back into the atmosphere. The fountain water sparkled where it rippled. She doubted the fae had similar traditions to the humans where they made wishes in fountains, but there was always a time to start.

Thinking of the look on Rowena's face when Brea asked for a small coin, she laughed. The servant couldn't understand what she'd need with money, but she'd brought her one anyway.

Brea flipped the silver coin over in her palm, feeling the smooth surface against her palm. Everything she'd ever dreamed of and more had suddenly come true. She had a family who cared about her, despite the fact they didn't know her. A palace surrounding her that no human girl dreaming of princesses could even imagine.

And best of all... no one doubted her. She'd spent her life seeing things others said couldn't possibly exist. The Clarkson Institute was a part of her past now.

But there was one thing this world still needed, one thing that kept her from the happiness she should feel.

Lowering herself to the short stone wall surrounding the fountain, she bent over and ran her hand along the surface, watching the disturbance the action caused. That's what Brea had always been. A disturbance.

But maybe that was okay. Her life wasn't normal by any means, and she didn't want it to be.

She brought the coin to her lips, pressing a kiss to it as she held the wish in her mind and heart. After a beat of hesitation, she lifted her hand and tossed the coin into the glimmering water, watching it sink down to the depths of the fountain.

A smile spread across her lips. "That wish was for you, Myles."

She patted the stone and stood, unable to stop the laugh bubbling past her lips. Because she knew without a shadow of a doubt now. Myles was alive.

"I'm going to see you again one day."

Brea Robinson wasn't a murderer. She hadn't killed her best friend. And he'd forgive her for everything else, just like she'd finally forgiven herself.

Guilt was a human emotion, one with no purpose.

And Brea wasn't human, not even a little.

She was no longer a lie.

She was fae, and she was home.

Alona Cahill

The constant drip, drip, drip noise drove Alona mad. Some days she counted the drips until she fell asleep only to wake up to another day of nothing but darkness, damp walls, and the constant drip.

Alona had never thirsted for magic the way some of the serving class did. But right now, she'd give almost anything to have been born with magic just for the ability to create fire for warmth and light.

"What does Regan want with me?" she asked the walls of her cell. "I am nothing but a useless princess destined to become a maid. I have no value as a bargaining tool beyond my mothers' love for me." And they would never compromise the future of Eldur just for her. That was too high a price to pay for their daughter's freedom. Regan had to know that.

The drip, drip, drip faded at the sound of footsteps approaching her cell. Alona hadn't seen a soul since her arrival in the dungeon. Her food and water appeared once a day on the table in the far corner of the cell. That was perhaps the worst part of her captivity. The solitude and the drip, drip, drip.

"Let's go, Princess. The queen has summoned you." A Fargelsi servant scraped a key in the lock and opened the heavy wooden door of her cell.

Alona scrambled to her feet, eager to leave the dungeon behind, if only to hear Queen Regan's grand standing about her plans for Alona.

The man was silent as he escorted her up the winding stairs to the servant's quarters and past the kitchens. Alona's stomach growled at the savory aromas wafting into the halls.

The Fargelsi palace was beautiful but a far cry from the one she grew up in. There was a cold, almost sinister quality about the palace that made her uneasy. Like the very walls were watching her every move.

The servant guided her into a throne room where the queen waited for her. Alona couldn't fathom what Regan could possibly want with her. Still, she stood proudly in front of the queen, refusing to bow as befitting her station. Alona was the princess of Eldur—at least for a few more months—and she regarded the queen as a rival and not a superior.

"You wanted to speak with me?" Alona was proud her voice didn't shake at all. The Gelsi queen was known for her cruelty and her ruthless magic, and here stood Alona, powerless in front of her. Her traveling clothes stained and torn.

"Welcome to Fargelsi, *Princess*." The queen's voice held a note of amusement.

Alona noticed the man seated beside the queen. "Callum O'Shea," Alona addressed him. "It surprises me to see you here in attendance of the Gelsi queen."

"You will address me as King Callum of Iskalt." His

demeanor was every bit as cold as the kingdom he stole from his nephew.

"I will call you nothing of the sort. Eldur recognizes no King of Iskalt other than the true heir, Lochlan O'Shea. You may have allied with Fargelsi, but your nephew will never allow it."

"You do not speak for Eldur, child." Queen Regan peered down her nose at Alona. "You are nothing to Eldur or any fae realm. You have no magic. You have no voice."

"Until I come of age, I am a voice of Eldur." Alona squared her shoulders. "And you have committed a crime by taking me from my kingdom."

"What do you know of the girl, Brea Robinson?" Regan asked.

"Who?" Alona hadn't known what to expect of this summons, but this wasn't it.

"She doesn't know." Another voice joined the queen's. Alona's eyes fell to the man standing in the darkness behind the queen's throne.

"Griffin?" She'd always felt sorry for Lochlan's brother, raised in the Gelsi court. If he was anything like his brother, he wouldn't condone any of this. "You know she can't be trusted, Griffin." She begged him with her eyes to end this. To help her escape whatever the queen had in store for her, but he refused to meet her eyes.

"She raised me, Alona." Griffin stepped forward. "Queen Regan is the only mother I've ever known."

"Speaking of mothers," Regan interjected, patting Griffin's hand as if to tell him he was a good boy. "Did you know you were a changeling, dear?" Regan batted her eyelashes.

"A changeling?"

"Of course, you little fool. Your mother is a weak queen, but even she would have given birth to a child with magic. She knew I would stop at nothing to take my brother's child so she switched her with a human girl. Her daughter has lived in the human world, leaving you, a human, to stand in as her only child who could never inherit her throne. She would have me believe Brandon's child was a weakling."

"No." Alona's legs trembled beneath her.

"Brea Robinson is the true heir of Eldur. The daughter of Queen Faolan and my late brother, King Brandon O'Rourke. She was to be betrothed to Griffin before she escaped the palace."

Alona gasped, realizing in an instant what the queen had planned. "You can't be serious?"

"You are smarter than your mother. Well, the woman who raised you." Regan smiled a cruel smile.

"I just don't get how this works in your favor." Alona stood straight. She could freak out later. "If this Brea girl is your niece and she marries your ward, Griffin, then Brea's child—a child who would share blood with you—would be your blood heir."

"Correct."

"You've gone a very long time without a blood heir, Regan." Alona smiled, crossing her arms behind her back. "This future child you've planned for would strengthen your reign and your hold on Fargelsi for years to come. But you've never been satisfied with just Fargelsi.

"If what you say is true, then Brea is my mother's blood heir. You intend to have her take Eldur and do your bidding? No, wait, that's not good enough for you. You've always wanted Eldur for yourself." Alona turned on her heel and paced across the room to pour herself a glass of wine, hoping Regan couldn't see the way her hands were shaking.

"By all means, help yourself." The queen chuckled. "I'm curious to see where you're going with your assumptions."

Alona took a sip of wine to strengthen her resolve. "With

Brea and Griffin's union you get a firmer hold on Gelsi and a foothold in Eldur. But we're forgetting Iskalt." She turned to the king and a cold sense of dread swept through her. This wasn't about Gelsi and Eldur. "You have an alliance with Callum, who has no heir." If she was right, they had a deal to make Griffin Callum's heir, and by default Griffin and Brea's child would be the future ruler of Iskalt as well as Fargelsi and Eldur.

"No wonder my mother went to such lengths to hide Brea Robinson from you. What an ingenious web you've spun for the future of our world. Your grand-niece or nephew will inherit half the fae realm. But what does that give the mighty Queen Regan?"

"Your speculations are quite impressive." Regan smiled, giving nothing away. "I called you here to make a bargain with you. You are a human without magic, caught up in the fae world where you can't hope to come out on top."

"What do you think you can offer me that I would accept?" Alona crossed her arms over her chest.

"I will set you free, and in exchange for your freedom, you will bring me Brea Robinson."

"Why would I ever do that?"

"Bring my niece home and I will allow you to return to the human world where you belong."

Alona shook her head with a grimace, her heart hammering in her chest. "I visited the human world once and I didn't care for it too much. I did meet a nice girl there though. She was good to me. It would be a shame for me to betray her now."

Alona chanced a glance at Griffin. He stood silently behind his queen, looking quite grave and uncertain. He might not be a lost cause just yet.

"If Brea escaped your clutches, you can bet Lochlan has

taken her to Eldur by now. She is beyond your reach, and I've grown weary of this discussion that doesn't interest me."

Without magic, Alona couldn't help her people fight against Regan's plans, but she could do one thing. She could be a prisoner. A prisoner who refused to be used as a pawn in Regan's schemes.

"Take me back to my cell." Alona turned to leave the throne room.

"Very well, show our guest to her new quarters," Regan called to Alona's escort. "We'll see how well she's ready to cooperate after she's grown accustomed to life in the bowels of Fargelsi."

The trip back to the dungeon was another silent one. But they continued down the stairs, far past the cell she'd spent her first week in. It was darker and colder. The smell of mold and rot made her gag as she slipped on the slimy stones beneath her feet. The walls closed in around her, and Alona began to panic. This would be far worse than the musty room with the constant drip, drip, drip.

The roar of the falls and the rush of the river sounded overhead. They were deep under the palace when her escort reached for his keys to unlock an iron grated door.

"I must follow my orders, you understand?" the man finally spoke, shoving the iron bars open.

"I hold no ill will for you, sir." She stepped into the larger hall on the other side of the door, and the stench of unwashed bodies assaulted her nose. Row upon row of filthy cells lined the corridor. Pitiful looking prisoners huddled in their tattered blankets and turned their dead eyes on her.

The queen's servant opened a cell door, and Alona stepped inside. The room was hardly bigger than a closet. More of a cage than a cell. A bucket sat in one corner, and moldy straw covered the muddy floor. There was barely enough room to sit, much less lay down.

Alona flinched as the iron bars clanged shut behind her. She sank to the floor, clutching her hand over her mouth to still her sobs. In one fell swoop, she'd discovered she was never fae born, and her mothers weren't her mothers after all. She would likely spend years, if not the rest of her life in this cell, paying the price for Faolan's attempt to save her true-born daughter from Regan's grasp. She was nothing more than a human stand-in daughter. But Regan couldn't take everything from her. Alona knew without a doubt in her heart that the mothers who raised her loved her every bit as much as they loved their true-born daughter.

A hand reached through the bars from the next cell and grasped hers. "Don't let them hear you cry, Alona." The filthy hand squeezed hers.

"Who are you?" She peered into the darkness, trying to make out the face of the woman beside her. She leaned against the bars, grasping the stranger's hand like a lifeline.

"My name is Neeve. I served the Lady Brea while she was here, and I helped her escape."

"She's in Eldur now?"

"I sent her through the southern Vatlands to Lochlan's camp," Neeve said. "It's only a matter of time before that girl gets her head on straight and strikes back."

"In the meantime, we need to plan our escape." Alona choked back her tears. She might be imprisoned and feeling lower than she ever had before, but Alona Cahill was a fighter and she wouldn't go down without an explosive battle.

"Fargelsi is no longer just a kingdom of the fae world, Alona. It is a prison. Those born of Fargelsi are prisoners of its queen—she holds our magic, only allowing us the faintest use of it. There is no joy here, only fake smiles and hidden agendas. For those without magic, there is no escape."

"Maybe for those born of Fargelsi and those born without magic. But I am human. I am not bound by the laws of this world, and I will find a way to fight back."

Want more from Brea's world?

Don't miss the free prequel,
Fae's Dilemma available at

https://www.subscribepage.com/faesdilemmanovella

Brea Robinson is a princess.

Ridiculous, right?

She's left her small Ohio town behind for an exotic palace beyond her imagination, trading old jeans for ballgowns and a drunken father for two Fae mothers.

Safe behind the power of Eldur, it's easy to forget everything that brought her here.

Like the two men who saved her that are now missing.

The abducted princess who should be roaming the palace halls instead of her.

The war coming for them all.

As Brea comes to terms with this new world and the web of secrets surrounding her, she realizes she stands on the brink of losing everything she never knew she wanted.

The mothers who would die for her.

The Fae who loves her.

And the people of her kingdom who trust her to save them.

Only, Brea can barely save herself. With uncontrollable magic warring within her, it's only a matter of time before she lets everyone down.

When the worst happens and the person she loves most falls into the enemy's hands, she has a choice to make. And if she bows to the enemy queen's demands, will she remain a princess or become a sacrifice instead?

ACKNOWLEDGMENTS

We had a ton of fun writing Brea's story, mostly because the entire time, we were waiting for the moment we could reveal the lies, that not everyone is who they say they are.

But with any new series, there are a lot of nerves, a lot of wondering if the story has merit, if we have done something that actually matters. Before a book gets into a reader's hand, there are many people who have eased our nerves and bolstered our confidence.

We find ourselves repeating the thanks throughout our books but it doesn't make it any less important.

First, we need to start with cover designer Maria Spada. For these stories, we didn't get covers designed to fit the book, we designed a story that would fit the gorgeous covers. She inspired our art with her own.

Cindy Ray Hale, our wonderful line editor. When we worried about the time crunch, she eased the burden by flying through the books with a speed that astounds us.

Caitlin Haines, our proof editor and all around cheerleader, meeting her in this business has been a blessing.

To our families who let us hide away while we write, we love you.

And finally, our biggest thanks to our readers. When you fall in love with our characters, it warms our hearts. Thank you for your continued support.

ABOUT MELISSA

Melissa A. Craven writes YA Contemporary and YA Fantasy (Contemporary fans will know her as Ann Maree Craven). Her books feature strong female protagonists who aren't always perfect, but find their inner strength along the way. Melissa believes in stories that make you think and she loves foreshadowing, leaving clues and hints for the careful reader.

Melissa draws inspiration from her background in architecture and interior design to help her with the small details in world building and scene settings. She is a diehard introvert with a wicked sense of humor and a tendency for hermit-like behavior. (She gets cranky if she has to put on anything other than yoga pants and t-shirts!)

Visit Melissa at Melissaacraven.com for more information about her newest series and discover exclusive content.

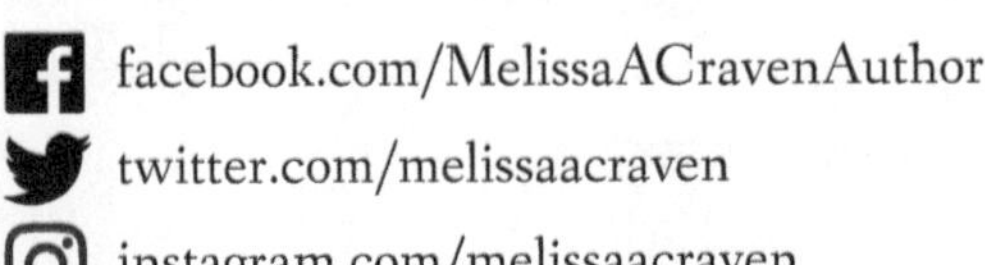

facebook.com/MelissaACravenAuthor
twitter.com/melissaacraven
instagram.com/melissaacraven

ALSO BY MELISSA

QUEENS OF THE FAE

Fae's Deception | *Fae's Defiance* | *Fae's Destruction*

CRIMES OF THE FAE

Fae's Prisoner | *Fae's Power* | *Fae's Promise*

IMMORTALS OF INDRIELL

Emerge (Book 1) | *Edge* (Book 0) | *Catalyst* (Short Story)

Judgment (Book 2) | *Scholar* (Series Companion) |

Volunteer (Short Story) | *Captive* (Book 3)

Assignment (Novella) | *Heir* (Book 4) | *Betrayal* (Book 5)

Runaway (Book 6) Coming soon | *Proving* (Book 7) Coming Soon

ASCENSION OF THE NINE REALMS

(Coming Soon)

Valkyrie | *Warder* | *Berserker* | *Druid*

ABOUT M. LYNN

Michelle MacQueen is a USA Today bestselling author of love. Yes, love. Whether it be YA romance, NA romance, or fantasy romance (Under M. Lynn), she loves to make readers swoon.

The great loves of her life to this point are two tiny blond creatures who call her "aunt" and proclaim her books to be "boring books" for their lack of pictures. Yet, somehow, she still manages to love them more than chocolate.

When she's not sharing her inexhaustible wisdom with her niece and nephew, Michelle is usually lounging in her ridiculously large bean bag chair creating worlds and characters that remind her to smile every day - even when a feisty five-year-old is telling her just how much she doesn't know.

See more from Michelle MacQueen and sign up to receive updates and deals!

www.michellelynnauthor.com

ALSO BY M. LYNN

QUEENS OF THE FAE

Fae's Deception | *Fae's Defiance* | *Fae's Destruction*

CRIMES OF THE FAE

Fae's Prisoner | *Fae's Power* | *Fae's Promise*

THE HIDDEN WARRIOR

Dragon Rising | *Dragon Rebellion*

FANTASY AND FAIRYTALES

Golden Curse | *Golden Chains* | *Golden Crown*

Glass Kingdom | *Glass Princess*

Noble Thief | *Cursed Beauty*

LEGACY OF LIGHT

A War For Magic | *A War For Truth* | *A War For Love*

A War For Love

www.ingramcontent.com/pod-product-compliance
Lightning Source LLC
Chambersburg PA
CBHW030529310726
48979CB00010B/1848/J

* 9 7 8 1 9 7 0 0 5 2 0 9 1 *